HER SILENCE

S. T. ASHMAN

For film rights, please contact: Joel Gotler: joel@ipglm.com

Print and audiobook rights: Ethan@ethanellenberg.com

To my son and daughter.
If you let me, I'll find you in every lifetime,
over and over,
and be your mom again.

CONTENTS

PART II

PART I

1

LACEY

The drawing in front of me was brutal. Absolutely brutal. …

My son Dylan and I were sitting in his classroom with his teacher, Mrs. Griffin. All three of us were looking at the drawing Dylan had made of his classmate Benny, who had become a joke on paper.

In the drawing, Benny sat on a toilet, diarrhea splashing into the bowl. His large body was grotesquely exaggerated. More monster than human. Bloated and slimy like that slug-thing from *Star Wars*. Benny held empty candy wrappers in his fists. Above his head, a speech bubble read: "Feed the beast."

It was childish and cruel. And I had no doubt that it had already gone viral here at school.

"It's … quite a drawing," I said as I shifted in the plastic chair. We were sitting in a typical public high school classroom. The walls were plastered with art and math posters. Everything looked old and worn. Almost the same way it did when I went to this very same school about sixteen years ago. I was barely older than Dylan was now when I became pregnant with him. Everybody thought I would drop out or get an abortion. But I finished school in these rooms and proved them all wrong.

Carried my belly like a badge of pride and determination. It was torture. And I came close to quitting many times. But, in the end, the bullying and jokes made me want Dylan and my diploma more than ever.

I looked at him as he sat next to me. Six feet two inches of sass. He'd become so handsome. Brown hair, a straight nose, and that athletic build. Girls already noticed him left and right. And even now, watching him sitting here getting scolded, I just loved him so much that it hurt.

"The whole school was laughing at Benny," Mrs. Griffin said in a stern tone. Her eyes settled on Dylan, who avoided her stare.

"Benny's parents are extremely angry about all this," she added. "Pictures can carry powerful messages."

She was right about that. And, at first, I sided with her. But then I realized who he'd drawn, and the lines between right and wrong blurred.

Benny wasn't just anyone. He was the school bully.

Like out of a bad movie. And his parents acting like victims after all Benny had done to the other kids was one of the reasons Benny was such a piece of work in the first place.

I looked down at the drawing in front of me. It was incredibly realistic, and I had to swallow a laugh the moment I first saw it. Dylan had always been good at anything he did.

"Well." I stood. Dylan and Mrs. Griffin rose too. "I see why Benny and his parents are upset about this. But Benny has been bullying Dylan and others for years. So this kinda looks like a cry for help from Dylan's end. To survive Benny's bullying. Is Benny's bullying getting addressed by the teachers and his parents?"

Mrs. Griffin's mouth tightened. "We ... are working with the family. But that's not the issue here. Today we asked you to come because of Dylan's drawing."

I was about to give her my two cents, when Mrs. Griffin added quickly, "Two wrongs don't make a right. And it's important we teach our kids that."

I sighed. She had a point there. And arguing more about this didn't help Dylan.

"Well, we have to go now. But Dylan will apologize to Benny. Right, Dylan?"

Dylan's whole posture tensed in defiance. Mrs. Griffin noticed and crossed her arms in response.

"Right ... Dylan?" I pressed.

Finally, Dylan rolled his eyes and exhaled. A teen's way of saying, *Fine, I give in, but under protest.*

"That will be the right thing to do, Dylan," Mrs. Griffin said.

"Thank you, Mrs. Griffin," I said, and we left.

We walked past lockers and more art and didn't speak until we were in the car.

"Why the hell do I have to apologize to him?" he snapped the moment the doors closed. "This is bullshit, Mom."

"Is it?" I couldn't keep my annoyance hidden any longer. Mrs. Griffin scolding us both kinda triggered the trauma of the few nasty teachers who tried to get me to quit school back then. Then Brian and the weekend also kept running through my head. We were supposed to leave for Zach and Amanda's lake house tomorrow. But if Dylan decided to throw a big teenage tantrum, I would have to cancel the trip. There was no way I would push an angry teenager on my mom.

"Yes, it's bullshit," Dylan insisted. His blue eyes were steady on mine. "Benny is a bullying asshole. He literally put dog shit in Connor's backpack. And he grabbed Anne's butt last week in the hallway. Like some pedo piece of shit. I can't just sit there and watch. I have to fight back. Make him the prey. Not the predator."

"The teachers can handle Benny," I said.

A sarcastic laugh escaped him. "The teachers? You mean the same teachers who didn't do shit when Ryan was bullied last year and killed himself? Did you all just forget about him already? Where were the teachers then, huh? Where were they when Ryan jumped off the bridge because he couldn't take the bullying anymore?"

I tried to say something rational, but his anger was more than justified. The town had lost Ryan last year to a bullying-related suicide. Despite multiple reports, the bully wasn't removed from the school until after it happened.

After.

And now Benny had taken over as the school bully.

I sighed. Schools just weren't what they used to be. Classrooms were now packed to the brim. Teachers were overwhelmed and underpaid. Parents were working themselves into the ground just to keep the lights on. Too tired to give their kids the attention and guidance they desperately needed.

"You always taught me to hit back," Dylan said. "Never hit first, but when a punch comes, you hit back hard or you become the target."

"But Benny didn't attack."

"Oh ... so you want me to be a coward? Someone who just watches *others* get bullied?"

I glanced in the rearview mirror. I looked so tired. Burned out. My brown hair hadn't been washed in who knew how long, and I had dark circles under my eyes. My brown eyes just stared back at me, dull. New wrinkles deepened on my forehead. My T-shirt and leggings looked more like a jogging outfit than real clothes. I had lost weight too. I'd always looked so young and was full of laughs. But now it seemed so long ago since people last asked if Dylan and I were siblings. There actually had been a time when people shook their heads in flattering shock when I said he was my son.

It felt like I was failing on all fronts.

A strained marriage.

A teenager fighting the world.

An eight-year-old with a million hobbies and a toddler who sucked the life out of me like a vampire.

Still, I loved them. So much.

My hand found Dylan's. "You're right. I'm sorry. You don't have to apologize to Benny. I'll handle Mrs. Griffin. But please try to talk to the teachers first when you see Benny bullying someone. All these shootings— The times we live in aren't safe. And your teachers are trying their best. But I got your back. I always do."

Dylan's eyes softened. He looked like he finally felt seen again.

"Thanks, Mom," he said.

Our family wasn't perfect, but we all tried our best.

"Let's go," I said. "Grandma is coming over tonight."

"I thought you weren't leaving for the lake house until tomorrow."

"I'm not. I'll leave tomorrow after work and carpool with Zach. But Grandma will keep Ethan home from daycare tomorrow because of his cough. She's staying the night to make things less stressful in the morning."

He offered a bored nod.

"You going to behave?" I asked. "Otherwise, I'll cancel the trip and—"

"Nah, you go. Dad really needs it."

I reached up and tucked a strand of his hair behind his ear. Kids were smart. Too smart sometimes. Especially Dylan, who was able to pick up on his dad's bad moods like certain animals that went still before an earthquake. Brian did indeed need the kid-free weekend. He had much less tolerance for stress than I did. And lately he looked so lost in life. Every evening, the moment he came back home from his HVAC business, the responsibilities of being a dad rolled over him like a bulldozer.

"Can you help Grandma with the little terrorists?" I joked. The younger kids listened to Dylan more than to us. His teenage sass kept Ethan and Lila in check.

Dylan grinned. "You make it sound like Grandma is some old lady with a cane. She doesn't need anyone's help. All Viking warrior woman 'n' shit."

I laughed. "That's true. But you know she has high blood pressure."

"Don't worry. I'll keep the little monsters in line."

I started the car.

"*If* you take me to Dairy Queen," he added.

"Deal. But we have to get rid of all the evidence before we go home."

He grinned. "Deal."

I sat there staring at him for a second. Dylan grew serious again.

"What?" he asked.

A fond, almost sad smile formed on my lips. "You know I'd do anything for you, right?"

He didn't smile back. Just nodded.

2

LACEY

The high-pitched screams from upstairs made my head hurt. From the street, someone probably would've thought a kid was being murdered. But it was just Brian, losing the bedtime diaper battle against an out-of-control toddler.

"No diaper!" Ethan wailed.

"Yes, you need a diaper at night." Brian was done. This fight had lined up right after the previous battles over brushing teeth and getting into pajamas.

"No diaper! Dada bad!"

I put a hot dog in the microwave.

Lila sat on the living room sofa watching a movie. Somehow she was hungry again after dinner. She wore her brown hair in a braid. A friendship bracelet was wrapped around her wrist.

"Maaamaaaa!" Ethan screamed, demanding I take his side in the diaper scandal. Dylan, of course, hadn't moved from his room.

I rushed up the narrow stairs and found Brian one second from losing it. He'd worked a ten-hour shift fixing people's ACs today. Then, the second he got home, his kid shift started.

When I reached the bedroom, Ethan balled his fist and swung at his dad.

"Ethan, no hit," I said and gently grabbed his wrist.

"I'll get a book to read." Brian hurried off.

"Mom!" Lila hollered from downstairs. "I'm still hungry!"

I could barely hear her over Ethan's shrieking.

"The hot dog is in the microwave!" I called.

"What?" she shouted back.

"The hot dog—"

"I got her!" my mom's voice boomed from the kitchen. Thank God. She must have just gotten here.

Brian came back from Lila's room carrying a stack of books.

"No book!" Ethan still howled. "No sleep!"

"These are Lila's special books," Brian tried to reason.

Every muscle in Brian's face tensed. He was done for the day. So was I. Exhausted.

"Damn it, Ethan!" Dylan yelled from down the hall. "Stop this toddler shit! I have to study for a test!" His door slammed so hard the pictures on the wall rattled.

And just like that, Ethan went silent.

Of course. The teenager accomplished in seconds what Brian and I had been failing at all evening.

Brian and I exchanged wide-eyed looks.

"Not exactly what the gentle-parenting book recommends, is it?" I said with a grin.

Brian grinned back. "No, but I'll fucking take it."

"You're terrible." I gave his arm a light smack. "Here." I grabbed the books from his hands. "Go take a shower. Relax. I got this."

"You sure? I can read with—"

"I said I got this."

I was just as wiped as he was. I'd worked all day at the pharmacy and gotten yelled at by a patient over a flagged pain-meds refill. Then I had to deal with the Benny drama at Dylan's school. But I had a higher threshold for stress than Brian.

"God, I need that shower," Brian muttered, heading for the master bath.

I scooped up Ethan, carried him to his room, put on that diaper, planted a kiss on his cheek, and crawled into his crib with him to read to him. I didn't make it two pages before he was out. His breaths fell into a slow, even rhythm, his curls plastered to his forehead with sweat. His cheeks still glowed red from his tantrum.

I played with his curls. These kids were killing me. But I loved them so freaking much it hurt in my chest. Literally. I always felt like a bad mom. For every time I'd yelled. For the small 1,300-square-foot house I had to offer. And the burned-out mom living in it.

I kissed Ethan and climbed out. In the hall, I ran into my mom, Lila curled in her arms.

My mom was the total opposite of what a grandma would look like in a Hallmark movie. She was only in her late forties, had shoulder-length brown hair, and didn't have a single gray hair yet. She was wearing skinny jeans and a striped sweater. She was attractive, and honestly, my two oldest could've passed for hers. Just like me, she became a mom very young. But while I got pregnant by accident in a teenage relationship with my now-husband Brian, my mom's pregnancy at seventeen was a bit of a mystery. I never knew my dad, and my mom always refused to talk about what happened back then. Knowing she would never keep a child from a father who offered more good than harm, I never pushed her for answers. In some ways, I admired her. Like me, she finished school and even went on to become a teacher. And, by God, she was good at it. All heart and fighting for her kids. In some ways, that's all she ever did. Fight for kids others gave up on.

"We're brushing teeth, then I'll tell her the rest of our bedtime story," my mom said.

"I can take over, Mom," I offered.

"No!" Lila protested. "I want Grandma to tell the story."

"Because you don't include any romance between a knight and a princess," my mom explained to me.

"Ah," I said. "That's probably because she's eight."

My mom smiled and rolled her blue eyes. Lately, they'd lost some of their spark. They looked tired. I didn't know if it was due to work or the high blood pressure that plagued the women in our family like a curse.

"They fall in love and hold hands in my story, Lacey," my mom scolded me. "So go ahead and call CPS on me."

With that, she left, Lila happily stomping after her to the small guest bathroom.

I watched them until they were out of sight. Then I walked into the master bath. Steam clung to the mirror. Brian stood in the shower. The water ran over his broad, muscular shoulders and down his back. He had the kind of body you only saw in movies.

I peeled off my clothes and stepped into the shower.

"Ah, that feels good," I said as the water slid down my body.

"Mmmmm," he groaned, eyes closed, soaking in the kid-free moment.

"We're about to have two kid-free nights," I said, hugging him. I loved this man just as much as I did all those years ago when we were barely older than Dylan.

"Heavenly," he muttered.

I pressed my bony body against his steel-hard chest. I'd lost weight lately, but not on purpose.

When I trailed my fingers down and wrapped my hands around him, I hoped for the old life. The fiery desire we used to have for each other.

I kissed him, trying to wake some of that with gentle strokes, but he got out of the shower.

"I'm tired," he said.

I watched as he toweled off. It had been ten months since we'd been intimate. And that felt long, even for tired married folks.

"But I'll give you a massage when you come to bed," he offered, pulling on pajama pants.

"Sounds amazing."

But I knew he'd be asleep by the time I got there. I still had laundry to fold and a bag to pack for the trip tomorrow.

"Are you all packed?" I asked.

"Gosh, I kind of forgot. Can you throw a few things into your bag for me?"

"Sure!" I called after him. "Hope it's warm enough to swim in the lake."

"If not, the indoor pool is heated."

"Yeah," I murmured. "The heated indoor pool."

Zach was loaded, and Amanda, my best friend since kindergarten, had the kind of life Zach loved: no kids, money, freedom. Amanda always wanted kids, but Zach didn't. And with her conflict-avoiding nature, that was that.

I stepped out of the shower, wrapped a towel around me, and crossed into the bedroom. Brian had turned the TV on but was already dozing off. The clock read 8:21.

I would also pass out on that bed the moment I lay down.

This was our life.

Some would call it pathetic. But to me it was everything.

My family and Amanda meant everything to me.

Everything.

3

LACEY

My mom was curled up on the couch under a blanket, watching TV. The room was dim except for the soft glow of the screen. I dropped next to her.

"Couldn't sleep, sweetheart?" she asked.

As if on cue, Ginny, the 140-pound female Doberman two houses down, started barking. She was the sweetest and kindest dog. Gentle with the kids and patient. Her occasional bark never bothered us, and the kids loved her. But most of the other neighbors didn't see it that way. She was one of the biggest Dobermans I'd ever seen. People judged her by her size, not her heart. And they constantly complained about her occasional barks. Treating her like a monster.

"Did Ginny wake you up?"

I shook my head. "No. Poor Ginny didn't do anything ..."

She lifted the blanket and pulled it over my legs. I tucked myself in.

"You're still picking up Zach after work tomorrow?" she asked.

I nodded.

She made that familiar "Hmm" sound of disapproval.

I looked at her. "What?"

"Make sure your car is spotless. No toys or crumbs. You know how he is."

"Well, that's his problem." I reached for the remote next to her. "He's the one who wants to save on gas and carpool. His office is right down the street from my pharmacy."

"He could've picked you up instead. Why do you have to get him and use your car? I mean, he's the one with trust funds and the fancy lake house." Mom shook her head. "Rich people are so stingy, it's unbelievable."

"We're staying at their place for free, Mom."

"Are you sure he's not going to ask you to chip in for electricity or sewage?"

I laughed. "Stop it."

"I really don't get how someone as sweet as Amanda married a man like him. He's a narcissist." She snatched the remote out of my hand. "Don't change my show if you're just going to fall asleep in five minutes. Remember that horror movie with the doll you put on last time? I was terrified but too invested to turn it off."

I grinned and leaned into her. She wrapped her arm around me like I was still a little kid.

"There are a lot of things that don't make sense when it comes to why we chose the people we do," I said. "But at least Zach is the only son of a big real-estate developer. No bills, trips to Europe, lake houses, boats, weekly massages. Amanda dries her tears wearing Prada in first class."

She frowned. "Well. When you put it like that …"

We went quiet. Her crime movie played in the background with dramatic music and cheesy suspense. I already knew the twist from watching two minutes of it. For a moment, I thought about blurting it out like I used to as a teenager when I wanted her to change the channel. Instead, I snuggled in closer.

My mom had me at a time when being a single mom was even shittier than it was today. She turned out all right. But, deep down, I always wondered if I was the reason she never fulfilled her dream of traveling the world. And when I got pregnant so young, I couldn't help but feel I'd let her down. Like she was hoping I would live my life to the fullest before settling down. For both of us. And here I was. A former teen mom with my firstborn and a strained marriage.

"Will you please try to have fun?" my mom asked. "And stop worrying so much about Brian?"

My eyelids felt heavy. I nodded.

"You deserve this more than he does," she said. "You always take care of everybody else and never do anything for yourself. And you look like you've lost weight aga—"

"I love you, Mom," I mumbled.

"I love you too, sweetheart."

Just like that, I started to nod off, knowing she'd wake me later after her movie was done and walk me to my room, just like she used to when I was little.

4

NICOLE

The night was giving way to a colorful morning sky.

Lacey had an early shift, so I got up to see her off while the rest of the house was still asleep.

I hugged her, kissed her cheek, and watched her walk down the driveway to her car.

She opened the car door and set her bag for the lake retreat on the passenger seat. Then she turned and smiled at me. For a moment, she just stood there, looking at me.

Then she gave a little wave and left.

I watched until she was gone, like I always did. Even when she was a child, I stood in the doorway and waited until the bus turned the corner. It was my way of saying, "I'm here."

Back inside, I made breakfast for the kids and Brian.

I grabbed eggs from the fridge and my thoughts drifted.

Brian would drive straight to the lake house in his work van so he wouldn't have to come back home. It made sense, but it was also kind of strange that he never wanted to drive up there with his wife.

Their marriage had been rough lately. Not because of money, or affairs, or the usual fights about kids. Lacey and Brian agreed on most things.

It was the marriage itself that weighed them down.

Brian wasn't the worst husband out there. And he was a decent father. But he was never strong emotionally. His moods were a roller coaster, and he was quite self-centered. Even as a child, when things hadn't gone his way, he threw huge tantrums and emotionally blackmailed people. Everything always had to revolve around him. He needed to be cherished, admired, and cradled like a toddler, or he would completely fall apart.

The girls didn't seem to mind. At six foot four, with a natural build like Superman, he'd win bar fights and have all eyes on him no matter what room he entered. And with that Hollywood face and that charm, the girls lined up and fought over him. Cherished the ground he walked on. Including Lacey and Amanda.

But it was Lacey who ended up with him when she got pregnant with Dylan at sixteen. She swore it was an accident and that the condom broke. But she wouldn't have been in this position in the first place if she hadn't let Brian pressure her to move things so fast, always worried he might break things off if she didn't make him happy.

Lacey still finished school and became a pharmacist. Brian, on the other hand, dropped out. Took an apprenticeship with an HVAC company.

I always wondered if this was the life he would have chosen if it weren't for Dylan.

Lacey was so happy when she got pregnant. But Brian always looked like he regretted having Dylan and only married Lacey because of his deeply religious parents.

I sighed.

Like every parent, I worried too much.

I worried when Lacey called too often or not enough. When she put on too much weight or lost too much. When she came home from a party too early or stayed out late. When she was trying too hard or when she'd given up.

I shook my head.

She'd be fine.

Lacey would find a way. That kind heart of hers was as strong as a lion's.

She would be fine.
She always was.

5

NICOLE

Ethan was home with me all day because of his cough. But Lila had to be picked up from her after-school science class at the town's recreation center, so Ethan had to come with me.

After that, I got Dylan from the mall. He'd wanted to check out shoes with his friends.

Of course, the kids didn't let me just get Dylan. Not when the mall had a candy store.

And, of course, they got their way. Three against one. I was a very young grandma, but a grandma after all; it was my job to spoil them. Each walked out with a bag of candy from the gummy bear bar.

Then we went back home, and I ordered pizza. Another pushover move, since I had planned to cook a veggie risotto. But they were so convincing, especially when they all fought for the same cause.

And, to top things off, they talked me into buying the new *Minions* movie even though I'd said no screen time today. Convincing Grandma of anything was their superpower.

But the house was a bit chaotic, so at least the movie gave me time to do laundry.

The kids sat on the couch, eating pizza for dinner and watching the movie.

I grabbed the laundry from upstairs and headed for the basement, peeking in on the kids on the way. Their eyes were glued to the screen. Even Dylan's.

The basement was colder and darker than the rest of the house. I set the basket on the dryer and accidentally clipped a candle off the shelf. The thing shattered across the concrete floor.

"Damn it."

I bent down and collected the glass pieces, careful not to cut myself. A large piece had somehow landed behind the dryer, glinting in the light. Then something else caught the light behind the dryer.

A vise squeezed my heart.

A glass bottle.

I stretched for it and pulled it out. It was a thin bottle of whiskey.

"I heard a noise." Dylan's voice came from behind me.

I turned, still holding the bottle. He noticed it before I could hide it.

"What's the date on it?" he asked, unfazed.

It took me a second to catch up. "Oh. Umm. Let me see." I squinted at the label. "The stamp says the bottle is ten years old."

He nodded. "Then it's an old one."

I looked at Dylan in a mix of admiration and sadness.

Admiration for how mature he was. Standing there like that. Calm and composed. So mature.

Sadness because that bottle was a reminder of darker times.

When Brian's parents died in their sleep from a carbon monoxide leak, it shattered the family. Brian fell into drinking, unable to cope with the loss.

It was Lacey, as always, who held everyone together and helped him through it.

"I'll throw it away," I said.

Dylan nodded again. "I better get back to Ethan and Lila."

He turned and headed back upstairs. I followed on his heels and tossed the bottle into the kitchen trash just as the phone rang.

Brian.

As if he knew we'd just been talking about him.

"Hello?" I answered.

"Hey, it's me. Did you talk to Lacey?"

I checked the clock on the kitchen wall: 7:01.

"Yes, she called me when she was finishing up her shift to check in on the kids. Is everything all right up there?"

"Yeah ... just ... just wanted to see how you guys are doing."

His tone wasn't alarming or overly sweet. Just neutral.

"We're good. Let me get the kids on the phone—"

"No, no. I'll talk to them later. Amanda ... she needs my help with something."

"Oh, okay."

"Talk soon."

"Okay. Bye."

I hung up and glanced toward the living room. The kids were still glued to the screen. Then I armed myself with a broom and dustpan and headed back downstairs to finish cleaning up the glass.

6

NICOLE

That standard cell ringtone, the kind half the world used, jolted me out of sleep. I sat straight up, disoriented.

It took a moment to remember where I was. My eyes adjusted slowly to the dark, and Lacey and Brian's bedroom came into view. The old TV mounted on the wall across from me. The cramped space, which that large wooden dresser filled—the one I bought them for their anniversary.

Early morning light came in through the window.

I reached for my cell, almost knocking over my water glass. I blinked at the screen.

Unknown number. It was 5:31.

My heart instantly started racing.

Nobody ever called me from an unknown number at 5:31 a.m.

"H-hello?"

"Are you Nicole Kolter?" a young man's voice came from the other end of the line.

"Yes. Who is this?"

"Ms. Kolter, my name is Officer James Nolan. I'm with the New Hampshire State Police. I'm calling regarding your daughter, Lacey Alderwyn."

I froze as cold terror struck me.

"Let me first say that Lacey is alive."

I gasped in relief. My child was alive. I would be able to keep living.

"She's currently receiving medical attention for a head injury. She's conscious but in shock."

"What … what happened?"

"She was found earlier this morning near Lake Seekonk. A man—Zachary Nabb—was found near the scene as well … deceased."

"De-wh-what?"

My hand shot to my throat. It was tightening quickly, making it hard to breathe or speak.

"Your daughter was found close to Mr. Nabb. Disoriented and injured. An ambulance transported her to North Pines Community Hospital in Cold Hollow. She's stable."

A strange silence seeped in. As if I was still sleeping and all this was just a terrible nightmare.

Only, it wasn't.

"Ma'am?"

"Y-yes, sorry. Umm … can I talk to Lacey, please?"

"She's currently being evaluated and isn't speaking much."

"But she's okay? What happened?"

"Yes. She's okay. But it would be better if you came up here so we can talk in person."

"I'm leaving right now."

"Thank you. If you need anything, please call me at this number. My name is Detective Nolan."

I cut off the call, already scrambling for my clothes. I felt physically sick. Like I might have a panic attack at any moment.

This couldn't be real. Zach dead? Lacey hurt?

"But how?" I said out loud.

My hands were now trembling so badly, I dropped my pants twice. But somehow I managed to dress quickly. Then I rushed down the hallway and tore open Dylan's door. He shot upright in bed with wide eyes.

"What's wrong?" he asked.

"We need to go," I said. "Your mom was in … there was … an accident. We have to get to her now."

"An accident?" His face paled.

"She's okay," I said fast. "But we have to leave right now."

He jumped out of bed. "I'll get Ethan."

"I'll wake Lila."

I stepped into the hallway, dialing Brian. No answer. I dialed again. No answer.

Where the hell was he? With her? At the hospital? Why didn't he call me?

I called Amanda. Busy signal.

My head spun. Zach was dead. But how? What the hell happened? What did all this even mean?

Lila was in her room. Her night-light glowed red against her face. I touched her shoulder and steadied my shaking hand as much as I could.

"Sweetheart, wake up."

"Mmm … what?" Her eyes blinked open.

"We have to go, honey. Your mom is in the hospital."

She bolted upright. "What? Is she okay?"

"She's fine," I said, even if I didn't fully believe it. "But we need to go see her."

She nodded hard and jumped out of bed.

In the hallway, Ethan was crying, calling for me.

Everything felt so unreal. Like I was wide awake but trapped in a nightmare.

My daughter was found injured in the woods.

Zach was dead.

I didn't understand yet what the hell was going on. But I had no doubt it was bad. Alarms weren't just going off. They were exploding.

Something horrible was happening. I didn't have all the details yet. But it was something that would change our lives forever.

Somehow, I just knew.

7

NICOLE

The lights buzzed in a cold white glow as the kids and I entered the hospital's ER. Sliding doors kept opening as nurses and doctors rushed into different rooms. Monitors beeped behind curtains. It reeked of antiseptic. People sat slumped in stiff chairs in the ER waiting area. Unmoving. Eyes blank and faces heavy with worry.

Brian and Amanda were among them.

He was wearing his khakis and shirt with his HVAC logo on it. The same clothes he'd left in yesterday morning for work. Dark circles had formed under his eyes, and his hair was unkempt.

Amanda looked wrecked. Her hands cradled her head, elbows propped on her knees, tears carving shimmering trails down her puffy face. She wore her favorite pink summer dress. The kind meant for something good. Not this.

"Dad!" Lila shouted and bolted toward him, followed by Dylan.

Brian's head snapped up, and he caught both kids in a crushing hug. He buried his face in their shoulders. The kids held on tight. Then they let go of Brian and wrapped Amanda in a tight embrace. The kids had always been so close to her. Amanda had practically raised them alongside Lacey and me.

Ethan shifted in my arms. Wide-eyed. Confused. Too young to make sense of all this, but old enough to know something was wrong. He stretched his arms toward Amanda. Of all people, he reached for her—another sign of these kids' love for her.

She grabbed him without a word, hugging him like he was the only thing keeping her from falling apart. Her lips pressed against his golden curls for a kiss.

"Where is Lacey?" My voice cracked. "How is she?"

"She's fine," Brian said weakly. "She has a head injury. Nothing serious, but they're running more tests just in case. She's in room 12, down the hall."

Relief hit so hard, it almost brought me to my knees. My lungs finally remembered how to breathe, and the invisible corset wrapped tight around my ribs finally loosened.

"And Zach?" I asked. The words came quietly. Carefully.

Amanda handed Ethan to Brian. Their eyes met for only a heartbeat before she looked away. Her tears poured, with no stopping them. I stepped in and wrapped my arms around her. A motherly hug. Fierce. Familiar. I'd known this girl nearly as long as I'd known my own daughter. And after the grandmother who raised her had passed, we and Zach were all the family she had.

She sobbed into my shoulder. Her body shook with every breath.

As I held her, my gaze drifted down the hall to room 12. A doctor was speaking to a detective in a suit. Both turned at the same time, their eyes finding mine across the corridor.

The detective was in his mid-twenties, with a gun holstered at his hip and a gold badge clipped to his belt. He was tall and athletic, with dark hair and hazel eyes, not handsome but not unattractive. He was quite young to be a detective, so he was probably extremely ambitious or incredibly good at what he did.

The doctor beside him was tall and thin, his face mostly hidden behind a surgical mask.

"What happened?" Dylan asked before I could.

Amanda took a step back. Her eyes stayed fixed on the floor.

"We don't know," Brian muttered, slowly shaking his head. His voice cracked again. "We … don't know."

Then his eyes locked onto mine.

This wasn't a conversation to have in front of the kids.

The police officer walked over.

"I'm sorry for interrupting you," he said. "I'm Officer James Nolan with the New Hampshire State Police Major Crime Unit. I think we spoke on the phone?"

I gave a small nod. "Major Crime Unit?" That part he hadn't mentioned earlier.

"Would it be all right if I ask you a few questions?"

I stared at him, trying to make sense of what the hell was going on.

"Come on, kids," Brian said. "Let's see if the cafeteria has some muffins and hot chocolate."

Lila slipped her hand into his. He hoisted Ethan, but after a few steps turned around and looked back at us. Dylan hadn't left my side.

"Dylan ... come on," Brian said.

Dylan glanced at his dad but didn't budge. His eyes met mine.

"Go," I told him. "I'll talk to the police. Then I'll get you to see your mom as soon as I can."

He held my gaze for a long moment, lips parting like he might protest, but then he turned and followed Brian down the hallway.

"There's an empty room over there where we can talk," Detective Nolan said, nodding toward an ER bay with glass doors.

But I didn't move.

"I want to see my daughter first," I insisted.

He paused. "I understand this is incredibly hard. But I promise you she's stable. They're just running a few more tests."

I thought about fighting him over this. But then Amanda and I followed.

We stepped into a small ER exam room with a hospital bed and machines everywhere.

He closed the glass door behind Amanda and me, then pulled the curtain closed.

"Again, I'm so sorry for what you're all going through," he said.

Amanda's face twisted, and tears poured out again. I placed my hand gently on her back, stroking it up and down in slow passes.

"This is something nobody should ever have to go through," the detective said softly, shaking his head.

"What happened?" My voice trembled. "None of this makes any sense."

His eyes bounced from Amanda to me. "Your daughter and Zach Nabb went missing last night."

"Last night?" I blinked. "Why didn't anyone call me?"

"Brian tried," Amanda mumbled through trembling lips.

I remembered his call. And the way he didn't want to speak to the kids. But it wasn't unusual for Brian to ignore the kids when he didn't feel like being a parent.

"We didn't want to worry you," she added. "We thought maybe they hit traffic. Or stopped to get snacks and drinks for the weekend. Something normal. Something harmless. Not … this."

Her voice shook on the last word.

"So what happened?" I asked as my jaw tightened.

"We're still working on the details," Nolan said. "But Mr. Nabb's car was found on a private dirt road this morning. The owner of the property said his dog had been nervous early in the morning, and when he let his dog out, it ran off barking. He followed the dog, found the car, and called the police." He paused for a moment. "Mr. Nabb was found murdered in the driver's seat."

The walls felt too close, and my ribs too tight.

"M-murdered?" The word stuttered out of me as Amanda put her face in her hands.

Nolan nodded. "Stabbed. Your daughter was found unconscious in the woods nearby. She had a head injury and was covered in blood from head to toe."

The room swayed. I couldn't breathe. My arms clamped around Amanda again, but this time to support both of us.

"I'm … so sorry," I whispered. "How unthinkable. Poor Zach." My words came out fast and raw. "Did you find who did this?"

"Not yet," Nolan said.

"Not yet?" My voice rose. "Somebody killed—" I choked. Swallowed hard. "Killed Zach. And tried to kill my daughter. And the person who did it is still out there? What if he comes back?" My words exploded. "What if he comes after my daughter to finish the job? Or Amanda?"

Detective Nolan stepped forward. Calm and controlled. He placed a hand on my arm like he knew me.

"I swear, we have every available unit out there. We won't stop until we find the person who did this. But, so far, it looks like a violent robbery gone wrong. Both of their wallets are missing. And their wedding bands. Mr. Alderwyn and Amanda confirmed that Lacey and Zach usually wore them. We have no reason to believe anybody will come after your daughter or Amanda. But it would really help us if you could answer a few questions."

I gave a small nod.

"Did Lacey mention anything unusual about the trip? Anyone else coming?"

"No." I shook my head. "All she said was she was carpooling with Zach."

He pulled out a notepad and started scribbling.

"Did they usually ride together?"

"Yes," I confirmed. "To the lake house, at least. Her pharmacy is just down the road from his office."

"Anything strange that morning? When she left?"

"She had an early shift. Grabbed her bag and left. Nothing abnormal."

My throat closed up as a terrible thought entered my mind. What if Lacey had been raped?

"My daughter," I started, but my voice was barely holding. "Has she been—"

I couldn't say it. My body trembled all over. The idea made me want to throw up.

"I need to see her," I demanded. "Now!"

Gently, I eased away from Amanda and stepped toward the door.

"Ms. Kolter, wait," Nolan called after me. "I need to tell you something."

But I was already opening the door.

The hallway blurred. Machines beeped.

I strode past carts and nurses, straight down the hall, and yanked open the door to room 12.

But I wasn't ready for what was waiting inside. My body jerked back as my hand shot up to my neck. "Dear God."

Lacey sat upright on the bed, wearing a hospital gown. A doctor stood over her, shining a light into her eyes. Two nurses flanked him.

I almost didn't recognize her.

Her hair was soaked in dried blood. Matted. Tangled with dirt and leaves. Thick blood streaks ran down her neck and across her temple like Viking war paint. Her face and arms looked like someone had tried to wipe her clean with a wet napkin and given up halfway. Just smears of pink and red everywhere.

The bandage on her forehead was already smudged with red too.

Her eyes met mine. Brown, blank, dull. Nothing behind them.

"Sweetheart!" My voice fell apart. Tears burst out of me as I crossed the room in two desperate strides and grabbed her. Held her. Pressed her to my chest so tight that nothing could tear her away again.

Not even the nurse who latched onto my arm.

"Ma'am, you can't be in here right now." Her voice was sharp and demanding.

I didn't move.

The other nurse came at me from the side. Hands on my other arm.

"You need to wait outside," she said, yanking at me.

"Get off me," I growled.

They yanked harder.

"Ma'am. Let go."

"No."

"I said let go."

"No!"

"Stop it," the doctor cut in. His voice was firm. "It's okay. Leave her be."

The nurses hesitated. Then released me.

I let go of Lacey just enough to cradle her face in my hands.

"Lacey. What happened?"

Her eyes didn't move. She stared straight past me.

"Lacey. Look at me."

Nothing.

"Sweetheart, please. Look at me."

Slowly, her gaze lifted. Met mine. But it wasn't her. Not really. Those eyes were empty. Dead.

Tears slid down my cheeks, as hot as fire.

"Sweetie, what happened? You can tell me."

But no words left her lips.

"What's wrong with her?" I asked, turning to the doctor.

"She took a blow to the head," the doctor explained. "Her CT scan shows no cracks or swelling. She was lucky."

I turned back to her.

"Then why can't she speak?"

"It's likely shock," he answered. "She hasn't said a word since she regained consciousness at the hospital. Medically, she's stable. But we'll keep her overnight for observation, just in case. Give her a bit more time. She should be examined by a psychiatrist as soon as possible."

I nodded slowly. Pulled her close again.

"It's okay, sweetheart. Mama's here. I'm here now."

Another tear slipped down my cheek. But this time I wiped it away and straightened. Calmed myself.

I needed to be strong for her.

"You'll be okay," I whispered. "Whatever happened, we'll figure it out. And you'll be okay."

8

NICOLE

The psychiatrist's office was a dim room with one of those glowing salt lamps in the corner. Probably to avoid overstimulating patients. The scent of lavender drifted from a nearby diffuser. Outside the door, a white-noise machine played a loop of ocean waves. Gentle and steady.

Dr. Sanchez was young for a psychiatrist but came highly recommended. And the way he spoke to us left no doubt that he cared. He sat behind his desk in black pants and a crisp white shirt. Lacey and I sat across from him on a small couch. Brian was watching the kids but, of course, avoided dealing with a therapy session, as he thought mental health professionals were a waste of time and money.

"Lacey," he said in a soft voice and leaned forward. "I know things have been so hard for you. And I know you went through something very, very terrible. But you're safe here. Can you try to look at me?"

She lifted her head slightly, but her gaze stayed fixed on the floor.

"Pumpkin, please try." I put my hand on top of hers. Her skin was warm, reminding me that she was still alive. "Try to look at Dr. Sanchez. He's trying to help us."

Lacey didn't move.

"It's okay," Dr. Sanchez finally said. I had no doubt he could sense my anxiety. "She's not doing this to upset anyone. This isn't stubbornness. What she's experiencing is called Functional Neurological Symptom Disorder. The body shows real, physical symptoms. In Lacey's case, her main symptom is loss of speech, but there's no damage to her brain or nerves. And the symptom appears as a response to overwhelming trauma. It's her answer to the terrible things that happened to her that night."

He let that sink in before continuing. "The brain essentially shuts off a function, like speaking, to protect itself. It's similar to when a circuit breaker trips to stop an overload. The system goes dark on purpose. With time, therapy, and a sense of safety, that function usually returns."

"And you're sure it's not permanent?" I asked. I tried to sound strong, but my voice trembled. It'd been a week since the incident. And that week had been brutal. The kids cried every day, wanting their mom instead of the silent body that stared out at nowhere. She was using the bathroom by herself—in silence like a robot. Other than that, I had to dress and feed her. Brian couldn't handle any of that emotionally, as if he were the victim.

"How long will it take for her to speak again?" I asked.

"It's hard to say. Some begin speaking again after a few days, especially if they feel safe. Moderate cases can take several weeks. And in more severe cases, where the trauma hit really hard and there is a case of PTSD, it could take months. Sometimes even a year or more. It really depends on the individual. And, of course, the support system."

I let that sink in while Dr. Sanchez pulled a set of headphones from his desk drawer.

"May I?" he asked, gesturing toward Lacey.

I nodded.

He rose slowly and approached her. "This won't hurt, Lacey. It's just calming music." She didn't flinch. Didn't blink. Not even when he placed the headset on her ears and stepped back to his chair.

"Did the police tell you any more details about what happened?" he asked. "It's important for therapy."

I tried to remember. My mind went foggy again, like it always did when I tried to put this horror show all together. "Not really. They said she was found unconscious, in a pool of blood. Not far from the car where Zach was murdered. He was stabbed. But we don't know if she saw it all. Or if she ran. Maybe she tripped. Hit her head on a rock."

"Did her injury match that explanation? A rock to the head?"

"Yes. But they haven't found the rock yet. So it's also possible the attacker hit her. And while he focused on Zach, she ran and—" My voice cut off mid-sentence.

Dr. Sanchez pushed his chair closer. Raised his hand halfway toward my arm. "May I?"

I gave a small nod.

His hand settled gently on my forearm. Something about this grounding gesture gave me just enough strength to continue.

"She was able to save herself. Somehow. We don't know much else." My eyes blurred. Tears again. I pushed them down. Crying wouldn't help her. I needed to be strong.

"So we don't know if she fought back and ran? Or if she watched her friend get murdered?" Dr. Sanchez asked.

I shrugged. "Only God knows." Or the devil, I thought. The silence that followed felt suffocating.

"How's the family holding up?" he asked.

"Not good."

"And you?"

"Oh, I'm fine."

His brow lifted.

I exhaled. "Struggling," I corrected.

"You know, you're allowed to be a normal human being too," he said. "You're allowed to struggle. To cry. To stay awake at night and spiral. And to come in here, talk it through, work through it with me. There's no shame in needing help. And there are medications too."

A faint smile tugged at my mouth. First one all week. "That's very kind. But I can't afford to be a normal human being right now."

He tilted his head. "What else would you be?"

I reached over and gave Lacey's hand a soft squeeze.

"A mother."

That got me a nod. And a smile. He removed the headphones from

Lacey's ears and placed them back on the desk. Then he scribbled something onto a pad.

"This is a psychological referral for the kids," he said, handing me the paper. "They should have someone to talk to. Learn how to cope. It'll help them, especially in the long term."

I took it. "Yes. Good idea. Thank you."

"I'm also calling in a scrip for an antidepressant and something for sleep. For Lacey. She needs to rest. I want to see her at least once a week. And if she starts talking again, call me immediately."

"I will. Thank you."

We both stood. Lacey didn't. I gave her a gentle pull. Like guiding a sleepwalker. Reminding her it was time to move. She stood slowly. Moved stiffly, arm hooked into mine.

I led her toward the door. "And if you ever need to talk"—Dr. Sanchez's voice was low again, steady, as he looked me in the eyes—"you can call me."

I gave him a tired smile. "Thank you for everything, Dr. Sanchez."

"Oh—and one more thing."

I paused in the doorway.

"The police are asking for your signature regarding our sessions. So they can get copies. And they're requesting access to all therapy notes moving forward. We call it a HIPAA release form."

"I can sign it for you now if you want."

He shook his head. "Let's wait. The police's interests aren't always the same as the patient's best interests."

My forehead furrowed. "What do you mean?"

"My notes can easily be misread. So let's hold off. We can talk about it more next week."

I stared at him, not sure I fully understood. But then I nodded. "Sure. Thank you."

9

NICOLE

I was driving in silence with Lacey. I wasn't silent on purpose. I was just so exhausted. But then I remembered what Dr. Sanchez said at the beginning of the session: try to talk to her as much as possible.

We turned onto Route 1 toward Peabody, and the colorful signs of shops zipped by.

"Oh, look, there's Dairy Queen," I said. "I think the kids deserve a treat, no?"

I smiled and glanced at Lacey, but she just stared out the window.

We hit the drive-through, and I ordered like a madwoman. Milkshakes, sundaes, fries. Chocolate. Vanilla. Whatever I saw on the menu.

"We're having a big party," I told the teenager at the window. She handed me the paper bags with a shy grin.

I put everything on Lacey's lap, then placed her arms around the bags so they wouldn't fall off.

Keep her body engaged. Keep her present. That's what the doctor had said. The more engagement, the better.

"Let's celebrate. You're still here with us. It's a miracle."

I paid and took the shortcut home. We passed wetlands, then rows of houses tucked away outside of Peabody.

"What happened was really terrible," I said. "And I probably wouldn't want to talk for a while either if I were you. But you're still here, Lacey. God, or whoever is out there, decided you should be here with your kids. With me."

I slowed at a stop sign, glanced at her again. "You made it through the worst. That night in the woods … that was the worst. But it's over now. You're safe. And we'll move forward together. At your pace."

I didn't let Lacey hear the slightest doubt in my voice. Even if I had it. What if she never spoke again?

I turned onto our street. It was a typical New England neighborhood. Leafy trees lined sidewalks. Old Capes and Colonials mingled with white modern farmhouses with black window frames. Prices had exploded like everywhere else in the country. And our little yellow coastal-style cottage looked like it didn't belong here anymore. Like we were being shamed for staying. For not remodeling. For still being here.

I waved at the Bristols, who were unloading grocery bags from their trunk. Sheryl just stared. No wave back.

Bob gave a tight nod. Nothing else.

Strange.

"What's wrong with them?" I asked Lacey, shaking my head. "I mean, I know rumors spread like wildfire, but that wasn't very kind."

We drove a few more blocks, but then I had to slam the brakes. The food bags tumbled off Lacey's lap and hit the floor with a loud crunch.

"What in the name—" The words slipped out as my hands clenched the steering wheel. Large vans were parked in front of our house, half on the curb, half on the street. One had *Seacoast News* in blocky letters. A camera crew stood beside it. More vans pulled up behind them. Reporters, cameras, mics. Women and men in sleek jackets and styled hair standing on the sidewalk, fixing their makeup, pointing at our house. I turned the car into a neighbor's driveway and pulled out my phone.

Nine missed calls from Brian. Three from Dylan.

I called Brian and backed out fast. I'd take the narrow private road that the trash trucks used behind the homes.

"Where are you?" Brian's voice jumped out at me through the speaker.

"My phone was on silent for the session. The psychiatrist took longer than expected. And we got takeout. We're coming in from the back now."

"You've seen the shit show then?"

"Yes. I have. What's going on?"

"We're becoming famous," Brian said, bitter. "And not in the good way. Talk to no one. Just come straight home."

10

NICOLE

When I got home, Amanda and the kids were sitting at the kitchen table, playing that pirate game—the one where a little pirate jumps out when you stick plastic knives into the barrel. Amanda had been with us every day since the incident. Being a mother to the kids seemed to help her just as much as it helped them. She was born to be the center of a large family but never got that wish fulfilled. Most of her relatives were either dead or avoided because of substance abuse issues. And Zach's family never liked her. They treated their marriage like it was a mistake.

All eyes turned to me when I entered the room with Lacey and the messy Dairy Queen bags.

"How did it go?" Dylan asked.

"Really well," I said, hoping to mask the lie. "The doctor says it's just a response to trauma. She'll be talking again in no time."

The kids exchanged glances. Then Lila jumped up, ran to her mom, and wrapped her little arms around Lacey's waist.

"See, Mom? I told you. You'll be better soon."

Lacey stared over her head at the wall. Not even a blink. The contrast between the two was insane. Life versus death. Lila beaming with light. Lacey's body bony and pale.

I swallowed. Pushed those thoughts aside before the tears came.

Lila didn't seem to notice my struggle and ripped the paper bags from my hands like a wild animal on the hunt. Ethan and Dylan rushed in next, each giving Lacey a tight hug before diving toward the food.

"Careful!" I scolded as one of the bags ripped open. Napkins were scattered on the floor while they bickered over who got what. But they were already halfway to the TV room before I could say more.

Brian walked up from the basement with a laundry basket tucked under one arm. He looked tired.

"Are the blinds down in the TV room?" I asked.

He nodded.

"I'll bring Lacey upstairs to rest for a bit," I said.

Brian and Amanda exchanged glances. Then nodded.

Amanda stepped forward and reached for the laundry basket. "Let me do that."

He held on. "What kind of man do you think I am? I can do laundry."

"Let go. You'll shrink everything."

"No way."

They went back and forth a few more times. It was so familiar. Almost like a married couple. Amanda always had that power over Brian. To soften him. Bring out his humor. As if he could finally breathe when she was in the room. They had gone to preschool together before Lacey met them both in kindergarten. Small-town stuff.

"Fine," she said, finally letting him win. "I'll cut up some fruit and veggies for the kids. They can't just eat ice cream and fries."

Brian headed upstairs. "That'll make you enemy number one," he called out.

"Only until the toys I ordered arrive tomorrow," she called back with a smirk.

"You bought more?" he countered.

"Board games and books!" she shouted, then turned to me and said in a softer tone, "And a few other things."

Amanda walked over, grabbed Lacey's hand, and held it tight. And just like that, the smile disappeared. Her whole face dropped. Grief hit fast.

"I don't know what else to do with the money Zach left me," she said. "Might as well spend it on my family."

I placed my hand on Lacey's back. "I'll take her upstairs and let her rest. I'll feed her in bed. Then we'll deal with whatever's happening out there."

But we all knew what was happening out there. There was nothing to figure out. We had become the big show in town.

Amanda gave a small nod and walked toward the fridge.

On my way to the stairs, I paused beside her and gently brushed a strand of golden hair from her pretty face.

"Sweetie ... we love you."

She didn't turn. Just nodded, eyes fixed on whatever she was doing inside the fridge.

LATER THAT EVENING, I turned on the TV. Lila and Ethan were upstairs, asleep, when Brian walked in from the hallway.

"Did Amanda leave?" I asked.

"Yeah. She'll call after she's done over at Zach's parents."

I nodded. They'd called and insisted she come. Said they needed to talk.

"Is Lacey asleep?"

"If you want to call it that," Brian said, flat. "Staring at the ceiling is more like it."

"She needs rest," I said, annoyed. "Call it what you want."

Brian never had much tolerance for stress. And when he was stressed, he got rude. Sarcastic.

Dylan walked in. His hair stuck up in the back. Dark circles shadowed his eyes.

"Lila crawled into Mom's bed again," he said. "I let her stay this time. Ethan's sleeping in his crib."

"Thank you, sweetie." I flipped the channel to the local news.

"Oh my fucking God," Brian breathed, right as we realized what we were looking at.

It was the front of our house. On live TV ... *live*!

A blond woman stood out front, overly styled, holding a microphone to her mouth. People walked by behind her. Reporters moved like ants, setting up cameras. Flashbulbs burst. Our house was the backdrop. Our home. And we were standing inside it. Watching.

"Why don't they just take a few shots and leave?" Dylan groused.

The volume was still on mute, but we didn't need to hear it. The reporter pointed at our front door.

"Dylan," Brian said in a stiff voice, "why don't you go upstairs and play the new video game Amanda got you? You shouldn't be seeing this."

"Dad," Dylan said calmly, "I'm a teenager with a phone. I can Google all of this shit."

"Language," I scolded him.

Brian glared at him. Then looked at me.

I said nothing. Just reached for the remote and turned on the volume.

The three of us stood there, shoulder to shoulder, the cold TV light glowing on our faces.

"... the murder weapon has still not been found," the anchorwoman said, "but when we inquired about the DNA results, Police Chief Henderson did confirm that the blood found on the female survivor was, in fact, not hers but that of the male victim. Making her one of the prime—"

I clicked off the TV. We'd heard enough.

The room went dark.

No one moved.

"What ..." Brian mumbled. "What is she talking about?"

He sounded like someone sitting on a train headed straight for derailment.

Inside, a tornado raged. My brain was spinning. Questions. Fear. Every thought knotted with panic. But then I remembered Dylan was standing right beside me. So I faked a calm I didn't feel.

I placed a steady hand on his shoulder.

"What does this mean?" Brian yelled, dropping his head into his hands. "Are they saying she killed—"

"It means we need to remain calm. And call a lawyer," I said.

"A lawyer?" Brian echoed, as if the word were foreign.

"Yes, Dad. A lawyer," Dylan said, annoyed. How was he so calm? So strong? "It means they're going to look at Mom as a suspect now," he added. "Have you never seen a crime show?"

"It's all going to be sorted out," I said, making myself believe it. "We have nothing to hide. Nothing will come of any of this nonsense."

Dylan nodded.

I smiled at him, but my mind flashed to that memory. Lacey sitting in room 12, covered in blood. Not hers … Zach's.

It made me sick.

If that was Zach's blood, she must've been right there when it happened. Probably screaming for help. Maybe she tried to help him fight back. But then fled when it was too late. Was she chased? Fell? Hit her head? Or was she struck?

So far, all the police told us was that they were still investigating, but it looked like a robbery gone wrong. To be patient. She wasn't raped. We knew that. And the bruises on her body could have been from a struggle or a fall. So as of now, we didn't know.

"Nicole!" Brian said in a stern tone.

I looked up. He had probably said my name more than once.

"Do you still have Jack Whitman's number?" he asked.

"The lawyer who read Great-grandma's will?" Dylan asked.

And handled your dad's DUIs, I almost said but caught myself.

"Yes," I said instead. "I'll call him right now."

11

NICOLE

It was late and dark outside.

Lila had woken up crying, so Brian read her a story to help her fall back asleep.

I was sitting with Lacey on the couch in the living room, both of us staring at the rolled-down blinds of the large window. Jack Whitman sat in the old TV chair, staring at the blinds too.

He wore an old suit, and his white hair was thinning. His wide nose cast a shadow over his lip. We'd known him for years. He had been my mom's lawyer at first, then Brian's after that.

It was dead silent.

Dylan stood by the window, peeking carefully through one side of the blinds.

"Are the TV crews still out there?" I asked.

He pinched his lips. "Yes. Most of them are still there."

I sighed. "Are you sure the police are going to come for Lacey?" I asked Jack.

"As sure as they say grace in church," Jack said. "You should have called me right away. Now we don't even have the coroner's report before the arrest."

Dylan walked to the couch and sat next to Lacey, gently taking her hand.

"And there is nothing we can do about it?" I asked.

"Nope. Nothing." Jack didn't even flinch. "If they have an arrest warrant, they can take her by force. If they don't have one, and we don't cooperate, they'll get one and we'll look guilty."

We sat in silence again. Waiting. Staring at nothing, just like Lacey.

Then a pounding knock rattled the front door, startling me.

"Police!" a man shouted from outside. "Open the door!"

I froze. Panic set my whole body on fire. Then I looked at Jack. But he just nodded once.

I rose with unsteady legs and made my way to the front door. My hand reached for the handle but stopped halfway. Trembling.

How did we get here?

A little over a week ago, we were all sitting here laughing at a funny cat video Dylan showed us. The same couch. The same home.

I took a deep breath, steadied my hand, and straightened. Then I slowly opened the door.

The front lawn was crowded with police officers. Their patrol cars lit up the dark street in red and blue. Behind them, near the edge of the lawn, camera crews pressed against a line of officers. Reporters yelled over one another, their voices sharp and frantic.

"Where is Lacey?"

"Why did she kill Zach?"

"Is she inside right now? Can we talk to her?"

Detective Nolan was there too, right at my door, looking the least intimidating of the bunch. Next to him was some buff officer. The GI Joe type. Broad chest. Tight jaw. Military haircut.

"May we come in?" he asked.

Jack stepped forward. "Do you have a warrant?"

Nolan's gaze locked on his. "Do we need one?"

"That depends on what you're here for," Jack countered.

Nolan gave a slow nod. "We're here for Lacey. To ask questions." His eyes found mine and held them. "Questions that really need answering."

"Well," I said quickly, before Jack could. "How about we just come with you and answer your questions. Warrant or not. We have nothing to hide."

Detective Nolan nodded.

"Can you please come around the back, though?" I asked.

"No," the tall officer next to Detective Nolan said.

Faint noises from upstairs reached us. The ABC song.

"So the kids don't have to see all this," I explained.

GI Joe frowned. "Ma'am, you're not in a position to make demands here. Step aside now."

He started forward, but Nolan lifted his arm, pushing the officer back a step.

"We'll meet her at the back door," Detective Nolan said. Brusque and firm.

"Thank you," I said.

I closed the door and leaned my back against it.

Jack and Dylan both stared at me.

Lacey hadn't moved. Still on the couch. Still staring at the floor like an empty shell.

"Well," Jack said. "Let's go."

He grabbed his coat from the hanger. I followed, taking mine, and was about to reach for Lacey's, but Dylan was faster.

I watched as he walked over and gently lifted her from the couch. Her body was limp, unresisting, as he slid her arms into the sleeves. Carefully. Tenderly. Like he was dressing a porcelain doll that might break if he moved too fast.

It broke something inside me to watch him do this.

"This is all a misunderstanding, right?" I asked Jack. "Lacey didn't do anything."

"That doesn't matter in situations like these," Jack said coolly, adjusting his tie.

"What do you mean? Doesn't it matter if someone's innocent?"

Jack shrugged. "Not really. What matters in the eyes of the court is what you can or can't prove. Let me do the talking. In the eyes of law enforcement and the world, your daughter is no longer a victim. Now we have to make sure the court doesn't get the evidence to prove that."

12

NICOLE

The interrogation room at the New Hampshire State Police Station was tiny. No windows. Gray walls. And a plastic table with four plastic chairs. A red light blinked on the camera in the corner as it recorded us.

Detective Nolan sat across from us. Lacey sat between Jack and me. A closed yellow folder lay in the middle of the table.

Nolan leaned on his elbows, hands folded, shoulders rounded. He looked a little lost. He had agreed to let me sit in. I told him I was staying for this, and he let it slide. Which was kind, considering it was his call, and he could have thrown me out.

"She hasn't said a single word since the incident?" he asked. He already knew the answer. He had been sitting here with us for over two hours. Going over everything. Over and over again. And Lacey hadn't looked up once. Her head was tipped down toward her lap. Her hands rested limp on her knees. Her face was so pale. How was this the same woman who used to wake up every morning with a smile?

I shook my head. "Not a single peep. The psychiatrist said it's Functional Neurological Symptom Disorder. He said the trauma made her brain shut off to protect itself from overload or something like that. Like an electrical outlet that trips when you fry it."

Nolan let out a slow breath through his nose. "How long will it take for her to talk again?"

"The doctor doesn't know." My voice came out thin. "It could be days. Months. He said it's hard to tell."

Nolan nodded once. "Okay. Are you at least willing to sign a HIPAA form to let me look at the psychiatrist's notes?"

"Yes," I said at the same time Jack said, "No."

Nolan's eyebrows lifted. His gaze went back and forth between us.

"We could have Dr. Sanchez share the diagnosis," I said to Jack. My hand settled on Lacey's knee.

Jack thought about it. Then gave a quick nod. "We can sign a release form for the diagnosis only. But nothing else."

The room grew quiet, feeling smaller by the second. Nolan stared at the yellow folder. His fingers brushed the edges. Then his gaze flicked from Lacey to me, back to the folder, then to Lacey again.

Then he shook his head.

"All right. For tonight, we'll leave it at that," he said. "But I need that confirmation of her diagnosis ASAP. An explanation from the psychiatrist would go a long way too."

"So, no arrest?" Jack clarified.

"No. You can leave. But stay in town for the rest of the investigation."

Relief hit so fast it made my shoulders drop and my head tilt back.

The door to the interrogation room opened before I could stand.

A woman walked in with two uniformed officers behind her.

She moved like she owned the room and everyone in it. Her red hair was pulled back tight in a braid. She had sharp cheekbones and sparkly green eyes. Her well-fitted navy-blue suit was expensive, no doubt.

Nolan moved his chair back and rose. "Kara. What a surprise to see you. Without any heads-up." Annoyance was in every word.

"That's because last time I checked, the attorney general's office didn't need a detective's approval for anything."

She grinned at him and dragged the extra plastic chair from the corner to the table.

"Deputy Attorney General Kara Belmont," she said by way of introduction. "I'm overseeing this case now, under direct instruction from the attorney general's office."

She grabbed the yellow folder from the table and pulled something out.

A photograph.

She held it up.

My head jerked back before my brain caught up.

It was an image of Zach. From the murder scene.

His eyes and mouth were wide open. Like his screams never fully made it out. He lay across the front seats of his car with his head tipped back. His chest barely looked human anymore. Just ripped flesh and torn fabric. His gut was hanging out too. Blood was everywhere. So much of it that my brain struggled to believe what I was seeing.

This wasn't just a murder. This was a massacre!

"Oh, God." I gagged on the words. I bent sideways and grabbed for the trash can on the floor, but it was too late. My stomach lurched up my throat, and I threw up hard. Acid burned the back of my nose. The room filled with the sour smell of vomit.

"Kara. What the hell are you doing?" Nolan snapped.

"You can shut up and stay or complain and leave," she said without even looking at him.

Her eyes stayed on Lacey.

"Does this man look familiar?" she asked. Her tone went flat and stern. "Might be a little hard to make him out under all this blood, but this is Zach Nabb. Stabbed over forty times. In your car."

"Stop this!" Jack's chair scraped loudly against the floor as he shot to his feet. "You may not use graphic crime scene photos to pressure my client. We're done here."

"No, we're not," Belmont countered. "Lacey Alderwyn, you are now under arrest. Before we continue, I'm going to read you your rights."

I wiped my mouth with my sleeve, tasting bile. "What?"

The deputy AG kept going with an iron facial expression, as if she'd done this countless times before in other vomit-filled rooms. "You have the right to remain silent. Anything you say can and will be used against you in a court of law. You have the right to an attorney. Looks like you already have one. But if you cannot afford one, one will be appointed for you by the court. You have the right to remain silent and stop answering questions at any time. Do you understand these rights as I've read them to you?"

Lacey kept staring into the distance. Blank. Pupils large.

Belmont seemed to take her silence as defiance and rose from her chair. "I take that as a yes," she said. Then she leaned forward and held Zach's picture inches from Lacey's face.

"Kara, stop," Nolan demanded.

"Look at your friend Zach, Lacey," Belmont demanded. "Why did you do this to him?"

"Stop it!" I shot to my feet and reached across the table to grab the photo out of her hand. One of the officers caught me from behind before I could grasp it. Strong hands clamped around my arms and yanked me back.

The room exploded.

"Stop it, Kara!" Nolan snapped.

"Let her go," Jack ordered.

"Don't look, Lacey!" I yelled over everyone. Over the chaos.

My heartbeat was up in my throat. Jack was fighting with the officer holding me, arguing and threatening. AG Belmont talked over him. The camera in the corner was recording as if all of this was just a TV show.

And in the middle of it, Lacey.

In all that noise, she moved her head.

Just a little.

Her chin lifted first. Then her gaze came up from her lap, inch by inch. But she didn't look at the photo. She looked straight at Kara Belmont.

The room went dead silent.

Everyone stared at her. Watching. Waiting.

For the first time in over a week, Lacey's lips moved.

Her mouth parted.

Belmont looked as shocked as the rest of us. As if her iron spine went soft. Quickly, she pointed at the picture again. Didn't want to lose the moment.

"Lacey, look at him," Belmont pressed. "His blood was all over you, Lacey. And your DNA was found on him."

"Of course her DNA was on him," Jack objected. "They knew each other and were in close contact."

She ignored him.

"Tell me why you did it," she pressed, "and I swear I'll make sure this is done quietly, so your family and kids won't be the center of a murder trial."

Silence again.

Then Lacey's gaze slowly moved from Belmont to the photo. Her pupils widened. Her lower lip trembled. She looked like a little girl for a split second, lost in a place nobody could reach.

"Sweetheart, no." The words ripped out of me.

But it was too late.

Lacey's eyes flew wide open. All white around the brown. Her whole face changed in front of us. Something tore loose in her, and her mouth opened, and the sound that came out didn't sound like her at all. Or human.

A high-pitched scream blasted out of her as if hell itself had opened a door under the table.

"Make her stop!" Belmont shouted as her hands covered her ears.

Lacey's scream intensified. The sound split the air. It wasn't just loud; it hurt. It drilled straight through the top of my skull and dug down into my spine. Like something from an exorcism movie.

"Lacey!" I twisted out of the officer's grip. He released me with a curse, and I lurched toward her.

The scream kept coming in jagged bursts. Lacey didn't blink. Her whole body shook as if possessed. She sucked in a ragged, choking breath before screaming again. And again. And again.

It was the worst moment of my life.

My ears rang. My heart pounded so hard my ribs ached.

"Get her out of here," the deputy AG yelled. "Now!"

The two officers moved quickly, as if they had finally woken up.

Cold cuffs snapped around Lacey's wrists. She didn't fight. She only kept screaming. They dragged her up from the chair, out of the interrogation room, and into the hallway.

"Let her go!" I shouted after them. I tried to grab her, but Jack caught me. His arm wrapped around me and held me tightly across my stomach.

"Let me go," I begged him. My throat burned. My chest burned. Tears blurred the hallway, where every door along it was now open wide. Officers stood there, curious, with wide eyes. Everyone watched as they hauled Lacey down the hall.

Even after she turned the corner and I couldn't see her anymore, she kept screaming. It bounced off the walls and came back to slam into me again, sounding like the end of the world coming from down the hallway.

Tears ran down my face. I kept shouting for her. My daughter. My baby. I'm here. I'm right here.

Lacey's voice bled out somewhere deep in the building, and I couldn't hear her anymore.

Then my knees gave out, and I dropped. The floor was cold on my legs.

Belmont rushed past me in panic. Her black high heels banged against the floor as she fled. No more sass now. She didn't even look at me.

"We'll let you know where they take her," she said in a shaky tone.

Then she was gone. Her footsteps faded. The hallway noise settled, and, one by one, officers slipped back into their rooms.

Finally, someone's hand touched my arm, steady and careful.

For a second, I thought it was Jack, but when I looked up through the blur, it was Detective Nolan.

"I'm so sorry, Nicole," he said quietly.

Jack wasn't done. He was furious. "You turned a voluntary interview into a shit show," he barked at Nolan.

Nolan kept his hand under my arm, keeping me from sliding onto the floor.

"You're charging a traumatized woman who hasn't said a word." Jack's voice was gravel now. "Based on circumstantial evidence and blood on her clothes. I assume there's no murder weapon, or that would have been mentioned. And without a weapon, you arrested and abused a mentally traumatized victim. Good luck explaining that to a judge. Let's go, Nicole. I need to call my assistant. We need to get an emergency hearing with the judge as soon as possible."

I nodded. Tried to stand. But my body didn't listen. My legs felt like gel, and I almost went down.

Nolan caught me before I hit the floor.

"I …" My tongue felt so heavy. My jaw shook. "I need a moment."

Detective Nolan walked me over to a bench set against the wall and helped me sit like I was an old woman who needed a walker. "You go ahead," I told Jack. "Call Susan. Every second matters. We need to get Lacey out of here. I'll be right out."

He narrowed his eyes at Nolan. That lawyer look. A warning.

"I'll be okay," I said. "Go."

"Don't sign anything or talk to anybody about the case."

"Okay," I promised.

Jack threw Nolan one more angry glare, then turned and headed down the hallway in long strides.

I thought Nolan would leave too. Go do whatever cops did after something like that. Write reports. Call superiors. Eat doughnuts.

Instead, he sat next to me.

"I know it doesn't mean much," he said quietly, "but I really didn't expect it would go this way."

He held out a handkerchief.

My sleeve was already soaked from wiping my face like a child. I hesitated and looked him in the eyes. And when I saw empathy staring back at me, I accepted the handkerchief.

It was still warm from his pocket and smelled faintly of aftershave.

"Thank you."

We sat in silence. Phones rang steadily in the background. The low murmur of officers behind closed doors drifted through the hallway.

"I never thought something like this would happen to you," he said, finally breaking the silence.

My brows pulled tight. His tone … he spoke as if he knew me.

"You were always so kind," he added. "God, you don't deserve any of this."

I shook my head, confused.

"You don't remember me, do you?"

I studied him. I sometimes ran into former students of mine. But I'd never taught a Nolan. I'd remember that name.

But when I looked into his kind, brown eyes, something started to stir. A memory fighting its way up through all the chaos.

"My first name is James. But the kids back then also called me—"

"Noodle," I said, the word slipping out before I could stop it. My cheeks flushed. "Oh my God. How did I not recognize you?"

He gave a dry, sarcastic laugh. "Noodle."

"I'm … so sorry. I didn't mean to call you that."

"It's okay." His smile was soft. "That was a long time ago."

"Well, they were cruel," I said firmly. "And it drove me nuts when they called you that. I had more than a few talks with parents to get their kids to stop ganging up on the smallest boy in the class and calling him awful names."

He shrugged. "It's the law of nature. Pick out the weakest. Pretend you're strong by torturing them."

I looked him over again. More intently this time.

He had to be almost six feet now. Broad-shouldered and fit. The kind of cop who looked like he could sprint across a parking lot and jump over a fence to catch a fleeing criminal.

"Well, look at you now," I said, nudging his arm with my elbow. "Not so small anymore, huh? Fighting crime. And you're already a detective? You must be really good at what you do. How old are you? Twenty-four?"

He smiled again. "Twenty-five."

"Good for you. I'm sorry I didn't remember you, but for some reason I thought your last name was Smith."

His expression shifted back to serious. "It was. Until someone finally called CPS and reported seeing my dad beating me and my mom."

Ah. Yes.

I remembered the bruises all over his back and arms. The sort of marks on a child that were unmistakable. CPS had told us that teachers couldn't intervene without a witness, despite the mother trembling in my office and confirming the abuse.

"We finally got the chance to leave after they arrested my dad," he said.

"I always wondered where you went. You just disappeared overnight that fall. We were told you left town with your mom. That your father was in prison."

"Yeah. We went to live with my grandma and took my mom's last name."

"So Nolan is your mom's name," I said quietly.

"It is."

He shook his head. "I'm really sorry you're going through such hard times," he said. "It's smart to get that emergency hearing with the judge."

"Lacey didn't do this." My voice trembled on the last word.

He pressed his lips together. "Funny. They all say that." Then his gaze lifted and met mine. "But if she's anything like you … then I believe it."

I placed a hand on his arm. "Is there anything you can do for her?"

He slowly shook his head. "Not anymore. Kara Belmont is taking over. And it's unusual for the AG's office to be this involved—unless it's a high-profile case."

"A high-profile case?"

He nodded. "We have so many murders and missing-persons cases. The Nabb family must be really important to get this much attention from the AG's office."

"I didn't know Zach's family was important. I know they're prominent real-estate developers, but powerful?"

"Where there's a lot of money, political donations are usually on the table. Especially with real estate. Developers are always trying to push zoning laws and building codes, get things rewritten for them. And from what I can tell, they seem dead certain it was your daughter who did this."

Silence. Again.

I gently squeezed his arm. "I better go. You take care of yourself, James. And thank you for your kindness."

He stood with me, staying close in case I lost my balance again. "I'll walk you out."

"No. If it's okay, I'd like to be alone for a bit."

He managed a sad smile.

I returned the smile. And for a moment, I didn't see that tall, young detective in front of me. I saw little Noodle. The skinny boy who'd once been a head shorter than everyone else. With his too-large backpack and crooked teeth. But he was a man now. Fighting for others. Surviving the kind of childhood most kids don't walk away from.

"Thank you again," I said and turned to leave.

His hand caught my arm. Not rough, but I could feel the urgency in his grip.

My eyes jumped to his hand. Then up to his face.

"Do you know who the attorney general is?" he asked.

I shrugged. "No."

"You might want to look into that."

"Why? Who is it?"

He stared at me for a long second. Something unreadable in his face.

"You'll see," he said. "I hope it's nothing, but there's a chance I'm not the only part of your past that's catching up with you, Mrs. Kolter."

My mouth opened, but before I could ask what he meant, his phone rang.

He glanced at the screen, and his whole expression changed.

"I gotta take this." He answered the call. "Hello?" A pause. "Shit. All right. I'll be right there."

He hung up.

"I have to go. Good luck, Mrs. Kolter."

"Thank you," I whispered, watching him rush down the hallway.

Then, suddenly, I felt lost again. Sad. Angry. Afraid. Numb.

The kids would have a meltdown when I came home without their mom. And Brian … oh God, Brian. He would spiral without Lacey.

And Amanda. Where the hell was she? I was sure someone had already told her lies about Lacey.

I wanted to sit. To collapse again. My legs were still wobbly, and my blood pressure was probably too high.

But I couldn't.

There was no time.

I had to find Jack. We needed to get Lacey out of jail as fast as possible.

And we also had a new assignment.

Look into the attorney general—to answer one very important question.

Why was this case getting his close attention?

13

NICOLE

It was dead silent in the courtroom.

The room looked smaller than it did on TV.

It was cramped and old, and the smell of mold clung to the red carpet. A dull New Hampshire state seal hung on the wall over the judge's head.

The judge's bench sat on a low rise at the front, directly across from Jack and Lacey and the prosecutor's table, where Deputy AG Belmont looked like a million dollars. Some young man in a suit sat next to her, his shoes way too shiny.

Brian and I sat in the gallery, directly behind Lacey and Jack. The aisle split us from Zach's parents and sister on the other side. The whole thing felt grotesque. Their hateful glares. Their crying. Every sound carried across the aisle and mixed with Brian's sobs.

Amanda wasn't with them. And we had no idea how she was doing or where she was. She hadn't answered any of our calls. Not even Dylan's. But she had texted him. Said she needed time. Said she'd always love us.

We all stared at Judge Rayner. An older man, bald, with hard lines cut deep into his face.

Papers crinkled as he turned a page, then another. A slight shake of his head. A frown.

I hadn't slept in thirty-six hours. Everything felt so unreal. Lacey looked totally detached from all of it. She stared at the floor like a broken robot. Like a thing. Something not human anymore.

Judge Rayner finally nodded. "This wasn't an easy decision," he said, "but considering there is no evidence tying anyone else to the crime scene, even without the murder weapon, I agree with the state's attorney to deny bail."

A wave of mutters washed over the room. Zach's family sobbed in relief as I gasped in horror. Brian grabbed my hand and squeezed it until it hurt.

Quickly, Jack turned to us. "Don't make a scene. Try to stay calm."

"What does no bail mean?" Brian asked, his eyes red from all the crying.

"I'm also ordering a more comprehensive mental health evaluation," Judge Rayner continued. "For the upcoming hearing."

"What does all this mean?" Brian asked again.

"Shh," Jack warned.

The judge gathered his papers. Then his gavel came down with a loud bang, and two officers grabbed Lacey. Her body was limp, and her movements were mechanical.

"Wait!" I shouted, but they dragged her out anyway.

"I'll get you out!" I yelled after her.

She didn't react. Didn't even blink. Just followed the officers like a puppet dragged by its strings.

"I'll get you out!" I shouted again, louder this time.

"Oh, God," Brian muttered as he buried his head in his hands.

Zach's family left quickly. No drama. No words. Losing a child was a pain no parent could ever recover from and, as a mother, I understood that. But their hate was aimed at the wrong family. Lacey didn't do this. And the real murderer was still out there somewhere.

The courtroom emptied until it was just us—Jack, Brian, and me, sitting in the heavy disbelief that followed.

"What now?" The words barely made it past my lips.

Jack adjusted the belt holding up his oversized suit pants. "To be honest, I'm shocked it went this way. Especially with her mental state and the psych evaluation we submitted. She's no threat to anyone. No motive, no weapon, no record. Not even a damn speeding ticket."

"Can't we appeal?" I asked.

Brian fell apart beside me, mumbling into his hands, "Oh, God, why! What are we going to do now?"

Jack grabbed his leather case. "I'm filing a motion to reconsider today. If that fails, we go straight to Superior Court. They've got thirty-six hours to rule once I file. Don't worry. I'll have her out in no time."

I nodded and rose. "Brian, did you hear that?"

He wiped his face with his sweater, nodding. "Yeah. That's a good plan."

We stepped out into the hallway … and I froze in shock.

Zach's family stood near the only exit, talking with Kara Belmont, who'd spent the morning painting Lacey as a monster. But that wasn't what stopped me cold. It was who they were with.

Thomas Harlow.

He stood almost a head taller than everyone else. He was wearing an elegant suit, and his silver hair was combed back. Every inch of him carried the same arrogance and entitlement I remembered from all those years ago. For a moment, he looked surprised to see me. Then the corners of his mouth curled into a grin.

"Hmmm," Jack murmured under his breath. "That's not good. Looks like the attorney general has taken a personal interest in Zach's case."

We watched as Belmont comforted Zach's mother with soft words.

I turned and rushed back into the courtroom. Jack and Brian followed.

"Nicole?" Jack called. "What's wrong?"

I sank onto the nearest bench, my head spinning. Out of all the things that could've gone wrong today, this might have been the worst.

"That's what he meant," I muttered. Suddenly Detective Nolan's warning about the attorney general made sense. And his statement about how my past might catch up with me. I'd been so busy, with everything falling apart, I had completely ignored his warning.

Jack crossed his arms. "What's going on, Nicole?"

I exhaled slowly. "That man out there. Thomas Harlow. That's the attorney general, right?"

Jack nodded. "Yes. The most powerful man in the state. And, hopefully, not our enemy."

A bitter laugh escaped me. "Well, I have bad news then. We can all stop wondering why Kara Belmont is so invested or why Lacey's case suddenly matters so much to the State."

Jack and Brian stared at me, waiting.

How the hell did I get here? How could things go from bad to world-shattering in just two weeks?

I shook my head and turned to Brian. "Do you ..." I had to take a deep breath before I could go on. "Do you remember that terrible incident with one of my students right after I got my first teaching job?"

He squinted. "You mean that kid from the high school football team who drugged a thirteen-year-old girl at a party? Then filmed her gang rape?"

I nodded. "The girl's name was Vivian Mercer. She came to me the day after it happened. I took her to the principal right away. But instead of calling the police, he pulled me aside and said one of the boys accused was Wade Harlow. The son of a New Hampshire Supreme Court judge. He asked me to convince Vivian to take his name out of her statement."

Brian's eyes widened. "Yeah, I remember. And you didn't."

"Of course not. Vivian refused. And I backed her. Took her straight to the hospital for a sexual assault exam. Wade Harlow's sperm was found in her and matched to the rape, along with ten other boys. They'd put socks into her mouth to keep her from screaming and also inserted a baseball bat into her."

Jack's expression darkened. The look of a man already identifying problems.

"Didn't the Harlow boy drop out of school after that?" Brian asked.

"Yes." My voice was soft. "After he dropped out, he spiraled. He overdosed on pain medication a few years later."

The silence that followed was thick in the air.

"Well, that shouldn't affect any of this, right?" Brian looked at Jack.

"There are laws, I mean. Laws guaranteeing fair trials. Constitutional rights."

Jack pressed his lips together. "There are."

"But?" I asked, already knowing.

"But some people think they're above the law," he said quietly.

"Think or are?"

"Both," he said. "Some people have enough power to keep someone locked up for years for no reason whatsoever. Long enough to drain you financially with lawyer fees until you're broke."

Brian sank beside me with a hollow stare. "So justice is only for the rich?"

"No," Jack said. "But it's hard for the rest of us to get it."

"What are the next steps?" I asked.

"Same as before," he said. "We'll file the motion to reconsider today. If it's denied, we go straight to Superior Court. The overall goal is to get in front of a jury as fast as possible. Take the power away from the judge and the AG."

That flicker of hope returned. Small, but enough to hold on to.

"Will she still be out in a few days?" I asked.

"It's possible," Jack said. "But even if it takes longer, don't lose hope. We'll get her out. And, who knows? Maybe they'll find the real killer in the meantime. Maybe another robbery gone wrong in the area that leaves somebody else dead. Then this will be nothing more than a terrible chapter of your lives. A test you'll all have made it through."

Brian and I stood and shook his hand.

"Thank you," I said.

"Thanks, Jack," Brian echoed.

He nodded. "It'll all be sorted out soon."

14

NICOLE - THREE MONTHS LATER

"Well, turns out Ethan had used permanent marker, and Brian couldn't get the fake eyebrows and mustache off for three days," I said, forcing out a laugh, empty and fake, as I shifted on the hard plastic chair in the visitation booth.

Across the glass, Lacey sat slumped in an oversized orange jumpsuit. Her hair hung in oily strands over her shoulders. Her cheekbones looked sharper. Kinda fallen in. She had to be down twenty pounds, maybe even more. Her skin was as pale as a ghost's, and the dark rings under her eyes made her look like the sad woman from *Corpse Bride*.

She wasn't even holding the phone. Just stared through the glass like she didn't even see me. Next to her, a female correctional officer in a black uniform was holding the phone to Lacey's ear. She had short black hair and a large nose. I gave her a grateful glance.

Two booths down, someone's mother sobbed into the phone.

"Well, we miss you so much, but we're hanging in there, so don't you worry about us," I said, lying.

We were falling apart at the seams. Dylan was a walking time bomb at school with Benny. Lila started wetting the bed again, waking up in the middle of the night in tears. Ethan had started biting at daycare. And Brian … God. Brian was a whole different story.

Three months. That's how long it had been. And Thomas Harlow had blocked every effort to get Lacey out.

Motion to Reconsider Bail—denied.

Motion to Reopen Detention Hearing—denied.

Motion for Conditions of Release—denied.

Every time, the AG pushed for preventative detention, calling Lacey too dangerous to be released.

"Jack filed another motion," I told her, keeping my voice hopeful. "This one will go to a different judge. Jack thinks he might actually listen. He also added a complaint about how the State keeps rescheduling your mental health evaluation. Jack said they can't demand a second opinion and then never schedule it."

She didn't blink or move. Her eyes were still locked on the same spot in her lap.

I hated them. All of them. Thomas Harlow. Kara Belmont. The police. The media. I'd never hated anyone in my life, but seeing my daughter like this ... it filled my heart with a rage as hot as the fires burning in hell.

My throat tightened. I forced my eyes back to the officer, catching her glance again. This one was kind. She held the phone for the full twenty-minute visit, unlike the last guard, who'd shrugged and said Lacey could "pick up her own damn phone or the visit was over."

"Two minutes," the officer said quietly.

I gave a small nod.

"Oh—I do have some good news," I said. "Jack was able to get the judge to grant me power of attorney. So I can meet with your psychiatrist and jail doctor. Maybe we can get you some protein shakes or powder, something to help with your energy. Nutrition is important when you're ... when you're trying to hold on. And we might be able to adjust your meds too. For the depression. And the nightmares."

No reaction.

"I already scheduled a meeting with the doctor this afternoon," I added. "They won't allow me to meet him here. But he agreed to see me at his clinic in Exeter." I rolled my eyes. "That's typical of the government, huh? Anything to make it harder on the people."

She didn't respond. Just stared at that same damn spot.

And seeing her like this made me feel something else too.

It was guilt.

So much of it I could barely breathe.

I knew Lacey always thought she had let me down. That I thought her pregnancy with Dylan was a mistake. Maybe even that she was a mistake.

"Pumpkin …" She kept her eyes down. "I …"

A tear rolled down my cheek. Damn it, I had to be stronger. For her. I quickly wiped it away and pretended nothing happened.

"I know you always felt like you let me down, but … that's just not true."

My hand pressed against the cold glass separating us.

"I'm so proud of the woman and mom you've become. Your kids adore you, especially Dylan. I know we didn't always see eye to eye when it comes to Brian, but I really need you to know how proud I am of you and everything you've accomplished and—"

"Time's up," the officer said gently, cutting me off.

"Thank you so much," I told her. "You were very kind." She gave me a curt nod.

"I love you, pumpkin," I said as they rose and walked to the door. "Hang in there. I'll have you out in no time."

But Lacey was led away before I could finish the sentence.

I stood and straightened my coat, trying to pull myself back together. I really had to meet Dr. Langford in Exeter. The way Lacey looked …

Jail was obviously taking a toll on her body.

"Time to go," one of the officers called. Someone else was already waiting for the booth.

I nodded and stepped aside, making room for the next crying mother to spill hope into a scratched-up phone.

15

NICOLE

I left the jail through the front door. The gray sky above only deepened my depression from my visit with Lacey.

I was about halfway down the concrete stairs when a low voice stopped me in my tracks.

"Hello, Nicole."

I turned around and froze.

There he was. In the flesh.

Thomas Harlow.

He was wearing an elegant suit and was extremely tall and skinny. His silver hair was combed back. His blue eyes were still as cold and as cunning as I remembered them.

I just stared at him, like a tiger zeroing in on its prey. Which seemed to amuse him, since he clearly thought of himself as the hunter here. Not the hunted.

My hand slipped into my jacket to reach for my phone. Maybe I could somehow record this conversation. But his eyes followed my hand.

A sarcastic laugh escaped him as he took a step closer.

"You think you're gonna pull your phone out and hit Record, pretending you're checking the time? Like I'm some idiot?"

I pulled my hand back out and stared at him in defiance.

"You haven't changed much, have you?" he added, taking another step. "When you look in the mirror, you still think it's David staring back. Slingshot in hand, all courage, strength, and that slight insanity needed to fight someone as big as Goliath."

I crossed my arms. "I didn't do so badly with that slingshot back then when you tried to silence Vivian Mercer to save your rapist son."

That washed the nasty smirk right off his face. He stepped closer, fast.

"Don't talk about my son," he growled. "You think you know what happened back then. But my son didn't do any of the things that lying whore told you and the police."

He was at the edge of the steps now. Towering above me like a master over his servant. I waved him off.

"Oh, stop this." I took the steps up and was now right in front of him. "You can play stupid with the morons who have to kiss your butt, but don't you think for a moment that you'll ever be able to convince me that Vivian Mercer wasn't gang-raped by your son and the other animals that were there that night."

His eyes widened. Obviously, he was still not used to people telling him how it is.

"How dare you, you piece of white trash."

I took another step forward, actually pushing him back a few inches.

"How dare I? Let me tell you how. I took Vivian to the hospital the day after it all happened. Right after she came to me. They found ten different semen samples in the poor girl, including your son's. Along with wood splinters from a baseball bat. She was torn up so badly down there, they had to fly in a reconstructive surgeon to make it look anything close to the female anatomy of a thirteen-year-old again. Did you not see the pictures the hospital took as evidence?"

His eyes were full of hate when he leaned over to whisper into my ear.

"Oh, I saw them. And I'll make sure your whore daughter's cunt will look just like that when she gets raped in prison by the guards someday."

My fists balled harder, and I was about to strike him, when I saw the jail cameras pointing at us. Their steady red blink meant they were recording.

Quickly, I stepped back. My whole body was trembling with rage. But somehow I had to control myself. He tried to upset me. Most likely even set me up to lose control. And he was almost successful.

"What happened to your son was by his own hand and his own doing," I said as I turned and raced down the stairs before I got myself thrown into the cell next to Lacey.

"Your daughter is lying, Nicole!" he called after me. "She comes from a line of liars and whores!"

I ran to my car. Resisted turning around. If I looked at him, I knew I wouldn't be able to hold back. And how would that help Lacey and the kids? They needed me to be strong.

My hands had a hard time holding on to the steering wheel. That's how hard they shook. For a moment, I was worried they might make a sharp turn and try to run over Thomas Harlow. As if they didn't belong to me anymore. But somehow I managed to leave the parking lot, not looking back once.

I had to talk to Lacey's doctor to get her weight loss under control. I needed one less thing to worry about, now that the fight to get her out had just turned from hard to total disaster.

And there was literally nothing I could do about this other than beat Harlow in court. Jack said that an AG was an elected official with broad prosecutorial discretion, meaning no judge could simply order him off our case. On top of that, courts set a very high bar for conflict of interest, so a personal grudge likely wouldn't be enough.

To get Harlow removed from Lacey's case, we would have to file a complaint with the governor, but that was as good as hopeless. The governor was a man in Harlow's own circle, and there was no public pressure to force his hand against Harlow. The public believed Lacey did it as much as Harlow did. Beyond that, I had no clear evidence of Harlow being partisan. I had no proof in writing, no witnesses, and even a face-to-face confrontation like this would come down to his word against mine in a world in which women who recorded their own rape were arrested for recording the rapist without consent. Where billionaires sex-trafficked women and kids and walked free.

And yet Jack filed the hopeless complaint with the governor anyway. Because in my mind, there wasn't the slightest doubt about Harlow.

He was settling old scores. And based on the hate I saw sparking in his eyes today, I knew he would fight to the bitter end to win. Just like me.

16

DYLAN

It was afternoon, and the school's bell announced that the long day was finally over. Usually, I would stick around a bit in front of school. Talk with some friends about teen stuff—like an old episode of *South Park* that reran late at night again. Or like Nate's driver's license struggles. He had literally managed to back into the same car seven times while trying to pull into a parallel parking spot downtown. Seven freaking times!

But today I said my good-byes quickly and fled the school as if I were being chased by one of the zombies out of *Dawn of the Dead*.

The cool fall air brushed my face as I stepped out and mingled with the students waiting to get picked up by their parents. I was usually one of them, but not today. My high school wasn't too far from my home by bike, maybe about fifteen minutes, and with everything going on, I told Grandma I was biking so she could go visit Mom in jail.

I didn't like riding my bike. But this wasn't the time to complain. This was the time to survive in whatever way possible. As crazy as it all was, considering we'd been just a normal family not too long ago, my life had turned into utter horror overnight. One day, I was a normal kid with school sweethearts and soccer practice, the next, my mom was in jail for murder. All while my grandma was trying everything she could to get her out. She barely ate or slept anymore. My mom was on her mind constantly, like an imaginary clock going on and on and on. *Tick-tock, tick-tock,* endlessly without the slightest break in sight.

I walked along the brick wall to the back of the school. Past the overgrown landscaping and dirty windows that screamed budget cuts at every corner. I knelt next to my bike to unlock it.

I was about to get on it, when my eyes locked with Benny's. He was lingering behind the school with two friends, and he instantly focused on me. His thin lips curled into a provoking grin, then he just stared. Like some alpha dog trying to warn me to look away.

I knew what this was about. My friends had told me he was talking shit about my mom behind my back. My misery and pain had drawn him to me like a bloodhound to a wounded fox. And why not? That's what piece-of-shit bullies like him did. Live off others' pain and struggles to make themselves feel powerful and important.

"Not with me, bitch," I mumbled and leaned my bike against the brick wall. My arms stretched wide open, and I waved him over for the whole school to see. "Come on, bitch. Come on. Make my day."

Little coward prick looked away instantly. Pretended he was in some deep conversation with his loser friends all of a sudden.

"Yeah, that's what I thought, coward!" I yelled over to him.

Six foot two at sixteen. Number one wrestler on my team. I would wipe the toilets with their ugly-ass faces.

When nothing else came from the loser trio, I got on my bike in one smooth motion and rode off.

I usually took the sidewalks and back streets home, but today I decided to take the longer way so I could stop at the gas station and get some chips and a soda. The good thing about all this mess with Mom was that I ate what I wanted when I wanted without an adult's eagle eyes scanning my world for sugar and artificial colors.

The gas station was only a short ride down the street, and I could already see its bright neon sign glowing in the distance as I approached Bubbles and Brews—the local dive bar—to my left. But there was nothing bubbly about it. The concrete in front of it was cracked, and some of the windows were boarded up. Faded posters from decades of this and that hung half-torn on its walls. Drunks were coming in and out to blasting rock music, smoking and vaping, stumbling and laughing too loudly about shit that most likely wasn't funny.

My bike rolled by, then I hit the brakes so hard it almost sent me flying over the handlebars.

I completely froze when I saw a man stumble out.

All six foot four of him.

Broad shoulders. Huge arms and muscular build. A baseball cap pulled into his face, like that would do the trick.

This man could just as well have been wearing a full biohazard suit. I still would've recognized him.

It was my freaking dad!

And he wasn't alone.

Some woman who looked barely old enough to be in anything with "Brews" in its name was laughing with him as they stumbled and swayed into the alley next to the bar. The woman was wearing tight jeans and had way too much makeup on. Her high heels scraped over the cracked street as Dad led the way, holding her hand.

Ice-cold needles stabbed me up and down my spine. Every inch of me told me to keep going, to go home. Told me not to follow them. But it was like I didn't have a choice. Like a moth that flies into a campfire knowing it will die but does it anyway.

Quietly, I pushed my bike up the small alley, but they weren't there anymore. When I walked all the way to the corner of the alley, I stopped and peeked around it. My bike almost slipped from my grip when I saw the woman on her knees right in front of my dad. He gripped her head with both hands, and his head was tilted upward with his eyes closed.

She was fucking giving him a blow job.

I tasted bile on my tongue. Bitter and sharp. I actually had to swallow not to gag.

Emotions pressed in on me from all sides. Sadness. Anger. Rage. Hate. And even shame.

I should have run over there and confronted him. Taken a picture with my phone. Posted it on TikTok for the whole world to see the pig as a pig.

But, as if my body wasn't my own, I jumped back on my bike and hit the pedals as fast as I could.

What the hell was I doing, riding off like a coward? I should have gone back there. Punched him in the face. Screamed at her that he was a married man. With kids. Who betrayed his mute wife and dropped her like she was trash.

But I didn't.

The road in front of me turned blurry as tears burned in my eyes. The wind bashed mercilessly against my face as I thundered my bike past stores and homes.

I hated him. I fucking hated this man so much.

The familiar oak trees on my street came into view. I took the back alley, where the trash trucks collected bins, to avoid any lingering camera crews.

When I made it to the back door, I didn't lean my bike against the wall; I just tossed it. No. Smashed it to the ground. It made a metallic clink, and the bell broke off, but I didn't care.

I walked to the door. My hand was already reaching for the handle when I froze.

I needed to calm the hell down. Ethan and Lila were in there. Most likely coloring with Anna, their babysitter. They asked for Mom day and night. All while Dad had completely abandoned us. Just like he did back then when Mimi and Poppy died. He spiraled instantly after losing his parents. And not in the usual way of grief—in some psycho way that would torch the whole world so it would suffer with him.

I'd been too young to make sense of all the details, but there were certain things I still remembered even now. Like when our neighbor rang the bell in the morning to tell us that Dad was passed out in his boxers on the front lawn, and the sprinkler was soaking him. Or the time Mom begged him to stay home, and he grabbed her by the wrist and threw her out of his way. To get more booze.

It took everything my mom had in her to save him. But, in the end, she pulled off the impossible. She got Dad sober. Got him on some pills or something and into treatment. All while she was nine months pregnant with Lila, all while attending college and working a real job.

However, unlike my mom—who seemed to see something in him I

didn't—I always knew he was a ticking time bomb. And today I understood that better than I ever had before.

I took a deep breath and steadied my shaking hands as best I could. Wiped the tears out of my eyes with my sleeve. Then I went inside.

But instead of Anna doing arts and crafts with the kids at the kitchen table, I found Lila on the couch, her eyes glued to the screen as the fast-moving lights from the TV reflected off her face.

I looked around. The living room was in total chaos. Toys and snacks were scattered everywhere. I picked up a stuffed unicorn and a fire truck.

"Where's Anna?" I asked.

"She left," Lila said, still staring at the screen as if hypnotized. Which she was. We kids and screens.

"She just left?" I sounded as outraged as I was. Lila instantly looked at me, her eyes wide with worry. Maybe thinking she'd done something wrong.

She nodded. "I'm sorry," she said, like the good girl she always was. Always taking the blame even if she wasn't at fault.

"It's not your fault," I said gently. "Where is Ethan?"

Lila jumped up from the couch. "He was playing over there." She pointed at the area where I had just picked up the fire truck.

A loud thud echoed from upstairs. Both of us froze for a second, then we thundered up the stairs.

"Ethan!" I yelled and stormed into his room. But he wasn't there.

"Ethan!" Lila called out and ran into her room, but he wasn't there either.

My heart hammered against my rib cage like it was about to break free. My little brother could be a real little shit sometimes, but I loved him with all my heart.

Lila checked Mom and Dad's bedroom while I stormed into my room, and, thank God, there he was. Relief hit me so hard, I actually stumbled back a step.

He was standing on my gaming chair, stretching his little arms high up to reach the shelf in my closet. His blond curls shimmered golden under the light, and, like always, he had smears on his cheeks, hands, and legs. Food stains, paint—who the hell knew. Next to him was my baseball bat, which must have fallen out of the closet.

"Ethan!"

I scooped him up quickly and hugged him so hard, the little rug rat actually said, "Ouch, too tight."

"He wanted to get your Halloween candy," Lila said and pointed at my pillowcase up there on the shelf. It was still filled with candy, and somehow Ethan knew this.

"Well," I said, reaching up to pull it out with one hand, still holding Ethan, "let's not let all his effort be for nothing."

"Really? We get candy?" Lila hollered cheerfully.

"Mmh-mm, but don't tell—" my voice broke off. I almost said Mom. "Anybody," I corrected quickly.

As we made our way down to the living room, Ethan and Lila both swore on their favorite toys that they wouldn't tell anybody.

I placed the candy on the carpet and turned on their favorite show: *Masha and the Bear*.

My heart broke for them as I watched them eat candy with big grins on their faces. How the hell could all this happen to them? And, even more so, how the hell could Dad do this to them? They needed him more than ever right now. They were just innocent little kids.

My hands balled into fists as the memory of him behind Bubbles and Brews flashed in front of my eyes. I shook it off and pulled my phone out.

"You wait here for me, okay? I really need to call Grandma. After that, we'll play some games and color."

Lila nodded. Ethan was too busy with the TV show to even notice I'd said something.

I stepped into the kitchen and was about to call Grandma, but then paused with my phone in my hand. Anna had just abandoned Ethan and Lila. And Dad was drunk at the bar.

But was I supposed to tell her all that? That Dad was getting BJs behind Bubbles and Brews? Grandma was barely holding on by a thread herself. And Mom needed her to fight for her. I was able to hold the fort with the kids here at home. She needed to know about Anna, of course. And we needed to get Dad back home before he drove drunk into some family and killed them. But the rest would stay with me.

I steadied myself as best I could. Told myself to be strong. That they needed me. Mom, Grandma, Ethan, and Lila. I had to place my own needs and pain behind theirs. Just like Mom always did for me and everybody else she loved. I would cry later. Alone in my bed. When everybody else was asleep and nobody could hear.

And, until then, I would fucking step up and be the man my dad would never be.

17

NICOLE

Dr. Susan Langford's office looked like any other private practice: clean and simple. Old carpet. The whole place smelled faintly of hand sanitizer. A few faux plants were scattered around the waiting room.

I didn't have to wait long before a nurse walked me back to see the doctor.

Diplomas hung neatly on the wall of her office. Family photos crowded her desk. Two little kids grinning with missing teeth, Dr. Langford hugging them in front of a birthday cake.

"Mrs. Kolter." Dr. Langford stepped into the office at the same time I did. Dr. Langford was tall and slim, with large blue eyes that pulled your attention away from her big ears. Her dark hair hung loosely over her shoulders.

The nurse slipped out without another word. Dr. Langford shook my hand, her grip firm, then sat in her chair behind the desk.

I sat across from her.

"Thank you for meeting with me," I said, handing her the power of attorney. She scanned it, quickly but thoroughly, then passed it back across the desk.

"Of course," she said in a kind tone. "I totally understand. I'm a mom too. I can only imagine how hard this must be for you."

I nodded, grateful for her kindness even though my stomach was twisting.

"I just wanted to see if there is anything we can do for Lacey. She does not look good, Doctor. It looks like she isn't eating. And since she's still not talking …"

Her expression shifted to sad seriousness as she leaned over her desk. "You have every right to be concerned. Especially when it comes to Lacey. Correctional facilities must provide medically necessary treatment, but necessary means the bare minimum."

"Yeah, that's what my lawyer said. But I was wondering if we could pay for protein shakes or talk about force-feeding meals. There has to be something we can do."

She shook her head. "Unfortunately, families can't pay for better medication or treatment, and they can't oversee the chemo treatment itself. But I was able to move her into the medical unit of the jail, which is a lot safer for her."

The air in my lungs turned heavy. What did she just say?

My head jerked back.

"I-I'm sorry … chemo?"

I waited for the correction. For the "oh no, you misheard." Some kind of misunderstanding. But her brows lifted instead.

"Yes, chemo."

"W … what?"

"Chemotherapy. For her clear cell ovarian carcinoma."

Every muscle in my body tensed. "I don't understand."

Her eyes locked on mine.

"I'm talking about Lacey's cancer."

Her words were like a punch to the face. A ringing shot through my ears, high and shrill. Cold needles rushed up my spine. Then nausea flooded me, and I swallowed so hard, I thought I would throw up onto her desk.

My hand flew to my mouth. A sound escaped anyway, broken and raw. Tears spilled down my cheeks in hot tracks.

"You didn't know?" she asked.

I managed a small shake of my head. Everything felt unreal. Like I had slipped into the wrong life. Or stepped into hell by accident.

"But," I whispered, "she was just in the hospital a few months ago. After the attack. They checked her. They would have found this."

She pinched her lips together before answering. "Hospitals don't usually screen for ovarian cancer after trauma, and a CA-125 isn't a routine test. They wouldn't have run it. They did the right labs for a trauma case. Blood count. Chem panel. Pregnancy test. Nothing in those tests screams ovarian cancer unless you're looking for it."

I tried to calm myself so I could listen to her. "And clear cell ovarian carcinoma is very hard to detect," she explained. "But a few years ago, I lost an inmate in a prison where I worked to this type of cancer. It was horrific. The prison refused to let me run tests and treatment, and we only found out about her cancer from her autopsy. The way she died …" Her voice broke off. "Horrific. So when I see inmates who are pale and extremely underweight, I run a few extra tests, including the CA-125, which is not a routine blood test. The jail lets me do screenings as I see fit. I negotiated this before accepting the job."

I listened as my world fell apart. Every word felt like someone was carving out my chest with a dull spoon.

"Lacey's CA-125 came back elevated, so I sent her for imaging immediately. And it confirmed my suspicion. I am so sorry."

I sat there and cried. How much more could I take?

"Why?" The word felt distant, foreign, like someone else was talking, using my body. "Why is all this happening to us? There are so many bad people out there. Rapists. Murderers. Which I swear my daughter isn't. Why is this happening to my daughter? To her sweet kids? To me? To good people? No parent should ever outlive their child."

Oh, God, the kids. How was I supposed to tell the kids? They loved their mother so much.

"I don't think I can keep going," I mumbled as my face fell into my hands. Then my gaze shot up to Dr. Langford. "How do people keep going in moments like this?"

She rose, walked around her desk, and sat in the chair next to me. Her hand grabbed mine, warm and steady.

"I know it seems impossible right now, but people do learn to live again after losing a loved one. With time."

Her kindness meant everything, but the words sounded empty. A Chinese fortune cookie sentiment.

"I know because I lost a child myself," she added.

My red, swollen eyes met hers.

"Our first child. She died when I was twenty-six weeks pregnant." Her gaze drifted for a moment, and her jaw tensed at the memory. "I had very high blood pressure during the pregnancy, and it was too dangerous to have surgery to remove my dead baby girl. So, for days, I had to carry my daughter after she'd already passed. Until my body was strong enough to survive surgery. It was the worst time in my life. I prayed my heart would stop so I could leave this world with her."

We sat in silence. My eyes wandered to the photos of her kids on her desk. Their smiles. Their missing teeth. Their whole lives untouched by grief.

"It might seem impossible right now to understand why such bad things happen, especially to good people, but with time, you can find happiness again, even if a part of your heart will always be missing."

Dr. Langford reached for the tissue box on her desk and handed me one. I dried my tears.

"I'll do everything I can for your daughter. For her chemo or imaging, I'll transport her to the hospital."

It took me a few tries to speak.

"It's serious, isn't it?"

She nodded. "It's very serious, Mrs. Kolter. Clear cell ovarian carcinoma is one of the more aggressive ovarian cancers. And because we caught it late, the options inside the system are limited. The jail will only approve basic chemotherapy. That might slow the cancer for a while, but it usually doesn't hold it back for long."

"How long?"

Dr. Langford looked as if she were losing her own baby girl again. Like a mother truly understanding the horror I was living.

"If she stays in jail," she said, "we're looking at maybe ten months. A year tops, realistically. I wish I could tell you something different."

"What if I could get her out?"

"If she's released, that could change things. She could see a gynecologic oncologist. Start the advanced therapies the jail won't approve. Avastin, PARP inhibitors, clinical trials ... treatments that actually work really well with this cancer. With full care, she could have years. Two, four, even five years. I've seen it."

That was all I needed to hear. I weakly squeezed Dr. Langford's hand. Looked straight at her.

"Thank you, from the bottom of my heart. Please do what you can while I get my daughter out."

She nodded and rose with me.

I didn't recall the walk through the parking lot back to my car, but I found myself standing in front of it. Time was jumping back and forth or sideways. The ringing in my ears was back. The sky looked warped, too bright.

I didn't remember getting inside my car either. But I was driving now, the wheels rolling, the parking lot shrinking in the rearview mirror like a nightmare dissolving behind me.

I whimpered. I gasped. I made it almost a mile before pulling into a parking spot next to a small bridge crossing a stream. Then I parked my car with my shaking hands and fell apart again.

"No!" I screamed, hitting the steering wheel so hard the horn blared beneath my fists.

"Noooo!" I screamed again, so loud my voice cracked. The pain flooded through me. I was losing my little girl not only to jail but forever to cancer. It was more than I could take.

Tears ran down my face as I broke into loud sobbing and screams, hitting things around me with full force. Whatever I could reach—the sideboard, the steering wheel—until I left a dent in the console.

I hated this world. My only child was dying in a jail cell, accused of a horrendous crime she didn't commit. All while the whole world hated her and would continue to hate her kids. We'd already gotten death threats via email and even one in our mailbox.

It all crashed over me. The court trial. The arrest. The constant fight with the prosecutors. All the friends and family who had turned their backs on us. The loneliness. The shame. The fear. For a moment, the unthinkable ran through my mind.

What if I just put the car into Drive? Drove down that hill into the stream? Ended this unbearable pain?

But even having that thought angered me. How dare I? I had to be there for the kids and Brian. Even if I didn't mean it, I couldn't let my mind go there again.

I grabbed the steering wheel and took a deep, shaking breath.

My phone rang, and I felt a flash of guilt, as if whoever was calling knew exactly what I'd been thinking of doing.

My shaking hands fumbled it out of my pocket.

Dylan.

I wiped the tears off my face, straightened up, and forced my voice to sound normal. "Yes, honey," I said.

"Grandma," he said in a somber voice. And somehow I already knew what would come next.

"Dad is missing again."

I sighed.

"I think he's at Bubbles and Brews again," Dylan added.

I nodded as if he could see me. Out of all of us, Brian had handled everything the worst. Instantly falling back into toxic coping mechanisms. And the fact that most of his HVAC clients had canceled jobs didn't help.

"Where's Anna?" I asked, trying to sound strong and unalarmed.

"She left a few hours ago. She doesn't want to babysit for us anymore. You know."

Yes. I did. I knew exactly what he meant. The murder family that nobody wanted to babysit for.

The younger kids were doing okay in school since they were shielded from adult gossip. Dylan, on the other hand, had a few incidents. He stood up to any bullying with his fists. And at six feet two, with his athletic build, he won. Plus, the girls at his school gave him support—mostly because they were in love with him. Just like his father, he was incredibly handsome. That gift would always give him an advantage in life.

But, at the end of the day, we were all alone.

I wiped my face dry with a napkin from my to-go lunch sitting on the passenger seat.

"I'll go get him, then come straight home."

Dylan was silent on the other end.

"What is it, sweetie?" I asked.

"How did it go with Mom?" he asked.

The unbearable pain almost took me out again.

Poor baby.

He would lose his mother.

How could I tell him that?

I steadied myself as best I could. For him. He needed me more than ever.

"It went good!" Fake happy. "She held the phone to her ear all by herself this time."

"Really?" He sounded hopeful.

"Yes. And remember—I got the power of attorney. I can talk to everyone at the jail now and make sure they'll take care of her. I enrolled her in the choir and even arranged for her to sit in some of the group therapy sessions with the others. To get her out of the cell, you know."

"Yeah, that's good."

"Well, honey, can you feed the kids, and I'll go get your dad?"

"Yeah, of course. They're doing good. Ethan is playing with Play-Doh here with me, and Lila is playing the princess dressing game on her tablet."

"That's good."

I felt horrible for Dylan. For him to be the man his dad couldn't be. But even if I tried to let him be a kid, he'd refuse. He was always right there to fight with me for his mom and siblings.

"All right, I'll see you soon, honey."

"Okay."

"Love you," I said.

"Love you too."

Then I hung up.

For how long I just stared at the trees, I had no idea. I just sat there, watching their lifeless branches reaching for the sky.

"Stop it," I scolded myself.

I had to get it together now. I had to get my daughter out of jail so she could get the treatment she needed. I had to save her life.

And Jack … his lackluster laziness on the case, which had started as soon as it seemed really hopeless, had also reached its limit. I would stop by his office and demand all the files he had. Read them over myself. Study them. The crime scene. The facts. The laws. There was no way the police hadn't messed this up. Or that Thomas, the AG, hadn't tried to hide evidence to make me pay for what happened to his son.

Zach had been stabbed forty-four times.

And my daughter was found in the woods, so traumatized she couldn't speak anymore.

Something had to be there.

I needed to get another lawyer. Someone a bit more engaged for $400 an hour.

My daughter wasn't a murderer.

I put the car in Reverse.

Jack's office.

Bars.

Home.

Then I would work on getting Lacey out of there. And that was the end of it.

18

DYLAN

The kids were in bed, and Dad was passed out drunk on the couch. I had just grabbed cold pizza from the fridge and put it into the microwave when Grandma's cell rang on the kitchen table.

The display read Principal Hoover. It was after eight p.m. This was a bit strange.

I picked it up for her before it could go to voicemail.

"Nicole?"

"No," I said. "I'm sorry, this is her grandson. Hold on a second. She's in—"

"No, that's okay," Mr. Hoover said. "Can you deliver a message to her for me?"

"Well, she's literally right down here in the basement. I'll get—"

"No, that won't be necessary. Just tell her not to come back to school. Take a break from teaching. You know, to rest and take care of you guys."

There was this strange silence. I bet he knew I saw right through his cheap attempt to make this look like anything other than what it really was.

They were getting rid of her. Because of Mom. And they knew the job meant so much to her. A lifeline still keeping her together. And now they were taking it from her, so they'd better make it sound like it was for her best … not theirs.

"I think she really likes going to work," I said, as if I could change his mind. "And her students told her the other day how glad they are that she's still teaching and helping them."

"Well, buddy …" Mr. Hoover sighed. He sounded like he was talking to a baby or a dog. In that weird kid-friendly voice. It was so fake it was insulting. "I know it's hard for a kid to understand adult matters, but I'm really doing this for your grandma and—"

"Fuck you."

"What?"

"I said fuck you. You're doing this for my grandma, but don't even have the balls to fire her yourself? You want to use her teenage grandson to deliver the bad news? My grandma has given your school everything, and you don't even have the decency to meet with her in person. Freaking coward."

"Ummm …"

"You'll hear from our lawyer!" I said and hung up.

Then I just stood there. I could literally feel my grandma's pain over losing this job running through me. She loved being a teacher. And she was so good at it. Many of her kids went on to college because of her and her alone. Now they were pulling this shit because of something someone else did and blamed my mom for.

I ignored my pizza and walked into the basement, which Grandma had turned into an investigation room over the last few hours. She'd hauled several side tables down the stairs and spread the files she got from Jack's office across them. She'd also sorted reports and evidence into little piles on the floor. Witness statements near the water heater and crime-scene photos on the cleaning-supply shelf. Everything else, including motives, was on the side tables.

"Grandma?" I stopped halfway down the stairs.

"Yeah?" She looked up, sitting on a chair in the middle of the chaos. Reading some document.

"I … have some really bad news."

She just froze and stared at me.

"Mr. Hoover called, and—"

"That's okay." She focused back on the paper.

I chose my next words carefully, suspecting she most likely misunderstood what I was about to tell her. But before I could say more, she shrugged.

"It was only a matter of time before they would fire me. But it gives me more time to get your mom out, so it's probably for the best."

My lips pinched hard. Her face didn't give anything away, but the way her hands clenched the paper told me that another piece of her heart had just shattered.

"How is it going?" I asked quickly, trying to change the topic. I took a few more steps, but she jumped up from her chair.

"Wait! Don't come down!" She rushed to the shelf. I caught a glimpse of the photos of Zach's mutilated body. My stomach clenched. They said he had forty-four stab wounds. His guts had spilled out. Literally. Whoever did this to Zach wasn't just angry. He or she was a monster.

"You can come down now," she said, after having flipped the images facedown so only the white backs showed.

I walked into the middle of all the piles, my eyes flicking over her setup. Then we locked eyes. She looked worried. Maybe she thought I'd tell her that she had to let the cops do their jobs. That all this was insane. And maybe it was. A teacher pretending to be Columbo in a basement filled with spiders.

But this woman was the strongest person I probably knew. So my doubts hardened into something else.

Determination and faith.

"How can I help?" I asked.

"Oh, honey … that's so kind. I really appreciate it, but—"

"All right, I'll just come back later," I said, already turning. "When you're in bed. Then I'll sit down here all alone and start with the dead body pictures. You know—like a totally stable teenager."

I wasn't ten. I was sixteen. And Grandma knew me. Knew darn

well the moment she left this room, I'd be back down here trying to piece it all together myself. I would crawl through fire for my mother.

And why wouldn't I? She would do the same for me.

I turned on the stairs.

"Wait." She let out a long breath of annoyance. "But just for a little bit. Then we both need to get some sleep. Deal?"

I nodded.

"Did you find anything yet?"

"Not really," she admitted. "Just got started. But the motive the police came up with is paper-thin. Basically nonexistent."

I reached for the folder marked "Motive" and flipped it open.

"Jealousy?" I scoffed, holding up the report. "Seriously?"

"Yup. They said your mom was jealous of Amanda."

I shook my head. "Mom wouldn't trade places with Amanda for a billion dollars. If anything, it's Amanda who was jealous of Mom."

Grandma cocked a brow. "And why's that?"

I shrugged. "Because of Dad. Amanda and Dad were childhood sweethearts, all the way through high school."

"How do you know that?" she asked, genuinely puzzled.

"Dad keeps her love letters in a box in the closet. I found them when I was digging for pictures of Grandpa in his military uniform. For that school project, remember?"

"Well, that was a long time ago, sweetheart."

"Maybe. But he still keeps them." My mouth tightened, and my tone was flat. "Dunno why Mom and all these other women fall for him. Remember when we went on that camping trip a few years back, and all those moths flew straight into the campfire? Literally getting torched to death. That's what it feels like with women and Dad."

"Dylan ... your dad is doing what he can."

"You mean getting wasted at bars?"

"No. I mean coping."

I pulled out a chair and sat at one of the makeshift tables. My fingers skimmed through the next stack of files.

"I guess," I finally muttered, softer this time. More for her than me. I didn't want to upset her at a time when she'd lost a job that was a huge part of who she was. All while reading murder files to save her daughter.

She gave a small nod. "Well, let's get to it. I've got an appointment with a new lawyer tomorrow morning."

I CHECKED the time on my phone: 11:51 p.m.

"God, we have to get some sleep," Grandma said as she stood. Papers were scattered across the basement floor, covering nearly every inch.

I didn't look up. I was focused on a report in my hands.

"Sweetie, let's go to bed. You have school tomorrow."

"Come look at this." I waved her over, my eyes still fixed on the page.

She stepped between folders and leaned over my shoulder.

"Here." I pointed at a police report. "It's from the police call logs the night Zach was killed. Officer Wrangler responded to a call from the owner of the SeaPort Gas Station, the one on the highway that leads to the dirt road where Zach was found. The owner called in at 9:42 p.m. to report a suspicious man pumping gas. Blood on his neck, jeans, and shoes. White male, late thirties, dark-brown hoodie, torn jeans, old white truck. Drove off westbound. The officer said in his report that it wasn't related to Zach's murder."

She took the paper from me and read it herself. The words were all there. Exactly as I'd said.

"We have him," I concluded, smiling for the first time in weeks. "Zach's real murderer. This is the proof we need to get Mom out!"

It wasn't that simple. But, still. Something in my chest lifted. That tricky, dangerous thing called hope.

She reached out and gently ran her hand down my cheek.

"Well done, sweetheart."

I got up so fast, I stumbled. "They must have missed this. We have to go to the police. Right now."

She shook her head. "Not tonight. It's too late. They already had this report. I'll go tomorrow. Right after I meet the new lawyer. Maybe he'll come with me, throw around legal threats if they don't follow up on this lead."

I nodded. "Good idea, Grandma."

"Bed?" she asked.

"Yeah. I can't wait to tell Dad all this in the morning. It'll help him. I think."

"It will," she said.

19

NICOLE

I was slumped in the driver's seat, parked right in front of the state police station where Detective Nolan worked. The engine was off, the windows cracked just enough to let in the cool air from the parking lot.

I'd been sitting here for at least three and a half hours.

If he didn't come out soon, I'd have to leave to pick up the kids from school. Brian could no longer be trusted to manage even the basics.

The lawyer appointment had been fast. The second he realized who I was and what I needed, he declined. The case was too hot.

I could crawl back to Jack, but after he'd billed us $84,897 and hadn't even bothered to read through all the files, I wasn't so sure that was the best idea. Because, at this point, it all made sense. Thomas Harlow and his bloodhound, Kara Belmont, didn't care about any leads that could prove Lacey's innocence.

I had to do more. I had to drag the real killer to them—served up on a silver plate.

I was about to leave and come back later, when the station door finally creaked open again and Nolan walked out.

I straightened immediately and got out of the car.

He moved quickly across the lot toward his SUV, but it didn't take long for him to notice he was being followed. He turned mid-step.

"Nicole?" His brow lifted. His brown hair looked a little tousled, and his suit pants were wrinkled.

"Sorry for ambushing you," I said. "But is there anywhere we can talk?"

He looked over his shoulder at the building behind him.

"Private," I added before he could say anything. That landed. I saw it in the way his gaze dropped, thoughtful, uneasy.

Talking to me out in the open was already a risk. Talking to me inside, where everyone could see, would be career suicide.

Nobody wanted to be seen as an enemy of the attorney general.

"Please," I said quietly.

It didn't sway him right away.

"Lacey, my daughter ... she has cancer. Did you know that?" My voice cracked, and I swallowed hard to stop the hot pressure rising in my throat.

He exhaled like the air had been knocked out of him. "God. No, I didn't. I'm so sorry."

I watched the tension tighten his face. He was doing the math, deciding whether to listen to me or walk away.

"It's not really my case anymore," he said.

"You're still listed as the detective."

"On paper." His voice lowered. "But the fact that you waited for me in the parking lot tells me you and I both know who's really running the show."

I nodded, stepped closer, and locked eyes with him. "I do. And that's the problem. Because whatever my daughter is accused of, this is still the United States of America. And the last time I checked, she has rights. Including the right to be presumed innocent. And the right to a fair trial. Now tell me—has this trial been fair so far, Detective Nolan?"

He looked away.

I nodded. "That's what I thought. Let me ask you something else. If you get into your car knowing all this, can you look in the mirror tonight and tell yourself you did the right thing? Maybe walking away from a mother asking the police to do their job isn't that hard. I give you that. But what about the chance that the murderer is still out there? Getting away with murder. Maybe killing again."

His sigh was heavy. But he was still torn.

"Do you …" My voice dropped as a pair of officers passed us, shooting curious glances as they greeted him. I waited for them to walk off.

"Do you remember that phone call? The one made to the police when you were little. About your father?"

He froze. "Oh no. Don't do that. That's below you."

I laughed, dry and bitter. "Look at me. There isn't much below me anymore. My family's financially ruined, thanks to a shitty lawyer. The government's blaming my daughter for something she didn't do just to settle an old score. And my only child is dying in jail of cancer. So, no. Telling you it was me who called the police on your abusive father and saved you is not below me. Not anymore."

He didn't speak.

"Did you know that I lied for you back then?" I added.

"What?" His eyes widened.

I shrugged. "I sure did. I mean, I never saw your dad hit you. I never saw any of what I told the police back then. But I saw your mother's bruises. And yours. I saw the fear in your eyes and the way you jumped at every little noise. I saw him grab her in the hallway before a parent-teacher conference and whisper something in her ear that made her cry."

He stared at me, wide-eyed.

"So I lied and told the police that he hurt you in front of me during a home visit. I said he threatened to kill me if I ever told the police. That's what finally got him arrested. And you all were able to leave."

He stared at me for a moment, nodded once, then turned and walked to his SUV.

"Meet me at the Hot Mug" was all he said and climbed in.

I rushed back to my car and typed the name into my phone.

A soup and coffee shop not far from here.

When I arrived, I spotted him parked in one of the spots at the edge of the parking lot. He waited until I pulled up before he got out and jogged to my door. I unlocked it, and he climbed into the passenger seat.

"Thank you for doing this," I said.

He nodded. Less bitter than I expected, considering I had just emotionally blackmailed him.

"Anything for my childhood savior," he said with a trace of sarcasm. "But I honestly don't know how I can help. Kara Belmont is running the investigation. Everything goes through the attorney general now. My name is just there for show."

"Attorney General Thomas Harlow," I said.

"Thomas fucking Harlow," he confirmed. "A real prick. I don't know anybody who can stand him. But he's the most powerful man in the state. And nobody wants to piss him off."

I let out a breath. "Life really got me good on that one."

"Yeah. It did. Which is why I don't think I can do anything. Even if I wanted to."

I reached into my bag and pulled out the officer's report from the gas station.

"Have you seen this before?"

He took it, read through it carefully, and shook his head. "No. I remember requesting the 911 call logs from the night of the murder when I started the investigation, but this report must have come in after I got pulled off the case. This has Kara Belmont written all over it."

"How do you know that?"

"I'm a detective," he said, a little too proudly. "Look at this last sentence in the report. Where it says there's no connection between the gas station call and Zach's murder."

He pointed at it.

"The gas station call came in before the body was found. So how could the officer say there was no connection to a murder he didn't even know existed yet? That line was added later to his already written report."

He flipped back to the top of the page.

"Besides, no patrol cop would take it on himself to call a potential lead to a murder unrelated. Not unless someone above him told him to do so."

His jaw tightened as he read the last lines again. "Goddammit," he cursed under his breath. Then he handed the paper back to me.

"Now what do we do?" I asked.

"We gotta go." He opened the door.

"Go where?"

"The gas station. Meet me there."

I glanced at the clock. I was more than an hour north of home and had to pick up the kids. But if I moved fast, I could do both.

I typed the gas station into my GPS as Detective Nolan got into his car.

I was anxious but also hopeful. For the first time, there might be real evidence—not just my word—that Lacey didn't do this.

Now all I had to do was find the real killer. And that was as terrifying as it sounded.

20

NICOLE

My hands clenched the steering wheel the whole time I watched Detective Nolan talk to the man inside the gas station. He was an older guy with a narrow face and a mistrustful stare.

Nolan nodded at something the man said, then they disappeared into the back for a few minutes before returning and talking a bit more. Finally, Detective Nolan rushed out of the gas station and hopped into my car.

He held a small piece of paper in his hand.

It read: MA 443FD.

I didn't know why, but I memorized it instantly before he slid the paper into the inside pocket of his suit jacket. Years as a teacher had taught me how to remember a few numbers and letters.

"Well?" I asked.

"Well," he said, "looks like you're in luck. The gas station owner is the distrustful kind and figured it was better to save a copy of that night's video recording before it got overwritten. Even after the police told him it was nothing."

"Smart man."

"Yup. He said something felt off about this guy. He was worried the man might come back someday. So he kept the video as evidence."

"So who is the man?" I pressed. "Do we have a name? Address? What was he doing here? Whose blood was on his clothes?"

Nolan lifted a hand. "Slow down. The gas station owner doesn't know any of that. And we don't either. But we do have a license plate."

My forehead creased. "And that's good, right? That means we can find the murderer?"

Nolan cocked a brow. "First of all, there is no 'we.' This isn't *Monk*. You're not the eccentric civilian tagging along, and I'm not the detective pretending that's normal. Nothing I saw on the recording proves this man is Zach's murderer. I need to be very clear about that."

He must have seen the disappointment on my face, because he quickly added, "But I agree the guy on the recording was acting extremely nervous, and he was covered in what looked like blood. So I'll run the plate and look into him."

"How long will that take? I don't have much time. Lacey's cancer is —" I couldn't finish the sentence. It hurt too much.

Detective Nolan looked at me, the hard lines in his face softening.

"I know," he said quietly. "I'll get to it the moment I'm back at the station."

I nodded. "Thank you. Will that get you in trouble?"

"I'm technically still on the case. I'm just looking into a lead. Can't get fired for that. But it can definitely make my life uncomfortable for a bit if the prick finds out."

I felt horrible. "I'm sorry."

He shrugged. "Hey, I wouldn't be able to forgive myself if the real killer struck again and I hadn't done anything about it."

He frowned, opened my car door, and stepped out. "I'll let you know what I find. But do me a favor."

Our eyes met. "What's that?"

"Don't put all your hope on this. I'd hate to see it crushed."

With that, he closed my door and walked back to his SUV.

I sat there quietly, letting everything sink in.

There was hope again.

It was only a spark. But even a spark could light up the darkness when everything around it was pitch-black.

21

NICOLE

"I'm sorry. That's just not a case I'm willing to take on right now," Mr. Bolter said.

Anger rose in my chest. A slow burn at first, then sharp: I couldn't take one more generic "Sorry, good luck" from any of these slimy lawyers. Not one more. They all wanted five hundred an hour but didn't want to do the slightest work for it. They all just wanted drunk driver cases, the sure bets, the easy cash. Besides that, people working in the system knew by now that the AG had put a target on my daughter's back. And nobody wanted to risk their relationships at court.

Not to uphold laws.

Not for constitutional rights.

Not even for the truth.

Like everything else, the court system seemed like another corrupt shit show designed for the rich.

So I hung up on slimy Mr. Bolter and stared out the kitchen window. The glass had a crack from one of the kids playing ball in the yard. Afternoon sunshine made its way inside. Outside, the trees in the backyard looked sad without their leaves. It was the kind of winter scene that matched my life.

The kids were playing upstairs with Dylan, thumping around like usual. It was good to hear their lively noises when everything else around me seemed dead.

I sank into thought, staring at nothing, when the phone rang.

Unknown caller.

My heart jumped as I picked up.

Brian walked in at the same time, rubbing his hands, as Detective Nolan's voice came through the phone.

"Nicole?"

"Yes," I said, locking eyes with Brian.

"I have some information on the license plate."

Hope and fear grabbed me all at once.

"The car belongs to a man in Peabody," he said. "He lives in a run-down trailer with his wife and kids. Says a guy he knows sometimes borrows his truck every few months or so. They're estranged friends from a construction job they did together about ten years ago. He said this friend just shows up out of nowhere and pays him a thousand in cash to borrow his truck. Then he uses the truck for a day. Returns it, then leaves."

"Does this guy from the trailer have an alibi for himself?" I asked.

"He does."

"Let me guess: his black-and-blue beaten wife?"

"No. Security camera. He has them inside the house and at his doors. I pulled the footage directly from the security company. He was home all night during Zach's murder. And that man he talked about really did show up. Matched the guy from the gas station. But he was wearing a COVID mask and a hoodie. Just like in the gas station footage. All we have on him is a disconnected phone number. And a first name."

"Which is?"

"I can't tell you—" He huffed, frustrated, like he already knew I wouldn't drop it. "Ah, fuck it. His name is John Myers. That's all we have. The truck owner's story is thin and not enough for charges. It's not against the law to rent out your truck as long as you have no knowledge of a crime being committed with it."

"So how do we find this Myers?"

"We don't," Nolan said.

"What do you mean?" My voice rose sharply. "We have to arrest him. Put a warrant out for him or something."

"Based on what?" Nolan said. "We have nothing. For all we know, this man could have been hunting, and the blood on him was from a deer. Or he cut himself on a jobsite. Hell, what if Myers says it was paint?"

"Paint?" I said. "Are you kidding me?"

"Nicole, I'm not sayin' I like any of this. But I'm speaking through the eyes of the system here. Every accusation needs evidence. Everything has to be proven in the eyes of the court, checked off like boxes on some shopping list. And, so far, we have nothing here. Literally nothing. Just theories and gut feelings."

"If we need evidence, well, what about DNA, then? Sweep the truck. There has to be something. Zach's DNA or something."

Nolan sighed, long and exhausted. "I … tried. But the judge denied the warrant, stating there's not enough evidence for that."

My jaw tightened.

Thomas Harlow.

My chest pinched with that old familiar burn of hate again. In the corner of my eye, I caught Brian rubbing the back of his neck, pacing up and down in the cramped kitchen. Another fire I had to put out. Another mess waiting for me.

"Listen," Nolan said quietly, "I'm sorry. I know this is not what you want to hear. But there's nothing else I can do. The AG shut me down. There isn't any more evidence to support pushing this lead. All we can do now is wait until this … Myers shows up again. The man from the trailer said he'd call me when he does. It might take some ti—"

"I don't have time," I cut him off, fingers pressing into the bridge of my nose as if that could stop the pounding inside my skull.

"I know. I'm so sorry, Nicole. I did refer Lacey to a somewhat decent public defender in the state. Figured you'd have a hard time finding someone willing to take her case. He said he would take it. Sean Holt. He'll call soon."

I wanted to scream. But it wouldn't change a thing. This was as far as Nolan was going right now. As far as he *could* go.

"Thank you," I said and hung up.

"Not good, huh?" Brian asked.

"Well," I said slowly, my thoughts racing in every direction. Something wasn't right here. This Myers and his friend needed to be looked into more. "Your old buddy," I said to Brian as an idea formed in my head. "The one who works at the DMV. Maybe you could ask him to do you a favor?"

"What?" Brian shook his head. Lost.

"I mean, I need the address of this man from the trailer." The words rushed out of me, fast and certain. "I have the number of the plate, just not the address. I feel like if I could talk to this man myself—"

"Nicole, stop," Brian said.

"No, wait." I insisted. "Hear me out. This Myers from the footage—even if Detective Nolan didn't get much out of this, there's more to it. I know it. And we can find out."

"Nicole. Stop!"

"I mean, people don't talk to cops. Especially not if your friend committed a crime with your truck."

Brian threw his head into his hands, shaking it wildly.

"Call your old friend. God, what was his name … Nick? Ask him if he still works for the DMV. You let him borrow money during his divorce, remember? That guy's license plate is MA 443FD. If we can get the address and talk to this guy, it can help us find the real killer and—"

"What if she did it?" he snapped, cutting me off. Tears welled up in his eyes. He looked so tired. So broken.

"Wh-what?" I mumbled, thunderstruck. My mind went blank. Shock. I was in total shock.

Brian shrugged. Red eyes glossy. "What if she did it?" he repeated, voice shaking.

I stood in stunned silence. This man— After everything Lacey had done for him, he showed no backbone. No loyalty. Nothing.

"I mean," he rambled on, taking advantage of me being frozen like an animal caught in headlights. "All the evidence says she did. There are no other footprints. No DNA but hers. Everybody says she did it."

He threw his hands up as he broke down. "So maybe she fucking did! Maybe Lacey fucking killed Zach!"

His trembling hand reached into his pocket and pulled out a flask. He took a long sip. Something about the motion felt unreal, like a shitty scene from a bad movie.

"Remember her pet hamster? Skibby?" He wiped his mouth with the back of his hand as a bit of liquor slipped out.

My head jerked back. I didn't see that coming. "Skibby?"

"Yeah. Fucking Skibby. Remember what Lacey did to him? In the backyard?"

"You're drunk," I growled. Furious.

"Oh yeah? Am I? Because I remember all too well when I came over to ride our bikes and saw Lacey bash Skibby's head in with a rock. Not just once. But over and over. Until the poor little thing was nothing but a ball of bloody fur. So what if she did Zach just like she did Skibby back then? What if she really was jealous of Amanda, just like the cops say? The kids love Amanda almost as much as they love her. Zach had all this money, and God knows Lacey and I weren't doing so good."

"What a bunch of horseshit!" I barked, not even bothering with that jealous-of-Amanda nonsense. "Skibby had been sick with cancer for weeks! Couldn't walk. Could barely eat. He was in so much pain that he squeaked every time he moved. Lacey did it to relieve him of pain. She'd seen your dad do the same thing for a raccoon he'd hit on the road. Lacey couldn't stand hearing Skibby squeal anymore. We'd tried to put him down, but the vet was on vacation that week. So she took matters into her own hands. After she told me about it, we buried him under the rosebush with flowers. She cried for weeks over that hamster. It broke her heart. That same big heart that forgave you when she saw you and Amanda—"

"You piece of shit!" Dylan's voice thundered before I could finish my sentence. Brian and I spun around to the doorway. Dylan stood there, trembling, fists balled tight. His shoulders squared as he stepped forward. Right in front of Brian. Eye to eye. Dylan over six feet. Brian barely taller than him at six four.

Dylan pushed his face into Brian's. Provocative. Alive with rage.

"What did you just call me, boy?" Brian's words slurred a bit, but his tone was sharp. He straightened his spine, squared his shoulders, and closed the last few inches between them until they were nose to nose.

I jumped forward, trying to wedge myself between them. "Stop it."

"I called you a piece of shit," Dylan repeated, ignoring me entirely. "Or do you prefer worthless drunk? Coward? Traitor? Or how about cheater?"

The first shove came from Dylan.

Brian snapped instantly and responded with a fast, aggressive grab of Dylan's hoodie, right at the chest. He yanked him forward violently. I got knocked aside in the scuffle, stumbling back into the counter.

"Stop it!" I shouted, but it was too late. Things happened so fast. I couldn't even tell who moved first. They both slammed into the kitchen counter, arms locked and legs shoving. The toaster crashed to the floor. A mug exploded near my feet.

"Stop it!" I screamed again.

That's when Dylan dropped low and used some wrestler move from the school wrestling team. He hooked Brian's leg, twisted hard, and sent him crashing to the floor.

"Don't ever talk about Mom like that again, you asshole!" he screamed, his face tomato red, tears streaking down his cheeks.

Brian was back up almost immediately. He grabbed Dylan with both hands, then flung him across the kitchen effortlessly. Dylan slammed into the kitchen table, its legs scraping loudly against the floor as it slid and tilted, nearly flipping over.

Brian charged again and got on top of Dylan, both fists gripping his sweater.

"I hate you!" Dylan screamed, not even fighting back anymore. "I fucking hate you so much!" He shouted like the words were burning their way out of his broken heart.

"Get off of him!" I grabbed Brian from behind. I yanked with all I had. It felt like this was all his fault. And none of it, at the same time.

"Daddy, no!" A high-pitched screech echoed through the room like shattering glass. Lila stood in the doorway. Her face was frozen in absolute terror.

Ethan was right next to her, crying already, wide-eyed and shaking. Both of them stared like they didn't recognize us anymore.

Something clicked, and Brian seemed to come back to himself. The anger drained from his twisted face, replaced by shock and shame. He looked down at Dylan like he hadn't realized what he was doing until just now. Then he let go and rose to his feet fast.

"Don't hurt Dylan!" Lila cried.

Ethan ran to me full speed and crashed into my arms. I caught him with one arm and dropped down to my knees beside Dylan, pulling him into the other. Lila came running too.

I held all three of them, trying to pull the broken pieces together.

"I'm so sorry—" Brian started.

"Get out!" I yelled.

Everybody was crying. The kids. Dylan. Brian. Me.

"I'm so sorry." Brian sniffled again. Then left.

"I hate him," Dylan sobbed.

"Don't say that," I countered gently. Not for Brian's sake—for the kids. So they wouldn't lose their father too. So they wouldn't carry that hate on top of everything else.

"How can he say that about mom?" Dylan cried harder. "I hate him!"

"He's hurt," I said, rocking all three of them like they were babies again. "Because he loves her so much. And he's not as strong as you. And what he said about your mom isn't true. I know it."

I nodded, firm. This conviction was rooted deep in my gut.

"And I can tell you why it's not true," I added.

A memory surfaced. Lacey when she was little, preparing my birthday breakfast as a surprise. The whole kitchen was a mess. The eggs literally on fire on the stove. A card that said "I love you with all my heart" on the table.

"Before I became a mom," I said, brushing a tear from Dylan's cheek, "I thought I understood what love was. Everyone tells you how much you will love your kids. And you think you get it. You think you know."

I looked down at Dylan, still holding him. "But then you have a child. And that love—it's … indescribable. It consumes you. It fills every part of you. It's so much more than you thought it would be. It's terrifying. You just can't grasp how it's even possible to love someone so much."

I paused, swallowing the knot in my throat.

"And when you love like that, that person becomes a part of you. Like your skin. And you know them better than you know yourself. I swear I know your mother. And she didn't do this. She didn't. I know my child."

I let that moment sit. It calmed us all. A little.

Dylan nodded. So did I. A slow, tired nod between two people who had nothing left to give but love.

"And you want to know something else?" I added in a soft voice. "I was blessed with that special kind of love all over again when your mom had you. When I became a grandma."

I squeezed them tighter, Ethan still buried in my side.

"I felt that same endless, bright, terrifying love consume me all over again when each of you was born. Every time. All three of you. It just swallowed me whole."

My chest burned with a mix of everything—grief, love, panic, hope. It hurt to breathe.

We just sat there. The four of us. Sniffling. Holding on to each other like the world might break apart if we didn't.

But despite everything I'd just said, despite the warmth in my voice and my arms around them, this was still rock bottom.

I wondered if Lacey was crying right now too. In that cold cell. All alone. Dying of cancer. Innocent.

I had to get her out.

The kids needed her.

By God, Brian needed her.

And even if we only got a few more years with her, at least we'd be together again for a little while.

It wouldn't be perfect. But nothing would be worse than her dying in jail for a murder she didn't commit. The kids never getting to see her again. Never getting to say good-bye. Never getting to know the truth. That their mom wasn't a murderer.

I had to find this man.

He had something to do with all this. I knew it.

I just had to prove it.

IT WAS two thirty in the morning when the back door to the kitchen rattled.

I sat on the couch, the TV flickering in front of me. My gaze had been empty, staring straight through the screen.

Keys scraped the lock. A clumsy pause. Then the lock finally clicked, and the door opened.

Brian stumbled in.

His boots dragged over the floor like he was a zombie. That alone already told me enough. His unsteady steps as he wandered into the living room sealed it.

Brian was completely hammered.

He made his way toward me, slow and swaying, as if the floor was uneven. Then he stopped in front of me and pulled a crumpled piece of paper from his pants. It smelled like cigarettes and cheap booze. He held it out like it was a diamond.

I took it without a word.

A name and address were scrawled in smeared ink:

Billy Dustin

36556 Moonlight Drive

Peabody

The second I read it, my spine straightened. My eyes shot up to meet his, which were now half-lidded and glassy.

"Can …" he slurred, lips heavy, "can you tell Dylan I gave you that? So he knows it was me who helped … you know … getting Lacey back home."

I nodded. "I will."

"This could be dangerous, you know."

I knew that. After everything had calmed down tonight, I'd done nothing but think about that. Turning it over and over in my head.

If this brought me closer to the real killer, there was a chance he'd come for me.

"I won't do anything unless I know it won't put the kids in danger," I promised.

And I meant it.

I had a plan. One with no second chances. And if it didn't work, then that would be it. The end of the road. I'd give up before putting the kids in danger.

Brian stared at me another long moment. His eyelids closed and opened slowly. Then he turned and made his way toward the stairs—and, of course, fell.

I was up in an instant and grabbed him under the arm.

"Why don't you take the couch?" I said, hoisting him back upright. He usually took the couch anyway, and I took the bed upstairs. Just not tonight. Tonight, I was sleeping on the couch, waiting for him.

I guided him over, and he collapsed onto the couch like a boulder. Passed out before he'd even taken his shoes off.

I pulled them off, one, then the other, then tucked the blanket around him. He didn't move.

With a sigh, I turned to go upstairs. But then his voice came low and slurred behind me. Barely more than a mumble.

"I love her," he said into the pillows. "And a love like that can destroy a man like me."

I turned back to him.

There he lay, all six foot four of him, sprawled across a couch too short for his body. His feet dangled over the edge like a child's. Even drunk, even wrecked, he still looked like the kind of man women would line up to ruin themselves for. That jawline. That body. The way he could talk to a stranger like they were already best friends.

When Brian was in a good place, you wanted to be locked in a cave with him. Everyone did.

But when he wasn't in a good place, which was most of the time …

"I love her," he muttered again, barely audible now.

"I know," I said quietly.

I did believe him. But a loving heart can still be a weak and selfish one. That was Brian's fatal flaw. He couldn't conquer even the smallest battles in life. Not without Lacey by his side doing everything for him like he was her fourth child.

And a man like that could wreck a family from the inside out.

Then it dawned on me.

If Lacey didn't make it back—if this whole thing ended the wrong way—it wouldn't be her who destroyed us.

It'd be him.

And standing here, smelling the booze as it filled the room, I couldn't help but resent him for that.

"Sleep now," I said, already walking halfway to the stairs when I heard him mumble one last thing. His voice was warped with alcohol and barely audible, but I thought I heard him say, "I swear … both of them. I love … them both."

22

NICOLE

I knocked at the back door of the modern waterfront home in Rye to avoid journalists.

Previously Zach's home.

Now Amanda's.

It was the nicest and largest on the street. Clean concrete, oversized windows, and towering glass railings. It screamed money and privilege. I could hear the sound of the waves breaking nearby.

A quick glance over my shoulder gave me strength. The kids were waiting in the car parked at the bottom of the solid stone staircase that led to the back door on a private road.

Above the door, tucked into the corner of the overhang, the little black security camera blinked red.

She saw me. She knew who it was.

If the door opened, that would be a good sign.

But it didn't.

I knocked again. Harder this time. "The kids are here."

Then I waited.

Still nothing.

But just as I turned to go, the door creaked open. Amanda stood there.

Her golden hair was twisted into a messy bun that looked slept in. The usual angelic glow was gone. No warm smile, just a woman who looked like she'd been dragged through hell over the last few weeks.

Every second counted now. I had to speak fast, speak from the gut.

"I know you wanted space," I said, raising both hands as if I could hold the space between us. "But I'm not here for myself. Or Lacey."

Her dull blue eyes looked past me. Locked on the car.

She crossed her arms, said nothing.

"Umm," I muttered, anxiety burning through me. "I walked through this conversation in my head a million times before coming here. I even made notes." I pulled the crumpled notepad from my jacket pocket and gave a pathetic laugh. "But now, standing here, I don't know what the hell to say."

Neither of us said anything.

But I was the one who came here. I was the one begging. So I forced myself to speak.

"I guess ... all I can say is there are three sweet little souls in that car. Three innocent kids who've never done anything wrong. And they can't be blamed for any of this. If you want to hate her, do it. If you want to hate me or Brian or God"—my jaw clenched—"be my guest."

That got her attention. Her eyes widened. "Brian isn't doing well?"

Her first words to me in weeks. And they were for him. The power this man had over women was unbelievable.

"No, he is not doing well," I said. "None of us are."

She nodded once. Still guarded.

"I understand if you hate me. Or Lacey. Or Brian. Or the whole damn world. I get it. But you've been part of those kids' lives since the day they were born. You're like a mother to them. And you made a promise. As their godmother, you promised that if the worst ever happened, you'd take care of them."

I let my hands fall to my sides, helpless. "Well. The worst is here. So I'm asking you for something now."

I looked her in the eyes. Her skin was pale. No makeup. Puffy eyes.

"Are you the second mother you made them believe you were?" I asked. "Or were you just a friend tagging along all those years?"

I gave her a second to let that sink in. Then added, "Because if you are who we thought you were, then you'll give these kids a place to feel loved and safe for a few days. If you're not, I'll walk away right now, and we won't bother you again."

Her pretty blue eyes narrowed again. Then drifted back to the car. A tear slid down her cheek. Then another.

She didn't speak, just wiped her face with the sleeve of her oversized sweater, breathing slowly and shakily.

For a second, I thought she was going to close the door, which would be Lacey's death sentence. I couldn't put those kids in danger. This was my only chance to find the killer.

Then, almost startling me, Amanda stepped forward.

She brushed past me, brisk and silent, and headed down the stone steps toward the car.

And as she passed, she muttered under her breath, "Just for the record—don't ever question my love for the kids again. That's the one thing nobody gets to touch."

23

NICOLE

I was standing in the fancy kitchen.

Sleek. Modern. Every surface wiped and spotless. The open-concept space spilled into a massive living room with fourteen-foot ceilings and a glass wall overlooking the beach and the ocean.

The kids were curled up on the couch, eyes locked on a movie, the noise blasting through the surround sound built into the walls and ceiling. Amanda moved through the kitchen. She slid frozen pizzas onto a baking tray, then quietly cut up organic apples and strawberries.

I didn't move. I stayed close to the hallway. My presence felt tolerated, not welcomed.

"I have a question," she said, peeling the skin off an apple with a knife. Her hands moved fast but steadily. I almost smiled. She remembered that Ethan would only eat them peeled.

"And if you don't answer it," she added, still not looking at me, "then you can just leave and never come back."

"I'll tell you whatever you want to know."

She still didn't look up. "Then tell me what the hell is going on. Why are the kids not safe at their home anymore?" Her voice was edged with something sharp underneath.

My eyes flicked toward the couch. Dylan hadn't turned around. The volume was too high. Good. They couldn't hear us.

"I don't think you're quite ready for—" I said, but Amanda looked up, eyes locked.

"Actually, Nicole, I think I'm quite ready for a lot of things right now. Including any information you might have that might help make sense of this all."

"Fine," I said. "I'm following a lead."

"A lead?"

I nodded. "To Zach's murderer."

I let that hang, watching her, seeing if anything flashed across her face.

Nothing. Just tension.

"That night, a security camera at a gas station nearby caught a man on tape," I explained, "covered in blood."

"What?" Her head jerked back. Then shook. "Why didn't anyone tell me?"

"Because of the attorney general. Let's just say he doesn't like me."

She raised a brow like I was wearing a tinfoil hat, babbling conspiracy theories about the government faking the moon landing.

"Remember that Harlow boy?" I asked. "Years ago. The case that almost got me fired for helping that girl."

"I … think so. Wasn't that the one with the group of boys at a party? They raped a girl, and you refused to stay quiet even though one of them was some important person's kid?"

"Yeah. That boy happened to be the AG's son. He died of a drug overdose later."

"So what lead are you following?" she asked. "Are you trying to find this guy from the gas station?"

"I have an address. It might help me track him down."

"The police should do that. What if he is dangerous?"

I skipped the whole Nolan backstory. Too much to explain.

"They won't help. And I don't have another day to waste."

She reached for her phone.

"What are you doing?" I asked, heart skipping a beat.

"Texting Brian," she said, thumbs already moving. "I assume he's at the bar?"

I nodded. She knew him so well.

Shame turned my cheeks red. What kind of family were we? Murder charges. Alcoholics. Beggars soon, if the lawyer bills kept piling up.

"He has a right to know where his kids are," she said, not unkindly.

"I would've told him," I said. "I just didn't know how you'd react. If you'd help us."

She picked up the apples and placed the slices neatly onto three separate plates.

"Just to be clear. I'm doing this for the kids. And having them here … honestly, it feels like I can breathe again for the first time in weeks. I missed them so much." Amanda kept her eyes on the counter, not blinking. "But none of this means I agree with anything you're doing. Or that I'll help Lacey in any shape or form."

It hurt to hear her say that, but I was too grateful to let that hurt last longer than a heartbeat.

"Thank you," I said quietly. "I'll call you later. It shouldn't take more than a few days. One way or the other."

She just kept her focus on slicing strawberries into neat halves.

I walked over to the kids, bent down, and kissed each of them on the cheek. They didn't flinch. Too focused on the movie. But Dylan looked up at me with that worried look in his eyes.

I gave a small shake of my head, reassuring him I would be just fine.

He knew what I was doing. He'd overheard Brian and me before the fight in the kitchen.

And he loved his mom enough to let it happen.

A soft smile curved across my mouth as I kissed him again. Then I turned and walked back into the kitchen. Amanda was still at the counter, scooping fruit onto plates.

She was family to us.

So how could she really believe Lacey did this?

"Funny," I said. "Last night, Brian reminded me of something."

"What's that?"

"He said something that made me think of that time Lacey ran into you two by accident. When she was pregnant with Dylan, and Brian had just dropped out of college."

Amanda froze mid-movement.

I kept going. Calm. Voice low so the kids couldn't hear me.

"You remember that restaurant in York? All the way up north? She was dropping off a college classmate at her parents' house and happened to drive by the Beach Shack, where she saw you and Brian sitting on the front patio. The odds of that …" I shook my head. "She was so sure Brian had told her he was visiting his aunt in the nursing home that day."

I let the words hang a moment before meeting Amanda's eyes.

"I know you both lied to her. But Lacey …" My voice cracked. "Lacey never questioned your story. That your car broke down in York. That you called Brian to get you. That you just invited him to lunch to thank him. Lacey didn't even question Brian when his strange late-night shifts just ended overnight after she saw you in York."

I blinked slowly. My throat was burning.

"She never doubted you. Even when I did. When the whole world did."

I took a deep breath, just to steady myself.

"Anyway. Thank you. For helping us. The kids love you. I do too."

I left it at that. I walked to the door, grabbed the cool metal handle, opened it, and pulled it shut behind me as I left. It closed with a thud.

Back in the car, the quiet hit hard. But, to my surprise, I welcomed it. Like the calm before another storm.

I took a deep breath.

I had work to do.

24

NICOLE

It was early morning and cloudy. The smell of traffic drifted through my cracked window. I sat in my car, staring at the Dustin family's trailer from across the street. Their white trailer with chipped paint was easy to monitor in the small trailer park.

A white truck sat in the driveway, next to a beat-up SUV. I had no doubt that this was the truck Zach's killer used. Some "Myers" showing up out of the blue, using his friend's truck for crimes. Then disappearing again.

And, still, the State acted like he had nothing to do with the murder, despite being caught on a nearby camera with blood smeared on him.

Bullshit.

If Nolan wanted to believe fairy tales, fine. But years of crime shows and real life had taught me better. Patterns mattered. People lied.

Billy Dustin knew more.

Which meant his wife knew more too.

I already knew which one would talk to me.

As if on cue, Mrs. Dustin opened the door. A baby on one hip, a four-year-old boy gripping her hand. Probably in her thirties. Like every mom I'd ever met with two small kids, she looked burned out. Sneakers. Leggings. A thick sweater that had seen better days. Her brown hair was pulled into a messy ponytail, loose strands sticking to her forehead.

She locked the door, walked to the SUV, and buckled her kids into their car seats.

When she pulled onto the road, I turned my engine on and followed.

We didn't drive far. Peabody's new space-station-themed playground came into view. Bright plastic rockets set against playground sand. A few swings. Children shouting and laughing.

I tried to look casual as I slowly approached the bench where Mrs. Dustin sat with her sleeping baby tucked against her chest.

I sat next to her, watching the kids as if one of them were mine.

We made eye contact, and I smiled. She smiled back. The kind of smile moms give each other.

For a moment, we just watched. Kids climbing the rocket tower, sliding down, hanging from the monkey bars. Laughter drifting through the air.

A million ways to do this ran through my head, but my mouth moved before my brain caught up.

"I can't do this," I said.

She turned, confused.

"What was that?" Her voice was soft. Careful.

"I said ..." I sucked in a breath and exhaled. "I said I can't do this."

Her eyebrows pulled together as I scooted closer.

"I mean, pretend like I'm just some grandma making small talk." I sighed. "Do you remember a detective stopping by your house not too long ago?"

The shift was instant. Her blue eyes narrowed. But for some strange reason she didn't ask who I was. Didn't question why I knew.

"Um ... yes. I remember," she said.

"Well," I continued, "I don't know if you overheard the conversation, but Detective Nolan came to ask your husband about a friend of his. Someone who borrows his truck sometimes. His name is John Myers."

Her gaze flicked to the baby in her arms. Then back to me.

"I think I have to go," she said, already grabbing her bag.

But before she could get up, I placed my hand on her knee. Light. Careful. "Please," I said. "I'm a mom too. My daughter is about to die in jail for something this *Myers* did."

She hesitated.

"You're a mother. Can you imagine watching your child die in jail for something someone else did?"

Her eyes met mine. Worried. Sad. And also scared.

It hit me all at once. What if she wasn't safe at home? What if talking to me could cost her everything?

"Do you feel safe at home?" I asked quickly. "Does your husband hurt you?"

She glanced over her shoulder. Then at her son, too far to hear us.

She sat there, staring at him as he climbed onto a plastic spaceship. A thousand thoughts must have been racing through her head. Her fingers tightened around the baby's blanket.

"I'm sorry," I said, standing. "I didn't mean to put you in danger. I'll talk to your husband directly. You don't have to worry. Just don't tell him I was here. I won't say a word either, I swear."

I had taken two steps when she spoke.

"That's kind of you," she said. "Worrying about me and the kids when you have so much to lose by walking away."

I sat back down.

"Billy is mostly harmless," she said in a dismissive tone. "A sweet idiot. Most of the time." She exhaled loudly. "But John. That guy." Her mouth tightened. "He's something else—I'll tell you that. He scares me. Scares the kids. Every time he leaves, I pray it's the last time we see him. But he always comes back. Sometimes it's months; sometimes years. It doesn't matter. He always comes back."

"Do you know anything about him?"

Her eyes scanned me. Thinking.

"You're the mom of that mute woman on TV, aren't you? That woman who was found with the rich dead guy in the woods."

I leaned back and sighed. Of course. My family was famous now, and not in a good way.

I nodded as my gaze dropped to the ground.

"That must be hard," she said. "For you. And her kids. I mean … your grandkids."

"Yes. It is. It's like drowning." The words spilled out before I could stop them. "Just to wake up underwater again. Like that Bill Murray movie in which the day repeats itself. Only, we just drown. Again and again. Nothing else."

My eyes burned.

Goddammit, Nicole. Not now.

She nodded.

"If it means anything," she said, "I don't think she did it. Your daughter, I mean."

My head snapped up.

"Do you know anything?" The plea was raw. I was clearly begging.

"I don't think so," she said. "I couldn't talk to the officer in front of Billy, but I also don't really have much. I woke up that night and heard Billy and John arguing in the kitchen."

Her jaw tightened.

"John showed up out of the blue after more than two years of absence. Borrowed Billy's truck. I hate it when he does that. It's never for anything good."

Her eyes drifted to her son. He'd found a friend and was racing him down the slide, both boys laughing hard. For a moment, warmth softened her face. Then it was gone.

"When I walked into the kitchen that night, John was there. Covered in blood."

My stomach dropped.

"They stopped talking the second they saw me. Something bad had happened. I could feel it. Billy told me to go back to bed. So I did. I'm scared of John. But Billy … he's too soft to cut ties with him. Says we need the money."

"Do you have his phone number? Or address?"

She shook her head.

"Anything else you remember from that night?"

Another shake. Slower this time.

"No. Nothing specific. Think he lives in Florida. Or North Carolina.

I'm not sure. But I know he did something really bad that night." Her arms tightened around the baby. "There's something wrong with him. He's the kind of man who could kill someone and then go watch a game at a bar, cracking jokes." Her eyes stayed on the playground. On her son. "I begged Billy to cut ties with him. But he brushes me off."

My hand reached for her arm.

"I'll put him behind bars," I said. The words came out steady, even though I felt so lost. "I swear it. Soon you won't have to be afraid of Myers anymore."

Something flickered in her eyes. Small. Fragile. Hope, maybe.

All of this made me so angry. What kind of idiot husband lets a man like Myers anywhere near his kids? And leaves it to his wife to keep them safe?

"I don't know if this helps," she said, leaning forward as her voice dropped to a whisper. "But Billy told me that some developer is paying folks in cash for some construction job in Newburyport right now. John sometimes drives up for these kinds of jobs. They pay more than jobs in the South. And whenever John is in the area, he stays at the Seacoast Inn near Manchester by the Sea. The owner owes him a favor. Keeps a room for him, off the books or something."

Seacoast Inn.

I knew the place. Rough didn't even begin to cover it. Hookers. Drugs. Guaranteed bed bugs.

I nodded and rose.

"This helps a lot," I said. "Thank you. From the bottom of my heart."

"Do you think you can really get him locked up?"

The fear in her voice was real. She wasn't just worried; she was terrified. And she had every reason to be. Unlike Billy, she understood what men like Myers were capable of. Borrowing a friend's truck. Killing someone. Letting an innocent woman rot in jail for it. Killing Billy someday over a lost bet or a debt or nothing at all was absolutely in the cards. And if she was unlucky, she and the kids would be in the way when it happened.

"I'll do everything I can," I told her.

I pulled a scrap of paper from my pocket, wrote down my number, then added *Mom from the playground* at the top. Just in case Billy found it.

"Call me if you need anything. Or if Myers shows up. If you feel unsafe in any way, leave and call 911."

"I'll be fine," she said.

She took the number anyway and tucked it into her coat pocket.

Before turning away, my eyes drifted to her son. He was still laughing. Still chasing another boy down the slide. Carefree.

"Thank you," I said again.

"Wait," she said. "John drives a red truck and has a long scar across his forehead. That's why he wears a baseball cap. To hide it."

I nodded.

For a moment, we just looked at each other. Two parents. Knowing exactly what needed to be done.

Then I left.

I hurried back to my car, fingers already pulling my phone from my pocket. Nolan needed to hear this.

But reality stopped me cold.

What could Nolan even do? He'd already said the Myers lead was closed. The DA's instructions. And this conversation, as important as it felt, proved nothing.

My car engine was running before I realized I'd turned the key.

I typed Seacoast Inn into the GPS.

I had no idea what I planned to do there. Of course, I wasn't going to confront the owner like this was some Chuck Norris movie. And Myers most likely wasn't even there. But maybe I could ask around a bit. Discreetly. And, who knew? Maybe life would show me an ounce of mercy for once and Myers would actually be there. Then I could get a picture of Myers' license plate. With his license plate, we'd have something. A real name. An address.

I was already on the road before it hit me how dangerous all of this was. But what choice did I have?

The Seacoast Inn sat right outside Manchester by the Sea.

The GPS read thirty-four minutes.

If I hurried, I could check it out before my visit with Lacey today.

25

NICOLE

I shifted in my seat. It was already getting dark as I sat in the parking lot of the Seacoast Inn. It was completely run-down. Moldy roof and siding. Chipped paint. A few cracked windows. The parking lot smelled of urine.

I'd already missed my visit with Lacey today, and that hurt a lot. I'd promised myself I wouldn't miss it. Ever. But sitting here, watching prostitutes and drug addicts come and go, I couldn't make myself leave before seeing Myers or getting a chance to talk to somebody.

Just one more minute. That's what I told myself. Minute after minute. Over and over again.

I huffed and did another dry run with the camera, practicing how to discreetly take pictures when Myers showed up. But the damn thing snapped a photo of the upper half of my face again. Third time. I'd hit the reverse camera by accident.

"Damn phone," I muttered, stabbing at the screen until it finally cooperated.

I held it ready in my hand and watched from my car as another woman stumbled out of her vehicle and toward one of the motel rooms. She wore a mini dress in this cold weather. Her makeup was too much, like she'd reapplied it for days without ever washing it off.

The woman swayed left and right and stopped in front of a room, digging through her purse. Probably for her keys. When she couldn't find them, she sat on the concrete and knocked her head gently against the door in frustration.

After all that, she just curled up and passed out on the ground.

I watched as a door slowly creaked open a few rooms down.

An older man stepped out in boxers and a white T-shirt. He looked at her. Then to his left and right. He hesitated, as if considering. Then he started walking toward her.

He checked the lot again, shoulders hunched, head swiveling. Making sure no one was watching.

He then nudged the tip of his slipper into the woman's back.

She didn't respond.

Then he grabbed her by the arms and started dragging her toward his room.

Jesus Christ.

"Hey!" I shouted and jumped out of my car.

He looked at me as I sprinted across the parking lot.

"Let her go!"

He dropped her instantly and bolted back toward his room. I chased him, just missing him as his door slammed shut in my face.

I turned around and rushed to the woman.

She smelled like a whole liquor store. Completely passed out, but her chest rose and fell steadily. Her skin was icy under my fingers.

I took my coat off and tucked it around her as best I could. My hands started shaking as reality settled in. Myers, this place, this woman on the ground.

It hit me all at once.

"Damn it," I mumbled. What was I supposed to do now?

At first, I wanted to run to the manager's office, but I couldn't leave her here. What if that man came back?

I fumbled for my phone and called Nolan's number.

"Hello?" he answered quickly.

"It's me, Nicole," I said.

"I know."

"I need your help," I said. "I'm in front of the Seacoast Inn—"

"The Seacoast Inn?"

Of course he was shocked. Everybody knew this place.

"Yes. I'm here with a blackout-drunk prostitute."

"A what?"

"I … I just saved her from a rape, I think."

"W-what?"

"The man is only a few doors down. I don't know what to do."

"Goddammit, Nicole! How the hell did you end up there in the first place?"

"That doesn't matter right now. Can you please come? The man might come back and hurt us both."

"Jesus Christ. Why didn't you call 911?"

"I'm not sure if it could hurt Lacey's case if I'm found here. Are you coming?"

"I can't. I'm escorting a murderer to the station."

I heard a pause, then Nolan spoke again, away from the phone.

"Dispatch, this is Nolan. Possible sexual assault attempt at the Seacoast Inn. Female unconscious. Suspect still on-site. Send a unit immediately." Another short pause. "Nicole?" He was back on the line.

"Yes."

"Can you get yourself to safety?"

I looked around. I could try to drag the woman around the corner.

"I think so. Hang on."

Quickly, I rose and shoved the phone into my pocket. Then I started dragging her. God, she was so skinny. How could this be such a workout?

Somehow I managed to pull her around the corner of the motel, all while Detective Nolan kept yelling my name through the phone, asking what was going on.

"I dragged her out of sight." I huffed, completely out of breath.

"Good. Stay there. A patrol car is less than a minute away. I'll stay on the line until they get there."

26

NICOLE

"Here," the officer said, handing me his card.

I glanced over my shoulder.

The motel was dead silent. No voices. No one in sight. Nobody wanted any contact with the police. Not a single door had cracked open when the police arrived—not even a curious peek. Except for the man's door. The one the police had kicked in when he refused to open it.

Apparently, there was a warrant out for his arrest—for drug trafficking.

He shot me hateful glares as the officers dragged him across the parking lot. They shoved him into the back of the patrol car and slammed the door shut.

The woman was already in an ambulance. Most likely just drunk, they said, but they wanted to take her to a hospital just in case.

The ambulance drove off. I watched it disappear and put the card in my pocket.

"Call us if you remember anything else," the young officer said. His face looked tired and bored, as if at the end of his shift.

He turned and walked back to the patrol car with the man in the back, who was grousing about something as the officer got in. Probably professing his innocence.

I walked back to my car too. The seat was cold when I slid in, and I couldn't help but feel like I had failed Lacey.

No red truck.

No Myers.

Exhaustion settled deep in my bones. The kind that made me want to sleep for days. For a second, the idea of getting a room nearby almost won. Just sleep. Just stop.

But the kids needed me.

And after missing my visit with Lacey, I needed to see them too. Even if it meant driving another hour. So I drove to Amanda's.

By the time I pulled into the driveway, it was pitch black. Only the narrow path to the back door was lit, small solar lights glowing softly.

The night smelled like the nearby ocean. It helped get the booze and urine stench out of my nose.

I had almost walked all the way up to the back door when my steps slowed. I looked through the large windows and saw Brian sitting at the dinner table.

When did Brian get here?

The kids were there too. With Amanda. All of them gathered around the dining table. Amanda rushed into the kitchen, grabbing a steaming bowl of something. I couldn't make out what it was.

There they were, sitting together like a family.

Lila and Ethan looked completely content, leaning toward each other. Dylan didn't smile as much, but he looked a hell of a lot better than he had in weeks.

The kids had missed Amanda. And Brian had missed her too. She had been a part of this family for so long. Her absence was a great loss to us.

I was about to knock but froze.

Was I even welcome here? Somehow, it seemed like I was the person connecting them to Lacey. Like I would drag murder and grief into a peaceful house.

So I stayed where I was. Watching. Maybe a minute. Maybe five. Ten. I didn't know.

Then Dylan pulled out his phone. Fingers moving across the screen.

A moment later, my cell vibrated.

A text. From Dylan.

Where are you? Is everything all right?

I typed back.

Yes. Everything is fine. Just busy.

The dots appeared. Disappeared. Appeared again.

Did you see Mom? She doing okay?

I'd never lied like this before. But that was before I had grandkids asking about their dying mother in jail.

Yes. She's looking good. She even smiled at me.

Even from here, I could see the smile on Dylan's face.

I'll stay the night at the house, I texted. *Too tired to drive back to get you. Is that okay?*

Yeah, sure, he wrote back. *Love you.*

He slipped the phone into his pocket and turned back to the table.

I turned and walked back to the car. The door shut with a thud. It was strange, but I felt happiness. Not for me—for the kids. They had laughed again. Had a proper dinner—even if it was only for a night. It was some kind of normal life again.

But then sadness pressed in just as hard.

For Lacey.

For myself.

For them too.

I started the car and drove back to Lacey's house. By now, it was the only place I had. I'd sold my own house. Every dollar had gone to legal fees, to keeping the kids fed, to keeping the lights on while Brian was out of work.

The street was quiet when I pulled up. The reporters were gone. No cameras. No voices calling out questions. After weeks of silence on our end, even the most stubborn ones had finally given up.

The door creaked as I opened it, and my hand lifted toward the light switch.

But then my phone vibrated in my pocket.

Dylan again?

Detective Nolan?

The bright white screen lit up the entryway from an unknown local number.

I answered. "Hello?"

The sound hit first. Crying, high and panicked. Kids. And, beneath it, a woman sobbing so hard she could barely breathe.

"Is this Nicole?" The voice was hard to hear over the crying kids in the background.

I knew instantly who it was. Mrs. Dustin.

"Yes!"

"It's Sam. Billy's wife. We met at the playground."

"What happened?"

A shaky breath. More crying in the background.

"Um … I don't know who else to call. I'm so sorry."

"No. No, it's fine. What happened?"

"Can … can you come get us?"

"Yes. Of course. Are you safe? Is he there?"

"No. He left to get cigarettes."

"Good. Do you have your car and car keys?"

"Yes."

"Listen to me. Get in your car right now and meet me at the playground."

"But I can't just take the kids away from him."

"Yes, you can. Grab your kids. Now. And meet me there as soon as you can."

More crying followed.

"Leave now. You hear me?"

No answer.

"Sam. Take the kids and leave. Do it for them. For you. And for him too, if you have to. Otherwise, nothing will change. If he really loves you, he'll put in the work. Maybe he'll be one of the few abusers out there who actually changes. But only if you stop putting up with this."

A long pause. Breathing. Sniffling.

"I'll meet you there," she finally said. The line went dead.

I was about to leave, when a sharp pain hit my chest. It spread quickly and cut off my air. For a second, I thought I was having a heart attack. But then I remembered this feeling, from a long time ago. When I found out I was pregnant with Lacey at only seventeen.

It was panic. Raw and uncontrollable. I was having a panic attack.

"Not now, Nicole," I scolded myself and clutched my chest. "Stop it. Not now!"

I slammed the door shut behind me and hurried back to the car.

The plan formed quickly. Playground first. I had to get them somewhere safe.

And after that, I would do the one thing I dreaded more than anything else.

But I needed help.

And doing this alone wasn't possible anymore.

27

NICOLE

We were all here. In my living room. Like some kind of broken family retreat.

Sam sat slumped on the couch, shoulders caved in, her body folded in on itself. Her eyes were swollen and red. One eye was half shut, purple and yellow already blooming where the prick had hit her.

The kids slept next to her, curled up together on the couch. Mouths slightly open. Faces smudged with dried tears. One small foot dangled over the edge.

I shifted closer to Sam, fingers wrapped around her hand, and squeezed it. She squeezed back without looking at me.

Detective Nolan stood in the middle of the living room. He wasn't sitting. He was just standing there.

His gaze moved slowly and settled on me. Then Sam. The kids. And back to me again.

The room was completely silent. The only sound was the clock on the wall, ticking loudly.

Then Nolan's shoulders sagged. His hands came up to his face, and he rubbed it hard. When he spoke, his voice was muffled through his fingers.

"Nicole, can … um … can I talk to you please?"

"Sure," I said.

His hands dropped to his hips. He straightened, then glanced past me toward the couch. Sam. The kids. Then his eyes locked back onto mine.

"Alone?"

"Oh. Yes. Of course."

The kitchen light flicked on as we stepped inside. He paused in the doorway, looking back over his shoulder again, eyes lingering on Sam. On the bruises. On the sleeping kids.

Then he closed the door and turned to me.

"Nicole … are you trying to kill me?"

"What?"

I scanned him head to toe. The dark shadows carved under his eyes. The way his hair stuck up in odd directions, like he'd been running his hands through it for days straight. He looked worn thin. So, so tired.

"I'm just asking," he said in a strained voice, "because you are literally putting me in the ground." A long breath escaped him. "Please tell me that isn't the suspect's friend sitting in your living room."

"It's not."

"Oh, so that's not Mrs. Dustin then?"

"Well … it … is. But she isn't the *suspect's* friend. Her husband is."

He bit his bottom lip, clearly swallowing a curse as he shook his head.

"Goddammit, Nicole." His voice rose a little. "Your grandkids are freaking sleeping upstairs, and you bring the murderer's friend's family into your house—"

"My kids aren't sleeping upstairs."

His head jerked back, confusion flashing across his face.

"I took them to Amanda's."

His eyes widened like he was watching a horror movie.

"You … took your grandkids … to the victim's widow?" His voice rose despite himself. "The State's main witness against your daughter? The murdered man's widow?"

He threw his hands up.

"I can't believe this," he snapped. "Does none of this seem like a bad idea to you? At all?" His hands flew up, then dropped hard against his legs with a dull thud. "The murderer's friends are sitting in your living room, and your family is with the victim's widow. You're the suspect's family, just in case you forgot."

"Well," I said quietly, "when you put it that way ..."

He started pacing back and forth. "I can't believe this."

"I'm sorry." The words rushed out of me fast. "Sam can't stand Myers. And Billy hit her. Sam's son, Henry, told his dad that Sam had talked to me on the playground. He told his dad I was the woman from the news. Gosh, kids are so observant. But now she has nowhere else to go."

"You talked to her on the playground?" His head snapped up. "Have you lost your mind?"

"I don't like any of this either," I said, heat creeping up my neck. "But my family is slowly dying. Literally." My fists balled. "I have to find the real killer myself because the AG would rather see my daughter dead than catch him. To get even for his rapist son."

He didn't answer. Didn't agree. Didn't disagree.

"What was I supposed to do?" My voice rose despite myself. "Just leave her there with Billy to beat her up in front of the kids?"

"Call 911."

"Why would I call 911 when she didn't? She wouldn't have talked to the police. And without her agreeing to leave him, you and I both know she'd still be sitting in that trailer. And don't act like you don't know how domestic violence cases are handled when the police are called. They'd tell him to sleep in his truck for the night, then he'd be right back inside the next day." I crossed my arms. "So, honestly, in all this madness, getting Sam and the kids away from that trash is the only good thing that has happened in weeks." My gaze stayed on him. Steady. "And if you see it any other way, there's the door."

Nolan stopped pacing. His hands dragged through his hair. A loud breath pushed out of him, full of frustration. Then his gaze caught mine, and he nodded.

"Has anyone ever told you that you're the most stubborn person on this planet?"

My lips curled into a smile. "You should meet my grandson Dylan."

"Rain check on that," he said, returning a tired smile before the moment passed.

"What can we do to help them?" My head turned toward the living room, toward Sam and the kids. "They can stay here for now, but what if he comes for them?"

Nolan shook his head. "They can't stay here. Mrs. Dustin might be a witness in your daughter's murder trial. Her testimony could be important. We can't have her look like your friend who lives with you." He exhaled. "And it's not safe. What if Billy comes for them?"

His jaw tightened.

"Fuck. I'll fix this. Somehow," he said, then went quiet, eyes unfocused, thinking. Then a nod. "Okay. I'll drive them to a women's shelter north of Boston. I know the director well. She's good at what she does. They'll get a room there. Food. Clothes. Money. Toys. Even a lawyer. If anyone can get Sam to leave that piece of shit, it's her."

I nodded.

"After that, I'll drive to Billy's," Nolan continued. "Let him know they're at a shelter. So he doesn't start looking for them here and cause trouble."

Another nod.

"And first thing tomorrow morning, you get your family back," he said. "They can't stay at the victim's widow's house. None of this helps you in the end. It could just cause more problems than you need right now."

I nodded again, even though I knew I wouldn't be able to follow that request. There was no law against living with the victim's widow when you were related to the suspect. No rule saying I had to tear my family apart just to make things easier for everyone else. My family had eaten a normal dinner for the first time in weeks. The kids had smiled again. Brian had looked sober.

The kids needed a mom. And Amanda could hold that place for Lacey while I tried to save her. Until Lacey could take it back.

"Are you going to look into Myers?" I asked.

Nolan cocked a brow. "So that's what you were doing at the Seacoast Inn."

"Sam told me that's where he stays when he's around," I said. "She also told me that the night of Zach's murder, Billy and Myers were arguing in the kitchen. Myers was covered in blood. Something felt off, she said. She just knew he'd done something really bad that night."

Nolan listened. His gaze stayed fixed and serious. Then he leaned back against the counter. "Fuck."

"What are we going to do?" I asked. "We need to find him."

"First of all," he said, straightening, "there is no *we*." His tone hardened. "You'll leave this investigation to me. If I have questions, I'll reach out. And that's it. No more playing Columbo or Miss Marple. This isn't a TV show. In the real world, people get hurt doing what you're doing." His eyes locked on mine. "And the last thing those kids need is to lose their grandma too."

I stared at him in silence.

He took it as agreement. And maybe it was. "Good," he said. "Now get some rest. I'll get Mrs. Dustin and the kids to Susan. She'll take care of them."

He turned toward the living room, but I grabbed his arm. His eyes dropped to my hand.

"Thank you."

For the first time since the murder, some of the weight fell off my shoulders. Like I wasn't carrying all of this alone anymore. Like somebody was fighting with me. Not against me.

"Get some rest," he said. "I'll text you once they're at the shelter."

He took another step, then stopped.

"And for Christ's sake," he added, "next time, call me before you do anything that, you know, a sweet teacher shouldn't be doing."

"I don't want to lie to you again," I said softly. "So I can't make that promise."

He blinked. "Wait. Lie again? When did you lie to me?"

I gently pushed him toward the living room. "Let's talk about that another time. I want to say good-bye to Sam. Then I need to get some sleep, or I'll end up in the psych ward tonight."

He let it go, barely, an annoyed look on his face.

"Fine. I'll start the car and carry the kids to their car seats."

28

NICOLE

A noise coming from the front door woke me up.

My body jerked upright. The couch groaned underneath me as I pushed myself up. I was still dressed. Same pants. Same wool sweater. Same shoes.

I must have passed out here after Detective Nolan took the Dustin family to the shelter.

I turned toward the hallway with a stiff neck and found Dylan standing in the doorway.

Tall. Too tall for sixteen. Just like his dad had been back then.

Fog clouded my thoughts. The room felt foggy, like I was still dreaming.

"W-what time is it?" I looked for my phone. The cushions must have swallowed it.

"Eleven in the morning," Dylan said.

My whole body went rigid. "Dear God, I never sleep that long."

I looked him over. Sneakers. Jeans. A baseball cap pulled low, the same way his dad always wore it. His school bag hung loose over one shoulder.

"Wait." I pushed myself to my weak feet. "Why aren't you in school, Dylan?"

He crossed the room and sat in the TV chair beside the couch. He leaned back, shoulders sinking into the worn cushion as his fingers played with the loose fabric.

"Because ..." The sentence died halfway out of his mouth.

"Oh, Dylan. Did you get in trouble again? Did you get suspended?"

"No." He shook his head. "It's nothing like that. Dad called the school for me. He told them I was sick today."

"Are you sick?"

"No."

His eyes scanned me, head to toe.

"Are you okay, Grandma?"

"Yeah." That came too fast. "Why, honey?"

He wrinkled his forehead. "You joking? Have you looked at yourself?"

My gaze drifted to the hallway mirror. Even from here, the reflection hit hard.

My hair was unbrushed, sticking out in uneven strands. Mascara was smeared beneath my eyes, black and harsh. I was still wearing the same clothes I'd been in for three days straight. I stank of perfume and sweat.

I looked like I'd escaped the psych ward and stopped here for a nap.

My throat tightened. "I'm just ... a bit tired, honey." I forced my lips into something that looked like a smile. "But why aren't you in school? Please just tell me. I don't want to worry for nothing."

"I ..." His gaze dropped to his shoes as his fingers went back to playing with the ripped piece of fabric on the chair.

"Dylan," I said. "Just tell me what's going on."

"Ah, fuck it." He lifted his head, and his eyes locked onto mine. "I'm going to visit Mom in jail today."

My body moved before my thoughts caught up, and I rose to my feet. "You're what?"

"Don't get mad." He stood up like he'd expected this. "I didn't want to do it behind your back. So I came here first. To tell you in person and ask if you want to come with me."

"But ... but you can't visit her!"

He straightened, squaring his shoulders. "Why not? She's my mom. I'm sixteen."

"I get that, honey, but your mom ..."

Your mom what?

Your mom looks like she's dying from the cancer I was hiding from him?

The words clogged in my throat.

"My mom what?" he asked, eyes narrowing like he could already hear the lie forming.

"She ..." I swallowed. "People don't just let kids visit jails. The jail needs to approve it. They need to run background checks. All of that. I don't even know if they allow minors at all."

His arms crossed over his chest. "Mm-hmm. Well, I have good news then. Dad called them first thing this morning for me."

My stomach dropped. "He did what?"

A humorless sound left him. "Yeah, he's actually good for something when he's sober." His mouth twisted. "Amanda somehow keeps him out of the bars. Not like we could."

"Amanda, huh? Well, I'm sure she told you it's better not to go and see your mom."

"Nope." He shook his head. "It was her idea. She thinks it would help me. Help me process things. Sort out all my emotions."

The room grew hotter suddenly.

None of this felt real. I'd been gone from them for what? Two days? Or was it three? Four? And then this?

"Well, that's very kind of Amanda," I said slowly. "But maybe Amanda isn't the best judge of things right now. Amanda isn't doing so well herself."

"So? None of us is," he snapped.

And why wouldn't he defend her? Even I knew she was right. Seeing Lacey might help him. Might ground him. But what none of them knew was that Lacey was dying.

In all the fighting to get her out, to stretch her time, to get her better medical care, I hadn't let myself think about the other possibility. The one where she didn't make it. The one where she died in there.

Without Dylan.

Without the kids.

Without good-byes and last hugs.

The idea pressed down on my shoulders until my body gave in and dropped back onto the couch. My breathing struggled to catch up, and I stared wide-mouthed into nothingness.

Dylan rushed forward to my side. His hand closed around mine. Warm. Strong. The only thing linking me to reality. To being alive at all. Without it, I might have slipped somewhere dark and hollow. Somewhere I'd already been visiting too often lately.

"Grandma, you all right?"

The sound of his voice reached me, but no words formed into an answer. My mouth opened, then closed again.

"If it upsets you so much, I won't—"

"No," I said, and pushed myself to sit upright. "No. You're right. You should see your mom. I'm sorry I didn't take you to see her sooner."

"It's okay." He placed his arm around me, protective. "I know you're doing all this for us. Even more than for her. You're doing it for me."

I looked at him long and deep. Those blue eyes were just like his father's. But Dylan's were stronger.

I smiled and rested my hand against his cheek.

What a man Dylan had become. Everything his father wasn't.

"I talked with the jail psychologist this morning," he said. "He was able to get me an emergency visit this afternoon. He said Mom isn't doing well."

I nodded, and my vision started to blur. My thumb brushed his cheek before falling back into my lap.

"He's right, sweetheart." I was barely holding it together. "And there's something else you need to know about your mom. But before I tell you, I need you to listen to me."

I gripped his hand tighter.

"I'm fixing this. I'm getting her out. So she'll have more time. With us."

His eyes never left mine.

He was so strong. Stronger than any sixteen-year-old should be.

Dylan nodded at me. Giving me permission to finally tell him the truth.

29

DYLAN

I was sitting in a dirty plastic chair next to my grandma in the jail visitation room. The stench of cigarette smoke and mold swallowed us and clung to my clothes. Across from me sat my mom.

She looked nothing like herself. I knew it was her, of course. The facial features were there. But the once so lively and sparkly person I knew was now nothing more than skin and bones. Her orange jail suit hung off her bony frame. Her collarbones jutted out sharply, and her hands rested limp in her lap. Her hair was wild, dull, and like hay, with strands sticking out at odd angles, like it hadn't been brushed in weeks. Her cheeks had sunken inward, creating spooky-looking shadows all over her face.

Her eyes stared past me, fixed on nothing. Like she was already gone and only her body was still here. Moving when told. Just a machine without a beating heart that would land in the junkyard soon.

As a teen mom, she always looked so young. People sometimes asked if we were siblings. Now that thought seemed crazy. Mom looked more zombie than human.

I could barely look at her. It was like my heart shattered into a million pieces, then somebody fed the pieces into a grinder so my heart could never be put back together again.

I wanted to scream.

Break things.

Punch a hole in the wall large enough so we could both escape.

But I had to be strong. For her. And as much as it hurt, I couldn't put into words how much it meant to me to be able to see her again. Talk to her again.

If you wanted to call this talking.

A female correctional officer stood next to her. She was kind enough to hold the phone up to Mom's ear so she could hear me.

"So, yeah," I said, leaning forward. "I guess I'm kinda dating, but I'm gonna break up with her."

I sounded casual. Like this was just another conversation at home before dinner.

"She's just kinda mean, you know," I continued. "I heard her make fun of this new girl at school. About her crooked teeth. And you know I don't like bullies." I paused, thinking, then shrugged. "She won't be heartbroken for long, though. She's the prettiest girl in school. She can have another boyfriend just like that."

Snapping my fingers, I nodded to myself, as if Mom and I had just come up with this plan together. "So yeah. I'll break it off."

My lips curled into a soft smile.

There was a time when Mom would've begged me for moments like these. Begged me to talk about school. About football. Soccer. Girls. Back then, she got little more than annoyed shrugs and clipped answers from me. It's nothing. It's whatever.

Now I offered her everything. Every detail. Like it might be the last time I could tell her who I was.

I glanced briefly at Grandma, who sank her teeth into her lower lip, staring at the floor. She swallowed hard as tears filled her eyes.

"Wrestling is going well," I said. "I made the team." I quickly pulled my sleeve over the bruise on my lower arm so she wouldn't notice. The one from my fight with Dad.

"Dad is doing good too," I said quickly, worried she might have seen the lie and suspected something. "Oh, and soccer is going well too."

Mom just stared past me, not even blinking.

"The last match we had, we won. And I kicked the winning goal."

My hands moved more as I talked. More animated. More effort for her.

"And there's this new girl on the girls' soccer team. She's kinda cute." A faint smile tugged at my mouth. "And she's, like, doing work with the homeless and stuff. You know. Good heart and shit."

I glanced at Mom, waiting for something. Anything. But nothing came, so I continued.

"I might ask her out once things are over with Amelie." I shrugged again. "We'll see."

There was an awkward silence. It was kinda hard to hold a conversation for two. When it got quiet, Grandma jumped in.

"Oh yeah," she said in an excited tone as she straightened in her chair. "Dylan got an A in math."

"Like, what the fuck, right?" I added.

"Language," she scolded me.

I waved it off. "You'd think with everything going on—" I stopped mid-sentence. Swallowed. Reset.

"I mean … anyway. Grades are good. Girls are still going. And soccer needs me so bad they're basically begging me to come to practice." My voice softened. "And the little monsters are doing well too. Ethan's using the potty now. Well, kinda. And Lila wants a horse." I paused, thinking hard. "Let's see, what else—"

"Five minutes," the guard reminded us.

"Dylan." Grandma reached out and placed her hand gently on my shoulder. "Could I have a moment alone with your mom?"

I looked at her. Then at Mom. And nodded.

"Well … I'll see you next week, Mom. Make sure you eat more. I love you. A lot. I always will. Okay?"

I stood up quickly, just in time before the first tear might roll, and handed the phone to Grandma.

Then I left without looking back. To make sure she wouldn't see me cry. To make sure my visit helped her. Not make her feel worse.

~

Nicole

My instinct was to run after Dylan, to make sure he didn't fall apart the second the door closed behind him. But I stayed. I needed to talk to Lacey. So much depended on it.

Quickly, I grabbed the phone and scooted my chair closer to the glass.

"Lacey," I said, leaning in. "Listen to me."

My eyes flicked toward the guard. She was distracted, watching another family two stalls down.

"I found him," I whispered. "I found the man who killed Zach."

I tapped my own forehead. "The man with the scar. Right here."

For a moment, her eyes moved. Just barely. But they moved. Up. Toward me.

My hands started shaking as I scooted even closer, pressing my knees into the wall separating us.

"His name is John Myers," I whispered quickly.

Her eyes locked onto mine. God, have mercy. For the first time in weeks, Lacey was actually looking at me. Really looking at me.

"He ... he—" I stuttered. Then got hold of myself. "He was seen that night. Covered in blood and—"

"Time's up," the guard barked.

"No, wait!" I shot to my feet so fast the chair tipped backward.

But the guard had already grabbed Lacey's arm, trying to pull her up, and she resisted. She actually resisted!

There was still life in her!

She pushed against the guard's grip, and her thin body went rigid.

"Wait!" I shouted. "I found him, Lacey. You hear me?"

Her eyes were wide now. She shook her head. Hard. Over and over. Like she was terrified.

"Wait!" I yelled again, barely noticing the guard next to me.

"Ma'am, you need to calm down," she ordered. She was a short woman with a tight, shiny bun. She gripped my arm.

Lacey was fighting now. Pushing against the guard, her eyes never leaving mine. Her head was shaking violently.

Another guard rushed in to help drag her away. It should have been easy, considering her weight.

It wasn't.

By God, my daughter was fighting.

"Please wait!" I shouted after them.

But the heavy metal door slammed shut behind her. The sound echoed back to me.

And she was gone.

I stood there, shaking.

"Ma'am, please leave," the guard next to me demanded. Her fingers dug into my arm harder.

I tore myself free. "I'll leave." I raised my hands in surrender. "I'll leave."

The guard walked me out of the visiting room. The heavy door swung open and heads turned, curious eyes following me as I passed.

Dylan was waiting in the hallway.

"Everything okay?" he asked the second he saw me.

"You good?" the guard with the bun asked me in a brisk tone.

I nodded.

She rolled her eyes. "Don't pull this shit again, or your visitation rights will be revoked."

Then she turned and walked back into the room without waiting for an answer. The door shut behind her with a thud.

I turned to Dylan.

He was staring at me. His shoulders slumped, and his lips started to tremble. Whatever strength he'd held onto in that room was gone. The strong young man who'd sat across from his mother was gone. And what stood in front of me was a hurting boy.

Then he broke. The sound came first. A rough inhale that turned into a sob. Then another. His body folded in on itself as tears poured down his cheeks. He cried and cried, shoulders shaking, face pressed into my shoulder as I wrapped my arms around him and held on tightly.

"I know," I said. "I know."

30

NICOLE

"You sure you don't wanna come in?" Dylan asked as we sat in the car outside Amanda's. "Ethan and Lila would love to see you."

I looked out the window, staring at Amanda's multimillion-dollar home. A mix of modern and colonial. Clean white siding and large stone steps. It screamed money in every inch of its perfect landscaping.

"I'd love to, but it's better if I don't come in."

I expected a "Why?" but, instead, Dylan's eyes dropped for just a second before he nodded.

He knew. He was too smart and observant not to. I was Lacey's fighter. The one who never stopped. And to Amanda, Lacey might still be Zach's murderer.

"Go now, before the little monsters see me. And kiss them for me."

Dylan leaned over and hugged me. I held him a second longer than usual. Then he pulled away and got out, his schoolbag slung over one shoulder.

I watched him walk up the path. Amanda had already opened the door. She welcomed him with a quick hug, one hand firm on his shoulder. He disappeared into the house.

She stayed in the doorway, staring at me. Her face was sad.

Conflicted. Like she wanted to say something but didn't trust herself. Then she turned and closed the door.

I put the car in Drive and drove home.

My thoughts wouldn't slow down.

Dylan. Then Lila. Brian. Nolan. Myers. But mostly Lacey.

She looked horrible.

The image wouldn't leave me. Her skin was so pale. Her eyes sunken and dull. Time was running out. Tomorrow, I'd meet with the public defender Nolan had recommended to see if there was any way to get her out on bail because of her cancer. She was barely a flight risk, dying like this. Anyone with eyes could see it.

But the DA. That prick. He'd do anything to see her die in jail. He would bend the law into whatever shape he could to deny her bail.

At this point, there was no doubt left in me that Myers had killed Zach. Lacey's reaction alone said it all. The way her body changed when I mentioned the man with the scar. She remembered him. She couldn't say it. The trauma was still running too deep to push past it.

Did he make her watch the murder?

My hands balled into fists as I remembered the police report. She'd urinated all over herself. Her clothes were torn. Maybe from a rape attempt. Who knew.

Damn this world. All of it.

I pulled into the driveway and noticed the reporters were still gone. That was great news.

I parked and saw the neighbors, Anne and George, pulling in with their kids. The moment they spotted me, their movements changed. Quicker. Tense. They rushed the kids inside like I was Jack the Ripper.

Then Mr. Warner walked past me on the sidewalk with Ginny, the huge Doberman. The moment she saw me, she pulled my way. She must have remembered the treats I usually kept in my pocket for her.

For a second, I worried he wouldn't let her come close. But quietly, without a word, he did.

Ginny stepped right up, sniffing my pockets.

"I'm so sorry, sweetheart. I don't have anything today."

She licked my hand anyway and leaned into me, asking to be petted. I stroked her enormous chest. It was like she knew. Like she could feel my pain. Maybe she wanted to show that she was here for me too, just like I had been there for her when the whole neighborhood called her the beast and ran from her.

"Thank you, sweet girl," I mumbled to her.

Mr. Warner gently pulled her back. He nodded once and kept walking.

Inside, I locked the door behind me and hung up my coat. I tried not to look in the hallway mirror. But I did anyway.

My brown hair looked like an oily bird's nest. My eyes looked tired and stared back at me like they had had enough of life itself.

God. I'd lost weight too. And I looked dirty. Absolutely homeless.

But even though a shower sounded amazing, it felt like more than I could handle right now. It would require energy I didn't have. And even bending down to take off my shoes was asking too much.

Somehow, the shoes came off, and I forced myself up the stairs. Each step felt heavier than the last. God, I was so, so tired. And what if something else happened today? Like Dylan showing up again. Would I just keep putting off basic hygiene forever?

So I forced myself.

I turned on the shower and got in. Then I just stood there under the stream. My legs felt weak, so I sank to the shower floor, sitting there while the hot water ran down my back.

I washed my hair and body, but now getting out felt so trying. Was this what burnout felt like? Depression?

I sat under the water until it slowly turned cold. Then I got out, dried off, and dressed slowly, like a zombie.

I made my way into the kitchen to get a quick bite. Crackers and cheese. Just enough to keep me alive for today.

After that, I walked to the bedroom. I wanted a real bed tonight. Sheets. Pillows. Something that felt normal.

It was barely late afternoon, but exhaustion already suffocated me.

I turned the TV on for background noise. I just couldn't stop thinking about Lacey and the kids. The same loop, over and over again.

Some crime documentary came on. Something about a crazy neighbor. I left it playing. Maybe watching someone crazier than me would make me feel less alone. Less unhinged.

But the moment I slid under the covers, my eyelids grew heavy. They shut on their own, and the voices from the TV blurred.

Everything faded.

Then darkness.

And deep sleep.

31

NICOLE

The noise of a soft scrape woke me.

It must have still been late. The house was pitch black except for the logo of the TV streaming service glowing on the screen.

I stayed still. Listened. Waiting for another sound. When nothing came, I turned my face into the pillow and closed my eyes again.

Then the hallway stairs creaked.

That sound. I'd heard it a million times before. A footstep pressing against the old wood of an old house.

Somebody was coming up the stairs.

My body jerked upright as adrenaline surged through me. Anyone I knew would just come up the stairs without trying to be quiet.

Another creak.

Closer.

An icy tingle flooded me like a tsunami wave. Quickly, I stumbled out of bed.

Another creak. Halfway up the stairs now.

Reality hit hard. Where could I go? The stairs were the only way down. I looked at the window for a second. But it was too dangerous to jump.

My eyes snapped to the closet. It had no lock.

The bathroom.

I rushed in and locked the door behind me, the click sounding too loud.

Shit.

My phone was downstairs on the hallway sideboard. Left there like an idiot. But what good would it do anyway? The police would never make it in time.

I stood in the dark bathroom. Motionless, I stared at the door.

The creaking stopped.

Right at the top of the stairs.

Then there was only quiet.

Had I imagined it all? Maybe it was just a nightmare? But just as I started to calm down, the bathroom doorknob slowly turned.

Just enough to meet the resistance of the lock.

I watched in horror as the knob eased back into place.

Then silence again.

I didn't breathe. Didn't blink. Didn't move an inch.

This wasn't a dream. Somebody was in my house. Coming after me.

SLAM!

Someone threw their body full force against the locked bathroom door. The white door rattled.

"Help!"

The scream exploded out of me. Raw and full of horror.

The person hurled himself at the door again. Harder this time. The impact shook the wood and my bones. I pushed against the door as hard as I could. But each blow came faster now. Stronger. Again and again. The door shuddered violently, and with every hit, it felt less like a barrier.

It would break and fall on top of me.

My eyes scanned the room for anything sharp to fight with. But there was nothing.

Then my eyes locked onto the window. As insane as it was, it was my only chance.

I launched myself toward it and yanked it open. Behind me, the pounding kept going like a countdown. And just when my hands grabbed the window frame, and I pushed my body through it, wood shattered behind me with a sharp crack.

I dragged myself onto the dormer and eased down toward the main roof. I was almost on the main roof when my attacker grabbed my nightgown.

I turned and caught a glimpse of him. He was wearing a black ski mask.

"Help me!" I screamed and pulled at my nightgown. It ripped, and my foot slipped. The roof's shingles burned against my bare legs like sandpaper as I slid down. I clawed at the roof, trying to stop the fall, but gravity owned me now, and I rolled off the roof.

The ground raced toward me, and the impact was unforgiving. It punched the air out of my lungs. My leg bent the wrong way and snapped. Pain detonated through me. The ground felt wet and cold.

This was pure horror.

"Help!" I screamed again. "Help me!"

My attacker jumped onto the roof. At the edge, he turned smoothly, dangled for a moment, then dropped to the lawn like it was nothing at all.

I tried to scramble up despite my leg's pain paralyzing me. But I didn't make it far. He was on top of me in seconds. His head snapped around, scanning the yard like he was looking for something he had dropped. A knife?

Then his hand closed around my throat and squeezed.

The pressure was crushing. No air came in or out. My eyes bulged, and bright spots burst across my vision.

My fingers desperately clawed at his arms, but his grip didn't loosen.

I tried to scream again, but only gagging groans made it past my lips.

Faces flashed before my eyes.

Lacey.

The kids.

Amanda.

Even Brian. Stupid, horrible Brian, collecting women like tourist-shop magnets.

I felt my body weaken. My arms slackening. The fight draining out of me.

Was this it?

Would it end like this?

The same hands that destroyed my daughter would now end me too, leaving the kids without their mother and grandmother.

I couldn't let that happen!

A different kind of strength rose within me. Ugly and desperate and furious.

"Ehhhbbb!"

My nails dug deeper, scraping harder, refusing to stop.

But his grip stayed tight.

My eyes burned with tears as a new idea emerged. Quickly, my hands shot up, scrambling for the man's ski mask. I needed to see his face so I could come back and haunt him. Follow him from the after-life. Make him pay for what he'd done to my family.

I gripped the mask tight and yanked it sideways.

And there he was.

A round, ugly face, barely lit by the weak glow of the streetlight. His eyes were dark and flat. The large scar on his forehead was impossible to miss.

My body went still.

Myers.

He looked shocked for a moment, and his grip on my throat loosened.

Finally, air filled my lungs in the form of a violent cough.

This was it.

My chance.

The only one I would get.

I gathered every last bit of air and strength. And screamed.

"HEEEEEEEEEEEEELLLLLLLP!"

The sound was so loud, I scared myself. It split the night. My ears rang from it.

A bark exploded two houses down. Ginny the Doberman.

Myers' eyes snapped toward the Warner house just as the porch light flared on and the front door flew open.

"Hel—"

I tried again, but Myers' fist slammed into my face.

There was a loud crack as a hot metallic taste flooded my mouth and poured down my lip.

The bastard broke my nose.

In the distance, Mr. Warner shouted Ginny's name. And I realized that her barking was surging closer.

Suddenly, Myers jumped off. I was free again and rolled onto my side. In the distance, Myers was already sprinting down the street like prey that knew it was being hunted.

"*Ginny*!" Mr. Warner screamed. "*Ginny, no*!"

She didn't listen.

Ginny launched herself at Myers, all muscle and teeth. She hit him hard, jaws clamping onto his leg. He went down hard, slamming onto the road as she shook him wildly like a toy.

Myers screamed. High-pitched and raw.

Moments later, Mr. Warner reached them, barefoot and in boxers. He grabbed Ginny's collar with both hands, bracing his weight back.

"Stop!" Mr. Warner shouted as he pulled at Ginny. But Ginny wasn't having it and dragged Myers violently over the concrete.

"No! Bad dog!" Mr. Warner yelled. "Let go or no treats!"

Finally, she released him just as porch lights turned on one by one.

Myers scrambled up and limped down the street as fast as he could. Mr. Warner was holding on to Ginny's collar as she strained after Myers, barking in short, vicious barks.

"Mr. Warner, help!" I called out.

He turned fast. "Oh my God," he shouted. "Mrs. Kolter!"

He rushed to me, pulling Ginny along.

"Emma!" he yelled toward his house. "Call 911!"

His hands were on me now. Steady. Helping me sit upright.

"Dear God," he said. "I'll get help. Here. In case he comes back."

He pressed Ginny's collar into my hand and took off. I held her in one hand and cupped my broken nose with the other.

She sat by my side, chest heaving up and down, her massive body still shaking with adrenaline. Blood streaked her mouth and teeth.

When my arms wrapped around her massive chest, Ginny leaned into me, solid and warm.

Of course she could run if she wanted. My grip would not hold her. But she stayed, guarding and comforting me all at once.

"Thank you," I cried into her silky fur. "Thank you, Ginny."

I was overwhelmed with emotion.

Relief. Gratitude. Love.

For Ginny. The Doberman everyone hated. The dog that parents pulled their kids away from. The one the neighborhood called the beast.

This queen had my devotion forever. What a hero.

Then the truth settled in. Myers had tried to kill me. And there were witnesses. There was blood. DNA. Evidence. The AG couldn't ignore this.

As crazy as it was, a smile split my bloody lips.

This night of horror was Lacey's chance to prove her innocence.

It was her way out.

32

OFFICER NOLAN

When I pulled up in front of Nicole Kolter's house, the street was the usual chaos of a nighttime crime scene. Blue and red lights reflected against siding and trees, turning a quiet neighborhood into something out of a TV show.

Police cars and EMT vans blocked the road. A few curious neighbors stood on their porches with messy hair.

What was unusual was the large crowd of officers and EMTs blocking the view of the Kolters' house. Just standing there. Shoulder to shoulder. No movement.

When I received the call in the middle of the night from local police to come to Nicole Kolter's home, I didn't know what to make of it. But as I got out of the car and slowly approached the crime scene, things started to make sense.

In all the worst ways.

I walked up and tapped the first officer blocking my path.

"Let me through, please," I said, keeping my voice steady.

He turned quickly. Late thirties. Tired eyes. Clean-shaven.

His gaze caught mine, then dropped to my badge as I held it up. He hesitated, then he stepped aside.

I had to repeat it a few more times. Over and over. An ocean of cops and EMTs slowly parting in front of me, like Moses with a badge instead of a staff.

I thought I was prepared for what I would find. By now, I knew anything involving Nicole Kolter meant a wild ride. That woman turned into a grizzly bear when it came to her kids.

But when the last row of EMTs and officers stepped aside and let me through, my body betrayed me.

I stumbled back in shock.

About twenty feet away, Nicole was sitting on her front lawn in a bloodied nightgown. Her leg was twisted at an angle no leg should ever be. Broken. No doubt about it. And blood drenched the lower half of her face, dripping slowly onto her chest. The pain must have been unbearable.

Beside her sat the biggest Doberman I had ever seen in my life. A beast. Maybe a hundred and forty pounds? More?

It was guarding her. Not letting anyone close.

Its mouth was covered in blood—but not Nicole's. If it were, Nicole wouldn't be sitting next to it.

The beast sat there perfectly still. Alert. Its eyes locked on me. Like it was daring: Do it and see what happens.

Right behind them stood a man in his fifties. Unshaven, in boxers. A down jacket zipped halfway. He looked small somehow. A kid trapped in a grown man's body with no idea what to do next.

I ran a hand through my hair.

This woman. Dear God. How the hell did she end up in this situation? She was one of the kindest souls I knew. Fierce and loyal. A nightmare when crossed, sure, but she didn't deserve this.

"Fucking Christ," I said.

I dragged my hand over my face, then looked up at her again.

"The EMTs can't help her unless someone gets the dog," an officer explained. "It looks like the dog won't leave unless the victim tells her to. And the victim refuses to do so."

I glanced over. His name tag read Mark Ellison. Low voice. Military haircut.

"We also can't shoot it as long as the owner and the victim won't move," he added.

My eyes snapped to his. "Shoot the dog? For what?"

He quickly added, "Of course we wouldn't do that." His eyes flicked to the other officers, a silent exchange passing between them. "We also thought about bringing in one of our K9 units."

I stared at him in disbelief. "And do what, exactly? Incite a dog fight?" My voice rose despite myself. "Are we all gonna place bets while this beast snaps our K9 unit in half?"

A few of the cops looked away. One EMT shifted uncomfortably. Nobody argued.

"Freaking idiots." I looked back at Nicole. Over the radio, they'd told me she'd been attacked but was doing fine.

This was not fine.

"Nicole, we need to get you to a hospital. Your leg and your nose look broken."

She winced as she shifted an inch. Her chin lifted, her eyes steady.

"They are," she said.

I nodded. I tried to stay calm and adjust strategies.

"Are you the owner?" I asked, turning to the man standing behind them.

"Y-yes."

"Can you please take the dog back to your house?"

He shrugged helplessly. "Ginny won't move. And I can't carry a hundred and forty pounds that far with my bad back."

I gave another nod. "Is there anyone who can help? Someone the dog will listen to?"

"My wife," he said, pointing two houses down.

I followed his finger. In the window, an older woman stood in a flowered nightgown, arms crossed tight over her chest, face hard as stone as she stared back at us.

"But?" I prompted.

"But she said she won't move Ginny until Mrs. Kolter says it's okay."

I exhaled slowly. "I see."

I took in a deep breath and exhaled slowly.

"Nicole," I said in a kind tone. "We need to get you checked out by the EMTs." I paused, choosing my words carefully. "Whatever happened here tonight, I need to get on it. Find who did this. And I need to know you're being taken care of while I do. So, please, can we send the dog back home?"

Her eyes lifted to mine. Sharp and clear.

"Well," she said, "first of all, Ginny can go wherever she wants. She's not on a leash."

That did nothing to calm me. Not with a dog that size sitting like it had been placed there with a death order.

"She's really friendly," Nicole went on. "She just wants to make sure I'm safe."

"You are safe," I said.

Her laugh came out dry and short.

"Yeah. Really safe. You all did an excellent job."

I pressed my lips together. "I mean, you're safe now," I tried again.

"Am I?" she asked. "Because the last time I checked, I was almost murdered by the same man who killed Zach. The one on the gas station video. Covered in blood. The one Mrs. Dustin warned us about." Her eyes never left mine. "The same man Thomas Harlow and his lap dog, Deputy Attorney General Kara Belmont, said shouldn't be looked into."

She didn't raise her voice. She didn't have to.

"The same man with the scar on his forehead." She tipped her head slightly toward Mr. Warner.

"The same man Mr. Warner saw here tonight. Brown eyes. Big scar on his forehead. And now," she added, petting Ginny, "he's got bite marks all over him. Makes him easier to find now, doesn't it?"

I held her gaze.

She wasn't ranting. She wasn't spiraling. She was setting the record straight.

The system had failed her. Failed her family. Failed in a way that couldn't be undone. And, if I was honest, it felt like I had failed her too.

I lowered myself onto the ground so we were level. The wet, cold grass soaked through my pants, but I didn't care.

"I'm sorry, Nicole," I said. No badge voice. No script. "I really am so, so sorry."

She looked at me as if she was weighing something. As if she needed to know if I meant it or if this was just a show. Then her iron expression softened a little.

"What can I do to help you?" I asked. "To get you taken care of?"

Her chin lifted, proud even as she winced in pain. God, she was so strong.

"I want the same thing I've been asking for since these useless idiots arrived," she said, nodding toward the police officers.

The idiot next to me, the one who'd wanted to shoot the dog, opened his mouth. I cut him off with a look.

"And what is that?" I asked.

"Do their job. They refuse to take Mr. Warner's statement about the man with the scar. Probably following the attorney general's orders."

I turned my head slowly toward Officer Ellison. His eyes dropped to the ground immediately.

"And as long as they refuse," Nicole continued in a calm voice, "I will sit right here with Ginny until the reporters arrive."

Officer Ellison threw a nod over his shoulder and asked, "Sir, can I talk to you in private?" But that wasn't necessary. I already knew what was up.

Thomas Harlow.

He was most likely getting informed about anything related to Nicole. Any police calls. Prison visits. He must have been informed the moment the call about this attack came in. Then gave his direct orders. Nicole was 100 percent right on this.

Damn it.

I let it all settle in.

This damn case could cost me my career. I knew that. But one look at Nicole, covered in blood, still fighting like hell for what was right, told me everything I needed to know. To finally do the right thing.

"Sir? Can I talk to you?" Officer Ellison asked again.

"No," I said.

Ellison blinked, thrown off.

"Take Mr. Warner's statement," I ordered.

"But—"

"I said take his damn statement," I cut in. "Or I will personally have you investigated for refusing protocol and crime scene procedures. Now get your fucking pen and paper out and do your job."

He glanced around for backup. None came. Every officer suddenly found something else to look at.

I turned back to Nicole. "Can Ginny please go home now?" I nodded toward the window, where the hard-faced woman was still watching. "So the EMTs can check you out while Officer Ellison takes Mr. Warner's statement?"

Nicole studied me for a long moment. Long enough to decide if trust was worth the risk.

Then she reached for Ginny, wrapped her arms around the dog's thick chest, and whispered something into her ear.

She looked up at Mr. Warner. "Please tell Emma she can get Ginny. Ask her to keep a cloth with some of the blood from Ginny's mouth for me in case the police do a shitty job with this as well. And please thank her for me. From the bottom of my heart. I'll never forget her kindness. Or Ginny's."

He hurried off, and a few moments later, a sharp whistle echoed through the night from the Warners' house.

Ginny lifted her head, then took off. She darted toward her home, startling the officers and EMTs.

Then she was gone.

The EMTs dropped to their knees next to Nicole, who was now groaning in pain as if she were finally allowed to be human again. Their hands were moving quickly now that the huge beast was finally gone.

I stood there and watched in awe. Nicole Kolter was a woman who made the saying "hell hath no fury like a woman scorned" feel painfully accurate.

She'd gotten her way. She could finally receive medical treatment and give her testimony that might tip the scales in the fight. Not just for justice but for survival. Hers and her daughter's.

But as happy-ending as it all sounded, I already knew what would come next.

Thomas Harlow wouldn't give up. Not quietly. He would fight her with everything he had.

And in this country, the court system didn't belong to the innocent. It belonged to those with power. And money.

But now he'd have to fight me too. At least with whatever authority and leverage I still had left. Whatever stood within my power to help Nicole find the real killer.

33

NICOLE

The hospital machines beeped rhythmically. I lay stretched out on the wide ER bed in a private room. Dylan and the kids hugged me clumsily. My leg was in a massive cast that ran from my foot all the way up to my thigh.

Broken.

Just like my swollen, crooked nose. The doctors said they'd have to wait a few days until the swelling went down. Surgery couldn't be rushed—not if they wanted it done right. And they also said they had to get my blood pressure down again, or I'd run the risk of a stroke during surgery.

Brian grabbed my hand the second the kids let go. He still looked like Brian. Broad shoulders. Thick arms. That worn, rugged blue-collar look that came from years of physical work and a naturally handsome face. But he was pale now, eyes rimmed red, jaw clenched tight.

"God ... Nicole ..." was all he managed before he turned and quickly walked out.

I watched him step into the hallway, hands on his hips, staring down at the floor like he was trying to hold himself upright through sheer force of will.

"Are you sure you don't need anything?" Dylan asked quietly.

He stood tall next to the bed, holding Ethan's hand. Ethan was wearing pajamas. Dylan was wearing a hoodie and worn sneakers. His hair fell into his eyes.

"They said they want to keep you overnight," he added. "And I know you need your pillow to be able to sleep."

I shook my head and gave him a soft smile. "No. I'll be fine. Thank you, sweetie."

"Can I draw on your cast?" Lila asked.

She was wearing mismatched socks and a pink sweatshirt that was inside out. Her eyes were big and wet.

"I can draw us," she said. "All of us together. So you know we love you."

"That would be wonderful, honey," I said softly.

My gaze drifted back to the hallway.

Brian was standing there with Amanda, who had just returned from the cafeteria. Her blond hair fell perfectly around her shoulders. Almost glowing under the harsh hospital lights.

She handed Brian the coffee. He barely looked at it before setting it on a side table. For a moment, they just stood there, like two people waiting to see who would move first.

Amanda stepped toward him and wrapped her arms around him. Brian's shoulders sagged instantly, and he pulled her into a tight hug. Much tighter than necessary.

Her hand pressed flat between his shoulder blades. She leaned in and murmured something into his ear.

He nodded.

The kids were saying something, but I didn't hear a word of it. My eyes stayed on the hallway. Nothing about that scene said friends.

It said everything it shouldn't.

God, I hated him in that moment.

While Lacey was rotting in a cell, this was what he was doing? Of course he claimed the moment. Of course he made himself the one who needed comforting the most. Like he was the one dying of cancer. Like he was the one who'd almost been murdered. Or the one who almost lost his grandma after essentially losing his mother already.

And of course Amanda was right there, holding him like he was fragile. Like something beautiful that couldn't be allowed to break.

But at least he was sober.

At least he was somewhat of a dad again.

Still, my hands started to shake. I couldn't tell if it was anger, left-over adrenaline, or the slow, sick realization that nothing was ever going to be simple again.

"Grandma," Dylan said.

"Huh?" I looked at him.

He flicked a quick glance at the kids. A warning. Not in front of them.

I smiled instantly.

"You know what," I said lightly. "Dylan, why don't you get us some coloring pens from the gift shop so we can all color my cast together? My credit card should be in my purse over there."

"Yay!" Lila bounced. "I want to come!"

Dylan hesitated for just a second. Long enough to glance back toward the hallway at his dad. At Amanda.

He knew.

Then he reached for my purse, pulled out the credit card, and nodded. "Sure."

"Can I come?" Lila asked again, hopeful. Probably already imagining a small toy along with the markers.

"Yeah," Dylan said. "Ethan?"

Ethan shook his head and climbed carefully onto the bed beside me. His body curled in close like he'd done a thousand times before. Way past nap time.

He was burned out the way kids get when their parents keep failing them.

His eyes closed almost immediately.

I scratched his back the way I always did. Slow and familiar. His breathing evened out within seconds.

Dylan and Lila watched for a moment. Then they turned and walked toward the door.

"Be right back," Dylan said.

Outside the room, he walked straight past his father. Lila grabbed his hand and followed along happily, oblivious in the way only a young kid could be.

Amanda and Brian loosened the hug when Dylan passed, and she looked straight at me like she'd only just remembered I existed.

Her face twisted into worry. She quickly stepped back, said something to Brian, then awkwardly placed the candy on the side table before leaving.

Her embarrassment didn't make me feel better.

But what did it matter?

Lacey would be free again soon. She would step right back into that role of wife and mother. The one holding everything together for this loser. I would hate Brian for the rest of my life. Not even so much for the affair but for hurting the kids. For saying he thought Lacey had killed Zach.

But I would never say a word of it to Lacey.

She had made it clear long ago that there were no boundaries for him. When she forgave him after he was caught with Amanda in that restaurant all those years back. When she forgave the drinking. The relapses. When she carried 95 percent of the work with the kids and around the house and listened to him with empathy when he complained about his 5 percent.

I loved my daughter and my grandchildren enough to accept her emotional dependence on him. As long as Brian kept it somewhat together.

What else could I do?

I didn't have the power to make Lacey leave him. He'd cast a spell over women that not even the Almighty could undo.

My thoughts drifted to the next court date. I would meet with the lawyer again this week. And this time it would be different.

The man who killed Zach had come for me. Most likely Billy Dustin had told him I was poking around. Or maybe he'd seen me near that motel where he usually stayed. Either way, we had him.

And the joy of my daughter's release would outweigh all of this.

But I had to be cautious. It would still be a battle with Harlow to get her out. I knew that.

But I let myself feel it anyway.

Hope.

Optimism.

Relief.

This nightmare might finally be ending.

And my daughter would finally be free. Not just from jail but from the world's judgment.

34

NICOLE

Brian and Dylan sat next to me in the public seating area. My broken leg lay stretched out in front of me, the cast cold and heavy.

Sean Holt sat by himself at the defense table, right in front of us.

He seemed to be in his mid-forties, thin, with gray hair at his temples. He had his papers lined up neatly in front of him.

Zach's family sat across the courtroom. His parents and his sister. They dressed as if they were attending a president's funeral. His mother and father sat perfectly still with their hands folded, while his sister stared straight ahead at Deputy Attorney General Kara Belmont at the prosecution table.

Belmont looked flawless in her cream-colored suit. Not a wrinkle in sight. Her red hair was pulled into a tight bun. Two male assistants sat next to her, both young and with cocky little smiles.

The courtroom was packed. Every seat was taken. Everybody was tense. Someone sneezed, followed by someone saying, "Excuse me."

Today was a big day. Sean had filed an emergency motion to reconsider bail based on new evidence. Officer Ellison's bodycam footage and the old gas station video of Myers were already all over social media, and public opinion was starting to support Lacey.

But that didn't mean she was going free. Not yet.

My head was pounding. The stress of all this made me physically sick.

Suddenly, the side doors of the courtroom opened.

Everyone stood when the judge entered.

Judge Harold McKenna looked to be in his late sixties. He had big, round eyes and short silver hair.

He sat, adjusted his glasses, and looked out over the courtroom.

"Be seated."

A moment later, the side door opened again, and two deputies brought Lacey in.

The orange jail uniform swallowed her. Her wrists were cuffed, and her eyes were empty like always. She looked terrible. Like a corpse with wild hair like an animal. And I had the horrible feeling that they made her look like this on purpose.

Sean rose. "Good morning, Your Honor. Sean Holt on behalf of the defendant."

Belmont remained seated, smiling faintly. Like she held an Uno reverse card and was just waiting to play it.

"Your Honor," Sean continued, "we are here because of an emergency motion to modify bail based on new evidence. Since Ms. Alderwyn's detention, Nicole Alderwyn was violently attacked in her home by the individual the defense has long identified as the real murder suspect of Zach Nabb. This attack was to silence her when she found out the name of the murder suspect, John Myers."

He let that sit.

"This attack supports evidence previously ignored by the State. We are asking the court to reconsider Lacey Alderwyn's detention in light of all this."

Simple. Direct. Almost modest.

Belmont finally rose. Her movement was elegant and deadly.

"Your Honor," she said, "the State has newly obtained evidence relevant to this motion as well."

Sean went still. "Your Honor, this is a discovery violation. We didn't receive any notice of this new evidence."

"Your Honor, the defense is arguing the identity of the murder suspect. We have newly obtained evidence that directly contradicts that claim. This is a proper rebuttal."

"I'll allow it," Judge McKenna said. "Let's hear what the State has, Mrs. Belmont."

Her grin widened. "Thank you," she said. "The footage came into our possession last week."

"Footage?" Sean repeated.

He turned to look at us, as if we knew what was coming. I shook my head.

Belmont nodded to one of her assistants. He picked up a remote and pressed a few buttons. The screen at the front of the courtroom turned on.

A grainy parking lot video came into view. It showed the Happy Rama Bowling Alley on Route 1. My heart almost stopped. There was no sound, but I knew exactly what I was looking at.

It was Lila's eighth birthday.

Lacey was wearing that bright yellow silk blouse. She'd bought it for $300 because she wanted to look pretty for Brian. But he was already pulling away, acting cold and withholding affection because he was bored with marriage again.

I remembered thinking that day how beautiful she looked.

And now that same sad memory was up on a courtroom screen, being shown to strangers as evidence.

"The woman in the yellow blouse is the defendant, Lacey Alderwyn," Belmont said. "The male with her is the victim, Zach Nabb."

Nobody challenged it, so the video kept playing.

The whole courtroom watched Lacey and Zach standing next to his Mercedes. He was vaping. She was talking. At first, it looked casual. Like two friends talking about nothing important. But suddenly Lacey's hands started moving faster, and Zach's face tightened. Even without sound, you could tell they were fighting.

Then Lacey shoved Zach. And he shoved her back.

I also couldn't watch. This was bad. No. This was catastrophic.

On the screen, Lacey and Zach kept going at each other. Hands flying. Screaming back and forth. Lacey grabbed Zach by his shirt. Zach shook her.

Then Dylan appeared at the edge of the frame, walking toward the Mercedes.

Lacey noticed him first and let go of Zach right away. She stepped back as if a switch had flipped. Just like that, she looked composed again. Sweet. Friendly. Smiling wide.

A second later, Zach noticed Dylan too. He froze. But, unlike Lacey, he didn't bother pretending. He turned and headed back into the bowling alley, knocking his shoulder into Dylan as he passed.

The video ended with Lacey placing her arm around Dylan and guiding him back inside.

Silence fell over the room as reality settled in.

The State now had something it didn't have before: a motive. The missing piece besides the missing murder weapon. I could already see what Belmont was going to do with this video. She would pull it apart. Twist it six different ways until Lacey stopped being a struggling victim and turned into an unstable woman full of rage. Belmont would reintroduce the old jealous-mistress theory. The State had floated the idea before but dropped it when it couldn't find any evidence.

But what Kara Belmont did next was worse than anything I could have imagined.

"The State calls Dylan Alderwyn to the stand," she said. "To testify about what he overheard in the parking lot that day."

Sean was up before the last word had even left her mouth. "Objection, Your Honor."

Dylan faced me with horrified eyes. "I didn't hear anything," he whispered. "I didn't. Please. I didn't hear anything." His voice was shaking now. "Everybody fought with Zach. He was a prick. He shoved a kid in a restaurant once because the boy was laughing too loudly. Did everybody just forget that?"

"Silence," the judge demanded.

"Your Honor," Sean said, stepping forward, "this is a bail hearing, not a trial. The State is trying to introduce testimony from a minor without notice. Calling witnesses here today serves no purpose other than prejudice and intimidation."

Belmont headed for the judge's bench.

"Your Honor, the State must insist. The safety of the Alderwyn children is at risk if a murderer is released back into their home."

"She's lying!" Dylan shot to his feet. "My mom would never hurt us!"

"Don't." I pulled Dylan back down.

Brian just looked stupid, like a man waiting for somebody to tell him he could leave.

"My client's son will not be testifying today," Sean insisted. "He is a minor. He has a choice."

One of Belmont's bulldogs rose immediately. Tall, slick hair. The kind of man who looked like he enjoyed being cruel in shiny shoes.

"No, he doesn't have a choice," he said. "That decision belongs to the judge."

"I'm not doing it," Dylan snapped.

The whole courtroom broke into restless chatter. Sean and Belmont's people were arguing back and forth in clipped legal language, talking over each other.

Then Zach's mother stood up.

She was crying, pointing across the aisle at Lacey with a trembling hand. "That monster killed my son! You people are insane if you let her go!"

The judge slammed his gavel.

"Order!"

For half a moment, things settled. But then Zach's sister shouted from her seat: "Thank God for cancer. I hope that bitch dies soon!"

Dylan was up again before I could stop him. "Thank God for hell too," he shouted at her, fists clenched at his sides. "Because that's where your narcissistic piece-of-shit brother is now!"

People gasped. Voices exploded all around us. Court officers rushed in trying to calm the chaos.

One of them stepped between our side and the Nabb family—a huge guy with dark hair. Hands up. "Enough," he barked. "Sit down. All of you. Now."

"Stop it!" I grabbed Dylan by his wrist, pulling him back as hard as I could, but the room was already spiraling.

Officers tried desperately to keep Zach's dad and Dylan apart as they were close to a fistfight. Brian just sat there staring, then he rose and left. People were yelling this and that. Lacey, on the other hand, sat frozen at the defense table. Her face blank, eyes fixed on nothing.

"Order," Judge McKenna shouted, hammering his gavel over and over again.

This time it worked. The courtroom calmed down.

But all of this was bad. Bail had become impossible at this point. And Kara Belmont's mocking grin confirmed it.

Judge McKenna looked down at the papers in front of him. He read. Paused. Read again. Then he shook his head.

My heart burst. Shattered into a million pieces as I watched the denial form on his tongue.

I grabbed Dylan's hand, holding it tightly. Both of us were shaking. Grief pressed in from every direction. Sadness. Anger. Hopelessness. Rage.

At the world.

At myself.

This had been Lacey's last chance. And she wasn't going to get it. She would die in jail.

"Under the current circumstances," Judge McKenna said in a firm voice, "I can't grant—"

The courtroom doors opened, cutting him off. All heads turned at once. A ripple of whispers followed as five men in tailored suits walked in. Confident. Cocky. They carried their briefcases with an attitude as if they were guns.

At the front of them was a shorter, older man. Round and bald with a long nose. His presence changed the mood in the room.

Everything stopped. We all stared at him in confusion as he walked straight up to me. Not the defense table. Not the judge. Me.

He stopped, pulled a pen from his jacket, and handed me papers.

"Sign this," he said.

At the same time, one of his associates rushed over to Sean and placed a stack of documents on the defense table.

I looked down at the papers in my hand.

Retainer Agreement and Substitution of Counsel.

My gaze lifted slowly over the man's golden silk tie until our eyes met.

"Robert Goldberg," he said. "Nice to meet you."

Across the room, Kara Belmont and her team recovered from the initial shock. Their murmurs turned frantic. Papers shuffled hectically.

"Mr. Goldberg!" Judge McKenna said. His tone had changed completely. It was warm and friendly now. "I think you might have the wrong courtroom," he added with a smile.

"I wish I had the wrong state," Goldberg joked. "We were supposed to be in the Hamptons with George, Betty, and the grandkids." He paused. "And I'd like the record to reflect that my wife is currently alone with toddler triplets. If her day doesn't end well, neither will mine."

Laughter moved through the courtroom. The attorney walked up to the bench and handed the judge a set of papers. "I've been retained to take over Mrs. Alderwyn's defense."

Kara Belmont was on her feet instantly. "Your Honor, that's not possible."

"Not possible?" Goldberg turned toward her. "This is America. And in America, people are allowed to change counsel at any time. So, the Alderwyns are changing counsel." He tilted his head. "Deputy AG Beemont, isn't it? Or close enough, I guess. May I, Your Honor?"

He gestured toward Sean Holt's table.

"Of course," Judge McKenna said, leaning back in his chair.

All eyes were on Goldberg as he crossed the room and picked up Sean's file, flipped it open, and skimmed it.

Once.

Twice.

Then his head shook slowly.

"Good God," he said. "Your Honor, is this case something else or what?"

Judge McKenna exhaled through his nose. Like someone finally understood him. "It is indeed."

Goldberg nodded, then turned toward Belmont and her team.

"Let's begin with the obvious," Goldberg said. "This court was ambushed with surprise evidence, a minor was nearly strong-armed onto the stand without a guardian's permission, and a documented, violent attack by the real suspect was treated like a footnote, despite nearly killing another victim."

He pointed at me, eyeing my cast and my swollen, bruised face.

"And months into this case," he continued, "the State still hasn't carried out the court-ordered psychological evaluation of a mentally suffering, dying defendant, who remains incarcerated. That order came from a judge. It was not unclear. It was not optional. And it was bluntly ignored by the State despite repeated requests from my client's family. At this point, Your Honor, we are no longer talking about mistakes. This isn't just disrespect toward the orders of this court and the judges who issued them. This is a severe violation of due process rights under the Constitution. And, dear God, let's not even talk about discovery, which was treated like an optional trip reimbursement insurance rather than a legal requirement. I'll be honest, Your Honor, I'm not even sure where to begin here."

He glanced at Belmont, a disgusted look on his face.

"But let's start by putting an end to the State's Wild West show."

Judge McKenna flipped through the papers in front of him. He stopped and looked up over his glasses.

"The court-ordered psychological evaluation still hasn't been completed by the State?"

"Your Honor," Belmont said quickly, "the State didn't refuse the evaluation. There were scheduling issues, and the medical transport presented complications. We intended to complete it soon."

The awkward silence that followed lingered just long enough for Sean to use it. "Your Honor, may I be excused?"

Judge McKenna nodded.

Sean stepped forward and extended his hand to Goldberg. The shake was firm.

"Good luck, Goldberg," Sean said.

Goldberg answered with a single nod.

Then Sean hurried over to us. He leaned in. "Sign now."

That was it. I watched as he turned and walked out.

Goldberg's team moved immediately. Two of the lawyers slipped into the public benches, ordering people to make room. The other two sat next to Lacey.

One of them reached out, offering his hand. But she didn't look at him. Didn't move. So he withdrew his hand as if nothing had happened. Like she was completely normal.

"Your Honor, may I?" Goldberg asked.

He stepped closer to the bench. Belmont moved at the same time, asking if she might join as well.

"May we speak in chambers for a moment?" Goldberg said. "I have serious concerns that need to be voiced."

After a beat, the judge nodded and stood.

"Good idea. Counsel," he said, "with me."

We all watched as the three of them left through the side door.

The moment they were out of sight, the room broke into loud conversations.

"What's going on?" Dylan asked.

"I'm not sure," I said. "But I have a feeling we should sign."

Dylan nodded.

I signed the papers quickly before I had time to second-guess anything.

Time slowed. Minutes passed. Or hours. It was hard to tell. It all felt surreal.

We spoke with our new lawyers quietly for a while. Asked questions, hoping for something to hold on to. All they told us was that Robert Goldberg would explain everything soon. They were now Lacey's new counsel. Things would be made right. And Goldberg was well-connected in the highest places. Places that could make or break judges and AGs.

Then the door opened again. Everyone stood as the officer said, "All rise."

Laughter came first. That was unexpected. The judge and Goldberg stepped back into the courtroom together, still laughing. Behind them, Kara Belmont followed. She looked pale.

The judge didn't sit right away. One hand rested on his bench as he looked down at Robert Goldberg.

"You may be seated," he said to the room in a conversational tone.

Everyone present followed his order. Belmont sat too, looking like a pouting child.

"I still can't believe he hit that hole from that far," Judge McKenna said.

"Well," Goldberg answered easily, "it was the only one he hit all day. A squirrel bit him in the leg two holes later, and he had to get a rabies shot at the hospital."

The judge laughed again, shaking his head.

Only then did he lower himself into his chair.

Goldberg's smile faded quickly.

"Anyway," Goldberg said. "I'll put together a full list of the new evidence when I get back to my office. Most of it is already sitting in police files that were never properly examined. Like the video footage of John Myers covered in blood at the gas station. That will have to be entered again. The testimony of the gas station owner too. Mrs. Dustin's statement will be taken formally." A pause. "We'll move immediately on DNA. John Myers' blood was recovered at the Kolter crime scene. We'll compare it to Zach Nabb's case." He shook his head. "The evidence is damning. The same man shown on the gas station video covered in blood tried to murder the victim's mother when she began asking the questions law enforcement should have been asking all along."

Judge McKenna nodded brusquely. "I'll ensure the court-ordered psychological evaluation is completed this week. There will be no further delays."

Goldberg gave a single nod and sat next to Lacey.

Judge McKenna waited until he was seated, then straightened in his chair and addressed the courtroom. "For purposes of today's hearing, this court is required to consider two things: new evidence and flight risk." He shook his head. "A mute, terminally ill defendant who can barely walk or speak doesn't present a flight risk."

"Your Honor." Belmont rose quickly. "Your Honor, may I?"

"No," he said. "You may not."

She stood there, dying a thousand quiet deaths.

"Given the newly presented evidence identifying an alternative suspect," Judge McKenna continued, "and given the defendant's medical and psychological condition, bail is granted and set at a hundred thousand dollars."

The gavel came down loud and clear.

And the courtroom exploded.

Voices rose. People surged to their feet. Somewhere near the front, Goldberg was moving toward the bench while Kara Belmont launched her plea with the judge.

My eyes went to the guards. Both of them were watching me now, as if unsure what to do.

One of the slick lawyers from Goldberg's team came up to me. He was young and polished with perfectly combed dark hair.

"Let me translate that for you," he said. "Your daughter goes home with you today. Right now, actually. You can hug her if you want."

Dylan and I were on our feet at the same time. He helped me limp around the bench, through the noise and the stares, and we wrapped ourselves around Lacey.

The cries that came out of me barely sounded human. Dylan was crying too. His whole body was shaking.

Hugging Lacey felt like hugging branches, and her skin was cold. She also smelled horrible. But it didn't matter. I loved her more than ever.

"We'll get you the best treatment," I sobbed into her shoulder, falling apart. "We'll take care of you. I promise."

But her body stayed rigid, her eyes empty.

"Honey," I said, pulling back just enough to see her face. "Can you hear me? You're free."

Nothing.

"Mom," Dylan said. "You're free."

Still nothing.

We held her anyway.

Behind us, Zach's family had come undone. His mother sobbed, hands clutched to her chest. His sister was shouting insults again.

Movement caught the corner of my eye. The judge and Goldberg were laughing again. Talking like men who played golf together. They shook hands, and the judge left. Deputy AG Belmont tried to stop the judge, but he was clearly done listening.

Goldberg walked past Belmont and said in that polished voice of his, "Tell Harlow he's done. Hate and lies go far in this country. But the almighty dollar goes farther."

Belmont's mouth opened wide, but nothing came out.

Then Goldberg came up to me.

I left Lacey in Dylan's arms and rose.

"Mr. Goldberg," I said, "I don't understand what just happened. But thank you from the bottom of my heart."

He smiled. "We'll have a real meeting soon once things settle. There's work ahead. I will push for police protection to make sure you're safe until they catch Myers. Although I doubt he will come anywhere near you now that they are looking for him. In all the years I've been doing this, criminals never come back once the police are hunting them. The benefit of killing you was to keep the police off his trail. Obviously, that didn't work. Now running is his only option. Also, the AG and his deputy will get ugly. But, for now, take your family and go home, through the back door. The front is already swarming with reporters." He lowered his voice. "I usually don't make promises, but I'm very confident we can get the charges dropped without ever going to trial. The evidence against her is weak, to say the least. No murder weapon. A suspect on the run."

A grin tugged at his mouth. "I've handled people in far worse positions than this."

"But the attorney general—"

He waved that off. "Thomas, that fragile-egoed prick. He is only an AG. Judges know that."

"Only?"

The grin widened. "There are people who answer to the AG. And there are people the AG answers to. I know the latter quite well."

My hands closed around his. I shook hard. Maybe too hard. But I was beside myself with joy. "How much do we owe you?"

I knew I couldn't pay his fees. The contract read eight thousand dollars an hour.

"Don't worry about a dime," he said. "It's already handled."

"What?"

"By Amanda."

He nodded toward the door.

I turned quickly. And there she was, tears streaming down her face as she watched all this unfold. One hand was pressed over her mouth as she tried to hold herself together.

My attention went back to Lacey as the guards lifted her shackled hands. One of them pulled out a key. His fingers hesitated for half a second. Then he set her free.

The cuffs slipped from Lacey's wrists and slid out of the officer's grip. They hit the floor with a hollow clang.

For a moment, Lacey just stood there, and it looked like nothing had changed. Like she would keep staring into nothingness forever.

But then her head moved.

And she looked up.

Actually looked up. Straight at me.

"Lacey?" I gasped.

Her eyes widened as if seeing me for the first time in months. Maybe she realized for the first time where she actually was.

Then her mouth opened wide, and a scream tore out of her. Shrill and uncontrolled. As if every possible emotion a human could feel was pouring out all at once. Relief. Rage. Grief. Hope. Loss. Sadness. Life. Fear. Love.

Every face turned toward her.

Her scream died with the last bit of breath in her lungs. Dylan and I were right there, catching her as her knees buckled. She collapsed in on herself, sobbing so hard her body shook violently. I tried to lower myself down with her, but the cast wouldn't bend, so I collapsed awkwardly next to her. Dylan went down with her, arms locked around her, holding her tightly.

It felt incredible.

My daughter was actually crying.

Real sounds. Real emotions. Real tears. She was alive again.

The officers had removed more than the shackles. Whatever had trapped her inside her body had finally broken free.

"Shhhh," I whispered into her hair, rocking her gently, back and forth. "It's okay. Mama's here."

We weren't out of the woods yet. There was still more fighting ahead.

But she was free. In my arms again. With her son. Feeling again.

My head lifted and found Amanda. She was still crying by the door. When our eyes met, I mouthed the words: *Thank you.*

She nodded once, then turned and left. Understandable. Zach's family would come for her. Hard. And when they did, we would protect her. She was part of our family, even if things were a bit messy. Like families always were.

Then the strangest thing happened. In the far back, between people coming and going, I saw Thomas Harlow. All dressed up in a fancy suit, staring at me with the face of a man who lost the war after winning a few battles. Even from this far away I could see the darkness and the hate in his eyes. Like he was making a promise. That this wasn't over. That no matter how long it took, he would find a way to destroy us. But just as I considered confronting him right there in front of everyone, he was gone. One second there, the next swallowed by the crowd.

My focus returned to Lacey. The cancer was still there. That truth hadn't changed. But now we could fight it head-on. Together. Every day would matter. Every moment would be a gift.

"Thank you," I said out loud, to nobody, to everybody.

Then my gaze drifted upward. To the ceiling. To God, maybe.

I was never religious, but I prayed anyway.

"God," I whispered. "If you're real … thank you. Thank you. Thank you."

35

LACEY – TWENTY-ONE MONTHS LATER

Our new house sat in the middle of a quiet, dead-end street in Jamaica Plain, Boston, surrounded by historic homes and old trees that gave Boston its charm.

Dylan and I sat next to each other, both of us in wheelchairs. Amanda, Brian, Ethan, Lila, and my mom were right behind us.

A warm summer breeze brushed my face. It carried the smell of flowers and fresh-cut grass. Somewhere nearby, a dog barked.

And I was still alive.

I turned my head toward Dylan. He sat in the second wheelchair, grinning, cheerful, excited. His hands rested on the large wheels. His fingers were flexing like he was already itching to go. Sunlight caught in his brown hair. His blue eyes were bright and alive.

We'd been racing up and down the street in my wheelchairs for almost an hour. The kids took turns racing, nearly crashing into each other. Lila pouted when she lost. Ethan had laughed so hard he'd peed his pants and had to take a break to get changed.

Brian started the countdown for this race, loud and dramatic, but I barely noticed him. My eyes were on Dylan. How beautiful he looked in the summer sun. The way the sunlight sparkled in his deep-blue eyes. He'd never given up on me, not even during the worst year of our lives. He never left my side. Not in jail. Not during my first chemo or surgery. Not during long nights when the pain felt endless. He fought for me. Always. Looking at him, I knew every breath I had ever taken had been for him. And every breath I had left would be too.

Since the cancer had returned a few months ago, I'd been in constant pain again. But it still didn't hurt as much as my love for my family did.

Dylan, my superhero.

Ethan, talking now, loud and sassy, always giggling.

Lila, nothing but pure kindness.

My husband. The man who didn't leave my side even when the whole world called me a murderer. He'd stayed and fought when he could have walked away, found comfort in another woman's arms, far away from all of this.

And my mother.

God. My mother.

The woman I owed everything to.

"Go!" Brian shouted, tearing me out of my thoughts.

But I didn't move.

Dylan's smile dropped instantly. His brows pulled together, and his hand reached for mine.

I shook my head, signaling to him I was fine. I pointed at him, tapped my heart, then pointed back at him again. The motions were clumsy but familiar. I still didn't speak to them. Not since that night in the woods.

My fingers curled, twitching. I wanted to write something. I wanted to grab a pen and explain. But my hand fell back into my lap. Writing wasn't an option either.

I'm fine, I mouthed, exaggerating the words.

It was a lie.

I'd been in deep and constant pain. The cancer came back after a year of something that felt like a normal life.

After my release, they took out as much of the cancer as they could. Platinum-based chemotherapy followed. A few months later, the cancer was gone. Like a miracle, considering I was stage four when my rotting body walked out of jail almost two years ago.

But now it was back, and my prognosis didn't look good.

I smiled for the kids. Nodded when they asked if it would go away like before. My stomach tightened every time. Because I knew it wouldn't.

"I think we should go inside," Dylan said, signaling my mom.

She nodded and walked over to me.

But before she reached me, my hands slammed against the wheels. I pushed hard, and the chair launched forward. I took off down the street like a storm.

"Hey!" Dylan shouted, faking outrage.

The kids exploded with cheers, running after us.

I twisted in my seat and saw Dylan chasing after me, laughing as his eyes locked on mine.

"Kick his ass!" Brian yelled.

"Go, girl!" Amanda hollered.

And for that stretch of pavement, with the sun warm on my skin and my family around me, I was alive again.

I'd made it just over the finish line, the driveway to our home, when a sharp sting sliced through my lungs. I hated that part about the cancer the most. The way my body betrayed me and ruined everybody's good time.

I folded forward, gasping for air, and just like that, Dylan was at my side. His arms slid under my knees and behind my back, and he lifted me out of the wheelchair as if I weighed nothing.

Which wasn't far from the truth. I was a skeleton.

"Time to rest, wild lady," he said softly.

He carried me to the front door. I wrapped my arms around his neck and looked up at him. I wasn't on death's doorstep yet. Some weeks were better than others. And I could have walked. But why take this from him? Or argue, when he would've insisted anyway?

And there was something so beautiful about it. Humbling. The endless love of my child. Being taken care of by him. At the same time, guilt pressed against my ribs. This was supposed to be my job. Not his. The roles had flipped, unfair and irreversible.

Brian jogged ahead and pulled the front door open. "Here, let me take her," he said, reaching for me.

But Dylan ignored him. He moved past him without a word, brushing him aside as he carried me through the doorway. Brian stood there like someone who had been left waiting at a restaurant after his date never showed up.

Dylan pushed the door closed with his foot and carried me down the hallway to my bedroom on the first floor. It resembled a full nursing room by now. Hospital bed, pill bottles littering every surface, and a TV mounted on the wall.

He lowered me gently onto the bed and adjusted the pillow behind my back.

When he turned toward the nightstand to grab the TV remote, my hand reached for his.

None of this is your dad's fault, I mouthed, hoping Dylan would understand.

The tension between the two had been going on for a long time. Dylan blamed him for everything the way teenagers do when the weight gets too heavy and the tools to carry it aren't there yet. Blaming a loved one was easier.

Dylan looked at me like he wanted to tell me something. His jaw tightened for a moment, and he turned serious.

But then he smiled.

"I'm sorry," he said softly. "You're right. I'll talk to the therapist again. It'll get better."

My hand lifted to my heart. Then turned toward him in a small, familiar motion. Reassurance. Love.

His eyes stayed on me, searching.

So I pointed toward his dad out there somewhere, then back to him. After that, I lifted my arm and bent it, holding the pose for a second. A strong arm. Just long enough to make the point about strength.

Dylan had more than enough of it. So did Brian.

He looked down for a second, jaw tightening. When he looked back up, his eyes told me he got it.

"You know," Dylan said, "if there's any strength in me, I didn't get it from him. I got it from Grandma and you."

My lips curved into a soft smile. One shoulder lifted in a small, playful shrug. I tipped my head, eyes warm, agreeing without words.

Grandma.

That woman was something else.

Then the worry crept back in. It always did. About Dylan. About Brian. Their relationship.

Dylan seemed to notice it right away. "I'll see if Dad wants to watch the game with me tonight."

The thought of them spending time together warmed my heart. My shoulders sank into the pillow.

I nodded slowly as I lifted my hand, palm up, then settled it against my heart.

"Glad that makes you happy," Dylan said. "But you need to rest now."

The door flew open.

"Moooom!" Ethan and Lila shouted together.

Lila rushed in first. "Can we watch a movie with you?"

Ethan launched himself onto the bed, all knees and wild energy. My fingers gripped the sheets as pain sparked sharply and suddenly. "Get off!" Dylan snapped, his patience gone in seconds.

"Where are the rug rats!" Brian said from the doorway, fake anger filling the room. "Your mom needs to rest."

He swept in, flexing his big muscles. One arm scooped Ethan up and tossed him over his shoulder like a sack of potatoes. Ethan laughed so hard he squealed. Then Brian grabbed Lila with his other arm, tucking her against his side.

Joy filled me as I watched them. Brian looked so handsome. Fit. Alive. Positive energy spilling out of him. A family man through and through.

How did I get so lucky?

Brian carried both kids out the door just as Amanda stepped into the hallway. She stopped short when she saw him.

"I'll give Ethan a bath," she said, taking him from Brian's arms.

Our eyes met, and I smiled at her. Gratitude welled up, for everything she'd done for me.

Their voices faded down the hall, and my mom came in with a

wash basin in her hands. It felt like something from another century. An old historical drama.

And we all knew what it meant.

Time for a cat wash.

I didn't shower this morning. And now it would be too much of a fall risk. Too exhausting. So we did this instead. A basin. A cloth. And soap.

Dylan leaned down, kissed my cheek, then slipped out, closing the door behind him.

I sat up and watched my mom place the wash basin on the nightstand like it was the most normal thing in the world. Her face stayed steady. Calm. Whatever pain she carried never made it to her eyes.

"Robert called. That lead in Florida wasn't John Myers." She shook her head. "I can't believe that monster is still out there. They should at least pretend to try to find him."

I pinched my lips. The first few weeks after my release were terrifying. Amanda had hired personal security when the State refused to protect us. But nothing bad happened, and weeks turned into months. Then a year, two. And with time came something close to a normal life again. One without the constant fear that Myers might come for me. Or my mom.

"Robert also said he wants to meet on Friday," she continued casually, as if talking about grocery deals. "That interview that Thomas Harlow did, the one in which he mentioned the bowling alley parking lot video and Dylan. Apparently, he said things he shouldn't have. Robert thinks it violated the settlement agreement, which means more money, he says."

The basin shifted as she dipped the cloth into the water.

We'd sued the State for a lot of money. Due process violations. A list of screwups as long as the Great Wall of China. They dropped all the charges. Then they settled fast. One point five million. Robert said it was low. But it meant no more fighting. All charges would be dropped. No time in court. He said that part mattered more than the money.

"Think about it," my mom said. "It's up to you if you want to ignore the AG or go after him."

I nodded.

"Lavender or lemon?" she asked, holding up the bottles of body wash.

I pointed at the lavender.

Brian's favorite smell.

Her eyebrows rose. Like she already knew.

"Dear God, Lacey," she said, scolding but amused. "You were born with the spirit of a horny old man."

A laugh shook out of me without sound. My shoulders bounced. I shrugged, as innocent as ever.

The doctor had said intimacy was good for me. Mom had raised concerns about health, safety, energy. All of it. But the doctor talked about how sick people were still humans. He said that, in some patients, desire didn't disappear just because they were ill. That wanting someone was still human. Still allowed.

Intimacy had been one of the hardest parts of this whole cancer nightmare. People didn't want to talk about it. Didn't want to picture it. As if sick bodies weren't supposed to love. Of course, everyone was different, and it also depended on how sick someone was. But I wanted my husband. I wanted him badly. Watching him stand by me when it got ugly, when it was humiliating, only made my longing for him stronger.

So the doctor prescribed Brian Viagra without flinching. And explained it was normal to struggle with erection issues due to feelings of sadness and stress.

A knock sounded at the door, and Brian came in.

"I'll take over," he said, reaching for the lavender bottle.

My mom rolled her eyes and turned to leave. As she passed the bed, my hand shot up, and I closed my fingers around her wrist.

Her eyes dropped to my hand first. Then her gaze lifted to mine.

I tried to be strong, tried to keep my eyes dry, but my vision blurred anyway. There was so much I wanted to tell her. How much I loved her. How grateful I was. How I would already be dead without her.

My mouth opened, but I closed it again.

The cold feeling of shame radiated through me. This woman had saved me from so much horror, and I couldn't even thank her and tell her I loved her.

My mom's hand lifted instantly, cupping my sunken cheek.

"I know, sweetheart. I love you too."

She held my gaze for a long moment. Her eyes filled with the kind of love only a parent carries for their child. Were there tears in her eyes?

She turned quickly.

"Well," she said, "I'd better make sure Lila is doing her homework. She got a C on her last math test."

Then she left.

Brian tipped the lavender wash into the bowl and then soaked the washcloth until it darkened.

"I love the smell of lavender," he said. "You know what it does to me, right?"

A wide smirk spread across my face, and I pointed toward his crotch, then mimicked swallowing a pill.

He understood, grinning as he helped me pull my T-shirt over my head and unclasp my bra.

His eyes cut to the door for a split second, then back to me.

"Took the little bastard the moment I saw your mom grab the wash basin from the bathroom."

A soundless chuckle shook my chest. I watched as he climbed into bed beside me and slid my pants down. For a moment, shame crept in at the ruined body I was offering him. It looked like something from a late-night horror movie—all bone and shadow. Bruises all over. A skeleton pretending to be human.

Doubt flickered across my face before I could stop it.

He saw it.

"You look amazing," he said, a little too fast, and quickly leaned in to kiss me.

Heat spread through my body all at once. Beautiful butterflies like I was eighteen again and didn't know better.

Brian moved between my legs as my fingers found the hem of his shirt. He lifted his arms without a word. The fabric slid away, revealing that perfect body. Strong. Familiar. Still solid in all the right places.

My hands traced over his broad chest before drifting lower. I undid the buttons one by one. Slow. Intentional. I reached inside, and he groaned when my fingers wrapped around him. I guided him closer, until he pressed against me.

He slid in with a push, then started moving slowly, evenly. Almost mechanical, like a robot.

Another quick glance at the door. So fast I almost missed it.

A few more strokes, and my body's aches finally eased off, slipped to the edges for a while. Love always did that to me. Blinded my heart, body, and soul.

My hands moved over him as he rocked back and forth. Over his strong shoulders, his muscular back.

His face stayed tucked against my neck, not looking at me.

I pulled back just enough to look at him. This loyal, beautiful man who was still mine. God, I loved him more than life itself.

And before I could stop it, tears ran down my face. I was so grateful.

In some twisted way, we felt closer now than before the cancer. He stayed when so many men would have left. Never doubted me. Never made me feel unwanted. Never made me feel small or cheated on me.

Dark thoughts still crept in sometimes. That maybe it was too good to be true. That maybe he was still here by my side because he was making up for something. Guilt. Or hiding something. But those thoughts were my own shame talking and unfair to this amazing man. So I shoved them away.

"Am I hurting you?" Brian asked, stopping cold.

My head shook fast. No, I shaped with my lips. I love you.

He understood and nodded once.

His eyes flicked to the door again, then he leaned in and pressed his face into my shoulder once more.

My nails dug into him, pulling him closer and holding him there. Pressure built inside me, which was surprising. Most of the time, my body didn't cooperate anymore. Most of the time, the closeness of feeling him inside me mattered more than the glorious end.

But this time felt different.

Today it would work.

He rocked faster, and as if life was granting me one last small gift, we came at the same time.

A silent scream escaped my lips, and my body tightened, then melted beneath him in hot waves.

His body twitched a few times, then he rolled off to the side, staring at the ceiling.

A tired laugh shook my chest. I tapped his shoulder, then pointed between us, trying to tease.

We still got it, I mouthed.

"Yuuuup," he said, eyes back on the ceiling. Empty, almost bored.

My fingers dragged slowly over his back.

Happy, yet also heartbroken.

I was dying. I knew it. I should have been dead a long time ago. So every second with my family, with this man, meant everything to me.

Guilt crept in when I thought about what they'd been dragged through because of me. Months of hell. The world branding me a murderer. My mother pushing herself to the edge of a heart attack just to keep me breathing. Almost getting killed herself. My kids never pulled away. Never stopped loving me. And Brian never doubted me either.

Then my best friend finally believed in me again. Paid for a lawyer who finally got me out.

The cancer brought a lot of fears.

But none bigger than those concerning my family.

Would they be okay? Would Brian fall apart after I was gone? Start drinking again? Would the kids lose their mother and their father too?

My mother had always struggled with her blood pressure. Would she have the strength to carry all this for years to come? Would they all become tragedies of the life I left behind?

My life was borrowed. An extension somehow granted by the devil or God. Who knew. It didn't matter. Because whoever had granted me more time also gave me one more gift. One I hoped for more than anything.

When I was gone, Brian would find happiness again, with another woman. Someone steady and kind. Someone strong enough to hold him together.

And that woman was Amanda.

I tapped Brian's shoulder. He looked at me, curious.

I pointed toward the door.

"Your mom?" he asked.

I shook my head.

"Dylan? Lila?"

Again, no.

"Amanda?"

The name came last. More careful.

I nodded.

Something shifted in his face. His eyes narrowed as he searched mine. I pointed at him first, then lifted both hands. One finger held up for Amanda. One for him. Slowly, deliberately, I hooked my two fingers together. Showing unity.

He stared at my fingers. Then back at me.

"No," he said, shaking his head. "Stop it."

My jaw tightened. I folded my arms across my chest. Then I repeated the gesture. Firmer this time. Insisting.

An angry huff slipped out of him.

He rubbed his palm over his mouth, exhaled, then nodded almost too fast.

"Okay," he said. "But only for you. If you really, really want this."

The tension drained from my face. My shoulders eased. A small nod followed, then a soft smile.

He smiled back. "Okay." Then he looked away. "Can you ..." he began cautiously. "Can you make sure you tell Dylan about this, though? So he knows it's what you wanted? I mean me and Amanda together."

I nodded, and Brian pulled me closer. His breath was warm against my skin.

My eyes closed, and for a moment it felt as if I could die right here, right now. In peace.

Knowing my kids and my husband would be okay after my death was the most precious thing a dying mother and wife could ever have.

I thanked whatever force was out there for every breath I still had in me.

Soon, I would die a free woman.

Declared innocent.

A victim, not a monster.

A loved and loving mother.

A loved and loving daughter.

A loved and loving wife.

And, maybe sometimes, when daylight faded and the night settled quietly over an endless sky, one of them would look up. Standing still. Hands tucked into their pockets as the stars glittered above.

Their thoughts would drift to me, wondering if one day we would meet again. Somewhere among the stars.

Then my last words would come back to them.

Just because my body isn't with you doesn't mean my heart and soul left too.

I'm right here.

And I always will be.

PART II

36

DYLAN - EIGHT YEARS LATER

My screams came out muffled, as if I were underwater. Swallowed by the walls of my mom's bedroom and the soft beeping of hospital machines. Dad had me locked against him. My arms strained forward, fingers stretching toward my mom lying still in the hospital bed they'd set up in her room. Her head rested on the pillow, turned slightly to the side. Her mouth was parted just enough to look like she might breathe again.

She looked asleep. Like if I waited a little bit, she'd blink and move. And tell me it was okay.

But she didn't.

"Mom!" I sobbed, the sound tearing out of my chest so violently it hurt my throat. "No, Mom, don't leave me here!"

Grandma was crying so hard her whole body shook. She pulled my mom's lifeless body into her arms, rocking her back and forth, pressing her cheek against Mom's head as if she could love her back to life. Like refusing to let go might change something.

I shoved harder against Dad, but his arms stayed tight.

"Let me go!" I screamed. "*Now!*"

His face stayed stiff and flat. "You need to calm down!"

Not one tear slid down his face. Not even a shine in his eyes. Just impatience. This was an inconvenience for him. Like Mom dying was something we needed to get over with quickly.

Piece of shit.

From the corner of my eye, I saw Amanda step closer and place a hand on his shoulder. Her fingers were steady and calm. She shook her head once, a slow and deliberate motion, and only then did he release me.

The second his grip loosened, my body lurched forward.

I fell against the bed so hard my hip hit the rail, but I barely felt it. I wrapped my arms around my mom's cold body, over Grandma's, and clung to her. She was so cold. Not cool—ice cold. The kind that told me, in the most horrific way possible, that she was really gone forever. That she would never smile at me again. Never hug me or kiss me again. Never hold me again when the world was falling apart around me and all I needed to survive was my mom's unconditional love.

"No," I choked out, burying my face against her shoulder. "No, no, no. Take me with you," I sobbed. "Please, Mom. Don't leave me here. Take me with you."

Ethan and Lila came in and screamed at the same time. Their voices bounced off the walls and stabbed me like knives. Dad just stood there, hands hanging uselessly at his sides as if watching strangers fall apart.

Amanda moved fast, scooping Ethan up. His small arms wrapped around her neck. Lila just stood there sobbing until my dad finally took her into his arms.

The cries.

The sobbing.

The screaming.

It felt like we would all suffocate.

My heart shattered so violently, I thought I might actually die right here with her. Maybe hearts really could break and kill people. Maybe mine was cut to pieces inside me, and I would just drop dead beside my mom and go wherever she had gone. The thought felt good in this moment. Like mercy.

How could life do this to me? How could life be so cruel?

Then, suddenly, the scene changed.

No warning. No soft fade. One second, the bedroom. The next, asphalt under my sneakers.

The bowling alley parking lot.

Lila's eighth birthday.

I was a teenager again. Black hoodie. Jeans. Sneakers.

Grandma had asked me to get Mom and Zach so we could sing "Happy Birthday" and cut the cake. I could still hear the noise from inside. Laughter and loud music.

Outside, everything changed and felt wrong somehow.

Mom and Zach stood next to his car and were arguing. She wore the yellow silk blouse she'd bought to please Dad, even though he couldn't have cared less. The fabric shimmered in the parking lot sun. Zach wore a pink polo shirt, leather moccasins, and that $200k watch. Smug as always. So freaking arrogant.

Each step toward them tightened something in my chest. Something really bad was going on.

The closer I got, the harder I tried to hear what they were saying.

Was it "If—" Zach said, right before she grabbed him?

Was it "But Amanda—" Mom shot back, just before he shoved her aggressively?

Anger rose. How dare he touch her! My feet kept moving faster.

But just before I got close enough, Mom turned toward me.

The moment she saw me, everything changed. Her hands dropped, and she smiled. Even after this fight with Zach, her smile was the most beautiful thing in the world to me.

Then, like always, things grew foggy. Voices blurred until they felt distant.

And I woke up from my nightmare. The same one that visited me in my dreams almost every night.

Hospital machines beeped in the distance as the room came back into focus. A phone rang nearby as I sat up on the lower bunk in the residents' room at the Mass State Hospital in Boston.

For medical residents, this place was a special kind of hellhole. The kind that offered old coffee and maybe a dry muffin after sixteen-hour shifts with no lunch breaks. Sometimes, if we got lucky, they stocked the countertops with ramen noodles, cookies, and soda.

But today was not one of those lucky days.

A few brown bananas sat on the counter, alongside the coffee machine that looked like it had given up on life sometime in the eighties.

After stretching the stiffness from my back, I walked over, passing the small table where two other residents sat scrolling on their phones. It looked like boredom, but I knew it wasn't. It was burnout. Months of six-day weeks. Twelve- to sixteen-hour shifts. Shit pay, less than minimum wage.

One of the two residents was Erin. Blond. Skinny. Came from Boston old money. The kind filled with expectations and pressure. She was an internal medicine resident.

The other was Jamal, late twenties. Emergency medicine. Permanent tired eyes.

This was my first year as an oncology fellow. Mid-twenties was absurdly young for that title. But everything had moved fast after Mom died. Nothing could stop me.

I got my high school diploma at seventeen. No college parties ever. No dating either. Just studies. I'd rather have died than failed.

I looked at the large clock mounted on the wall—nine thirty. My twelve-hour shift should have ended four hours ago. Technically. But reality laughed at that. We were short of physicians. Short of nurses. It was Thanksgiving week. And, as a resident, you lost all human rights anyway. Complaining was frowned upon in a culture that felt closer to a Navy SEAL training camp than a hospital. Be tough, take the pain, or get the hell out.

"Dr. Rothchild is looking for you," Erin said as I grabbed the coffeepot.

"Dear God," I said. "Did I forget to line up his Sharpies in order of the color spectrum?"

Both of them laughed.

"I am sure it's something like that," Jamal said. "The bastard made me write a full-page apology letter to my badge when I forgot it the other day. Like, to my actual fucking badge. Started it with Dear Badge, I'm sorry—"

"No way," Erin gasped, eyes widening.

"Yep. I'm not kidding."

Listening to them, I poured myself a cup of coffee. Paper cup, of course. Real mugs were apparently too much to ask for.

One sip was all it took to make my face twist.

"Damn," I said, staring down into the cup. "This should be illegal. I'm going to the cafeteria for something close to the dark drink the world calls coffee."

Erin stood, already grabbing her badge. "I will come with you."

"Sure. You coming too?" I asked Jamal.

"Nah. I'll take a nap." He was already walking toward the old bunk beds.

Out in the hallway, the hospital was in full motion. Nurses hurried past us with clipboards tucked to their chests. Low voices mumbled patient updates and complaints about coverage. Phones rang. Monitors chimed from behind closed doors. It smelled like chlorine and the nasty coffee I'd sipped.

"Is Rothchild forcing you to cover the Thanksgiving shift on Thursday too?" Erin asked as we walked. "Because, you know, I'm still kind of undecided if I'm going to take a shift. So, you know, if you are taking it, I could take it as well and give you some company."

Of course I knew why she asked.

I called it my father's curse. Women were drawn to the Alderwyn men like moths to fire. Nothing good ever came from it. In Erin's case, it explained why she bought something at the cafeteria every single time I did. Why she always asked, casually, whether we could meet outside the hospital for a drink. A walk. Anything.

But, unlike my father, I didn't drift wherever the wind pushed me. I wouldn't float from woman to woman like a snowflake with no direction. Until I had time to actually be present with someone, I chose to stay alone. Medicine came first. Everything else had to wait.

"I might do the Thanksgiving shift," I said. "Today is my grandma's birthday. We all get together on her birthday and are a bit more relaxed about Thanksgiving."

Erin nodded, excitement flickering in her eyes. "I'll tell Dr. Rothchild I'll take the shift as well."

We were just about to take the stairs down, when Tessa nearly collided with me. The friendly older nurse smiled up at me, like always. She had that warm aura of a grandma.

"Ah, there you are," she said.

"I know," I said. "Rothchild is looking for me."

"I'm sure he is," she said. "But I'm here for Mrs. Gonzales. She wanted to see you before you head out. Also, there's some guy waiting for you in the waiting room."

My brow lifted. "Some guy? Is he a patient?"

She shrugged. "He said it wasn't anything important. Just that he needed to talk to you."

"Any name?"

"Didn't want to say."

A slow breath slipped out of me. Probably an unhappy patient. Or a family member.

"You go ahead," I said to Erin. "I'll check in on Mrs. Gonzales, then deal with the mysterious man."

Erin's face fell for just a second before she smoothed it out. A polite smile took its place. "Sure. See you later."

I returned the smile. "Later."

Tessa led me toward the ICU floor and took her usual seat at the nurses' station.

Mrs. Gonzales was in the third room down. When I entered, she was asleep in a large hospital bed, surrounded by machines that hummed and beeped.

Twenty-five years old.

Younger than me.

She was a single mom who owned a car repair shop in a small town just outside Boston. And actually fixed the cars as well.

A thin oxygen line rested under her nose. The IV pump was right beside her bed, clicking softly as it delivered fluids and pain medication. Near the foot of the bed, a catheter bag hung low.

Her skin looked pale and washed out, but the freckles across her nose and cheeks still stood out. Dark circles pooled beneath closed eyes, matching her black hair pulled back for surgery, with a few loose strands slipping free.

A whiteboard hung at the foot of the bed, listing goals for the day and diet restrictions in blue marker. I had checked her vitals on the computer about an hour ago. Everything looked amazing.

Dr. Rothchild had been able to remove the entire tumor. He was an asshole but also one of the best surgeons in the nation. And, luckily, her ovarian cancer had been found just in time.

I was turning to leave, to let her rest, when her brown eyes opened and settled on me.

"There you are," she said in a weak but warm voice. A small smile tugged at her mouth.

I pulled the chair closer and sat beside her bed.

"Everything still looks great," I said. "Your vitals are fantastic, and Dr. Rothchild got all the cancerous cells out."

Her hand lifted slightly, and she pointed toward the nightstand.

I rose and walked over to the nightstand. Tucked between a water glass and a stack of get-well cards was a drawing in bright colors. I picked it up and looked at it.

It showed a woman in a bed and a man beside her, dressed all in blue. Both of them were smiling, and they were holding hands. Beneath them, written in crooked letters, were two words.

Thank you.

"My daughter drew this for you," Mrs. Gonzales said, smiling. "You saved my life."

"God." My head shook on its own. "I didn't save you. Dr. Rothchild did the surgery. And you're the one who fought through all this."

She reached for me. Her hand settled around my arm in a weak grip. The touch was cool. A little rough. Callused from years of working on engines and tools in her shop. Her eyes held mine. Brown. Tired. But still carrying that familiar, stubborn strength I knew from my mom and my grandma.

"I know it was you who fought for my surgery with Dr. Rothchild," she said softly. "The nurses told me. The doctors wanted to put me on a months-long waiting list."

That part was true.

What they didn't tell her was that the fight had mostly been about reimbursement issues with her insurance, not about skipping the line ahead of other cancer patients. After a few arguments with the billing department, I got her approved for the hospital fund. It covered what the insurance didn't. Which was most of it.

"I..." Her eyes grew teary. "I don't know how to thank you. I always thought my biggest fear was ending up all alone. Then I became a mom and realized my biggest fear is my child ending up all alone in a world like this."

I didn't know what to say for a moment.

"Well," I finally said, "it's my job."

Her smile widened.

"What a beautiful job," she said. "Saving single moms from the pits of hell so they can be with their kids. Like a white knight in shining armor."

A laugh escaped my lips as heat crept up my cheeks. A faint blush I hoped she wouldn't notice. Something about Mrs. Gonzales stirred strong emotions in me.

A woman who'd fought. A woman who'd carried weight. A single mom working with her hands in a male-dominated field. She carried the weight of an unfair world all on her own like a superhero. Strong. Stubborn. Kinda like my mom and grandma.

"There you are," Dr. Rothchild said as he walked in.

He was short and thin. His glasses sat low on his nose, and his white coat hung stiff on his shoulders.

"Your shift is done. You can go home," he said. "We're slammed all week, so I need you back tonight at eleven for the night shift." He glanced at his watch. "If you want to shower or sleep, you should leave right now. I don't want to hear whining later, understood?"

Mrs. Gonzales and I exchanged a look. The kind that said asshole.

"I'll check in on you again when I get back tonight," I said to her.

She nodded.

"Please tell your daughter thank you for this beautiful picture," I added. "I love it."

I really did. It was the kind of thing I'd hang on my fridge. Right next to thank-you cards and family pics.

Her smile lingered as I tapped her leg. "You get some sleep."

Rothchild joined me and we left. He was probably heading to the cafeteria.

The elevator doors closed behind us and silence settled in.

I stared down at the drawing in my hand, taking in the crooked lines and bright colors.

Then Rothchild cleared his throat.

"Alderwyn," he said, nodding at my name tag. "That's a really rare name."

A small frown pulled at my brow. Small talk. That was unexpected from him.

"Yeah," I said. "I don't think I've ever met another Alderwyn."

He nodded. "I actually met another Alderwyn before. A cancer patient."

My head lifted. "You met someone with the name Alderwyn?"

"Yeah. During my first year out of residency. In this very hospital. I remember the name. I'm into names and their meanings, so I looked up what it meant."

"Really?" A pause. "What does it mean?"

He scratched his head. "I think it comes from the old Germanic alder tree or something. Means endurance. Someone who survives hardship. Also means protector."

I nodded. Stunned.

The elevator stopped with a *ding,* and the doors opened. He stepped out.

"See you at eleven," he said. "Don't be late, or I'll fail you this semester."

The doors were about to close when I put my arm between them.

"Wait."

He turned around.

"How long ago was that?" I asked. "I mean, when you met the other Alderwyn?"

He thought for a moment. "God. I don't know. Maybe ten years or so."

"Was it a woman?"

He shook his head. "No idea, kid. It was a long time ago."

Interest gone, he turned and walked off.

The doors closed again, and this time I let them.

By the time I reached the waiting room, it was nearly empty. An older woman was flipping through a magazine. A mom nearby tried to keep two bored kids quiet. That was it.

I walked up to the front desk.

"Was there a man waiting for me?" I asked Kelley. Her glasses slid down her nose as she typed.

She didn't look up. "I think so. But I'm not sure."

A small nod. "Did anyone ask for me?"

"Nope."

I sighed. How strange. "If he comes back, can you please write down his name? I don't want any patients' complaints to go missing."

She nodded.

Then I left.

37

DYLAN

I left the hospital parking garage looking over my shoulder a million times, like I always did. Most of my family acted like John Myers was dead or had given up on us. That's also what the police had told us.

But I never believed that. A man like Myers was unpredictable. Even if he was on the run, his circumstances could change. He might then have a reason to come back. To seek revenge. To finish the job. Or God knew what else.

I pulled out into busy Boston traffic. The early morning sun sat low, flashing between buildings as glass and brick slid past my windows.

At the first traffic light, a black SUV idled behind me. Matte paint. Dark tint. No plates that I could see from this angle.

The light turned green, and traffic rolled forward. Cars thinned as I merged onto the highway. From there on out, it was a traffic-free ride to my grandma's. Somewhere past the malls and large apartment complexes, the road opened up.

That's when I noticed the same SUV was still behind me. Not too close, but not that far either.

I took my exit. Relief hit when I no longer saw the SUV in my rearview mirror.

By the time I reached Wellesley, everything looked so different from Boston. Old trees lined the streets. Big houses were tucked behind stone walls and perfect landscaping. Many of those mansions were worth several million.

At the highway exit, I slowed. My stomach dropped when the black SUV appeared from behind a truck and took the same exit I did. The damn thing was still behind me.

Alarm bells went off. No way someone had followed the same route all the way from the hospital by coincidence. Right?

The light turned green. But I hesitated. Horns blared behind me, angry and impatient, forcing my foot back onto the gas.

Usually it was a straight drive from here, but I took the next left into a mall parking lot, just to see what would happen.

The turn signal of my car clicked. Once. Twice. And I turned.

The SUV slowed, hesitated for a bit, then continued straight. I watched it disappear down the road, the dark shape shrinking in the distance.

Strange.

Maybe I was just being paranoid. It had been so many years since Myers had vanished. He never came for my grandma. Or Amanda.

Of course, we wanted him caught. Wanted him to face justice and rot in prison forever. The utter incompetence of the authorities in failing to find him was unbelievable. And, to this day, we were convinced the DA, Thomas Harlow, that prick, never truly pushed to find him, hoping Myers would finish the job and kill my grandma.

But maybe, in the end, they all were right, and Myers had died of some overdose somewhere.

The rest of the drive was peaceful. No SUV.

I slowed when I saw the large nursing home sign about fifteen minutes from my dad's house: Senior Flower Gardens.

It sounded amazing.

It wasn't.

If a train station bathroom and the motor vehicle administration had a child, this would be Senior Flower Gardens. Crowded to the brim. Dirt and stench everywhere.

The parking lot was a mess of cracked concrete and had a rodent problem. The building itself looked like it hadn't been cared for in years. Even the windows looked dirty and old.

Some guy was smoking weed near the entrance, stinking the place up.

The glass doors opened automatically as I stepped in. As usual, the front desk was unmanned. Jill was most likely helping out with seniors again.

The air inside was horrible. The neglect of old bodies, smoke, and mold wasn't something anybody should have to smell.

But, like most state-run nursing homes, this place was underfunded and barely hanging on by a thread.

Down the hallway, a cart sat parked against the wall with old food trays.

I turned into the last room on the right, my grandma's room.

When I entered, I thought I'd find her in her wheelchair looking out the window. But she wasn't. She was still in bed, right next to her roommate, Nancy, who was still in hers. Both of them lay there, staring at the ceiling with wide, empty eyes. Not sleeping. Not talking. Just ... there.

My hands curled into fists. They both should've been out of bed hours ago. Instead, they lay there like nobody had even checked whether they were alive today. And the room smelled like feces and urine.

"Good God, Grandma." I rushed to her bed.

The stench of her diaper hit me instantly. Sour, foul, and unbearable. Her silver hair was flat on one side, no doubt from having her lying in the same position for too long.

Her eyes shifted toward me, slowly, with effort.

"Please tell me they at least changed you this morning," I said, although I knew better. God ... I hated this place.

The second I pulled her blanket and nightgown up her legs, I realized how bad it really was. Her diaper was swollen to the rim. My stomach turned, but my hands didn't hesitate. They never did. Not with her. Not after everything she had done for Mom and me.

But it hurt to see her like this. It hurt so freaking much. My jaw clenched hard as hate poured through me, hot and endless. And it landed where it always did.

My worthless dad.

The man who did all this to her.

Ever since Grandma's stroke, about three months after my mom died, Grandma had been trapped inside her own body. Her mind was still in there, somewhere, but the rest of her had turned into a prison. She seemed to be holding herself together for as long as she could, using strength she didn't really have. And once my mom was gone, her body had given in. Like it had been waiting to make sure my mom could leave in peace first. And only then would the curse of high blood pressure finally claim her. Not even sixty years old.

"Let's get you clean," I said, forcing my voice to sound calm. Grandma didn't need my anger. She needed my love.

I walked to the closet and yanked it open. Inside sat the usual stack of supplies. Diapers. A few folded clothes and sheets.

I grabbed a fresh diaper and fresh clothes. Today was her birthday, and I refused to let her look like this place had finally killed her. So I chose the pink silk blouse. Something that still felt like her. I paired it with the black skirt. The one she'd worn to my graduation.

I grabbed the hairbrush from the bathroom too so I could make her look like a million bucks. Even if it was just for a few hours.

On the way back to the bed, my fingers trembled around the folded blouse. Just a little. Enough to notice. Enough to piss me off.

That hate for my dad was still there.

He could pay for the nicest nursing home in the state for my grandma. The same woman who'd kept his kids alive when he was a drunk. The same woman who'd sold her house for us and stepped in when he disappeared into bars and lies. But even when Amanda wanted to help, he overruled her with a huge fit. And sweet Amanda didn't stand a chance. My dad took over her fortune like it was his. And refused to spend a dime from it on my grandma. Left her to rot in here. So this place was her only option, since she'd spent most of her money on my mom and on keeping us afloat when my mom was in jail. She'd burned through savings like it was firewood. The house she sold was worth about $450,000. Jack, the lawyer before Amanda had stepped in, took a lot of it. The rest went fast. It went to my parents' mortgage. It went to groceries and bills. Then, after my mom's death and my grandma's stroke, my dad just kept the rest, since we were still minors.

Now I was too poor as a resident to help financially, and that truth sat in my chest like a sharp knife. But I'd sworn I'd get her out of here the moment I made money. I'd sworn it so many times it had become a spell.

I pulled off my grandma's diaper and dropped it in the trash. Then I used the wet wipes and cleaned her carefully.

"You could also take a quick bath," I said, keeping my tone light, like this wasn't humiliating for her.

She blinked slowly. That usually meant no.

I nodded. "Okay. We won't."

"Nancy," I said to my grandma's roommate. "I'm so sorry you have to wait. I'll get to you in a second, ok?"

Nancy made a sound that wasn't a word, more like a rough groan, but by now I knew her sounds. It meant thank you.

Suddenly, Nurse Carol stormed in with flushed cheeks like she'd been running from room to room. She was a stocky woman with oily short hair and tired eyes that had seen too much for too little pay.

She stopped short when she saw me, and her eyes flicked to my grandma's bed.

"Oh, God, Dylan, I'm so sorry."

"What the hell, Carol?" I shot back.

I pulled clean underwear up my grandma's motionless legs. "They're lying in full diapers, and they're still in bed. This is unacceptable. What the hell is wrong with this place?"

Carol's mouth tightened. For a second, she looked like she might get mad. Instead, she swallowed it.

"I know," she said. "We're short two nurses. They quit last night."

The words should've made me soften. I understood staffing shortages. I did. But my heart couldn't take the sight of my grandma like this.

Carol rushed to my side, but I shook my head.

"Nancy needs help. I got my grandma."

Carol nodded and wiped her brow with the back of her wrist. She quickly moved to Nancy's bedside.

I finished with my grandma and dressed her in her blouse and skirt. Then I combed her hair. It had turned silver from the stroke. Some strands fell into place, neat and soft, and finally she looked like herself again.

"You look beautiful," I said.

I carried her over to her wheelchair, gently set her down, and got her the hell out of this shithole.

For a few hours, at least, we'd both step into a different world.

Into a world of wealth and narcissism.

My dad's.

I PULLED through the automatic gate of my dad's home and onto a long, curving driveway that hugged the edge of Lake Waban. The house sat back from the road, built of old stone and wide glass. A massive colonial mansion. Over ten thousand square feet. Floor-to-ceiling windows caught the morning light. Everything about the place screamed money. Pure luxury.

We had no idea how rich Amanda really was until she married my dad without a prenup. Zach had left her an insane amount of money. Once my mom was gone and the wedding was over, my dad stopped pretending. He sold Amanda's old house and made her buy this one. Triple the square footage. Triple the statement.

He said it was for us kids. For my mom. So she could watch us from heaven, happy. He also said a bigger house meant space for a new beginning. The shameless bastard even mentioned a baby—Amanda's ultimate dream. Becoming a biological mother, finally. Zach had never wanted kids. He hated them.

The driveway was crowded with Dad's toys. A Porsche, his truck, and the black Mercedes were parked there like they owned the place. Amanda's minivan was pushed to the side like the maid's car.

Ridiculous.

As I pulled up, rage climbed up my throat.

Hot. Bitter. Sharp.

My dad had taken all my grandma's and my mom's money, even our shares, and made us beg for everything. And he was now letting my grandma rot in that hellhole.

I also never forgave him for all the other shit he pulled.

He cheated on my mom while she sat in jail, dying of cancer. Turned on her the second it became convenient. Accused her of murder. Planned his escape. Lined up excuses in case she was convicted. So he could walk away from us too.

And now he lived here. His dream life. With an angelic wife who went along and somehow managed to be more of a mother to his kids than he'd ever been a father.

For years after my mom died, sleep was impossible. I woke up gasping, images of my dad killing Zach burning behind my eyes. Some days, the thought followed me long after the nightmares faded. Felt more real when I was awake than it ever did in my sleep.

I moved out the moment I turned eighteen and tried to take care of my grandma as best as I could.

But even if hate twisted my stomach, I never let it show.

For my grandma. For the kids.

Even for Amanda too. None of this was her fault. Like my mom, she was powerless against this man. And when my mom needed her most, Amanda was there for her. For us. She never treated us as less than her own two kids. Sometimes, it even felt like she loved us more because we reminded her of my mom. And her biggest shame.

So, like always, I took a slow breath in. Another out. Long enough to steady myself. Long enough to make sure I didn't walk inside ready for a fight.

I got out, walked around to the passenger side, and opened Grandma's door.

"Let's get inside, birthday girl." I unbuckled her and lifted her into the wheelchair I'd pulled from the trunk. Her hands lay still in her lap as I tucked the blanket around her.

Then I closed the car door and pushed her toward the back entrance.

The designer kitchen waited on the other side of the back door.

And we went inside.

38

DYLAN

"Happy birthday to you," we all sang together, voices overlapping and out of tune.

"Happy birthday to you. Happy birthday, dear Grandma, happy birthday to youuuuuuuuuuu!"

Claps and cheers filled the dining room as we stood crowded around my grandma's wheelchair.

"On three," someone said.

"One. Two. Three," we all said at once and blew out the candles for her. Applause followed. Louder this time.

You could tell Grandma was happy. Not by words or movements but by the slight lift of her left hand. And by the way one side of her mouth pulled upward into an uneven smile while the other stayed still. Frozen. Caught where the stroke had left it.

Amanda carefully sliced the cake. She barely looked like herself anymore. The overdone lip fillers. The facelift my dad insisted on right after Markus was born. Even the way she dressed sexy now didn't belong to her. And all of it was for my dad. He demanded it from her, constantly dangling the threat of cheating or leaving for a younger woman.

I pushed Grandma closer to the table.

"Grandma, I drew this for you—it's us!" Elizabeth said, holding up a drawing that looked exactly like something a five-year-old would make. She wore a pink dress that already had a chocolate stain on it, although it was brand-new. Her blond hair was pulled into an uneven braid.

"Blink twice if you like it!" she said, rocking on her heels.

Grandma blinked twice. Fast. Deliberate. Her eyes stayed on Elizabeth the whole time.

"Yay! I'll add a unicorn!" Elizabeth thundered down the hallway into her room.

Markus, my little brother, barely three now, clung to Lila like peanut butter to jelly. His arms were wrapped tight around her as he demanded cake. Lila didn't hesitate. She scooped some onto a plate and handed it to him. She wore an oversized sweater, sleeves pushed up, hair pulled back in a lazy bun. She was close to graduating high school and wanted to take a year off before college to travel in Europe. Just like my grandma's dream before she had my mom. And maybe my mom's too, before she had me. Lila would live that dream for both of them.

Ethan was sitting at the table as well, cake half gone, crumbs on his shirt. His hoodie hung loose on his shoulders. His eyes glued to the screen, and one hand scrolled through his phone while he chewed. Detached and checked out. Like most boys entering their teenage years.

Dad lowered himself into the chair next to Lila. He was wearing a jersey.

"Can you put down that phone and have a conversation with us like a normal human being?" he complained to Ethan.

Ethan rolled his eyes and set his phone down with a little too much force. The thud echoed on the tabletop. He stared straight ahead, jaw tight.

I sat next to my grandma. "I have something for you," I said and pulled a small gift from my pocket.

"We're doing gifts later," my dad said.

"Gift or cake first?" I asked her, ignoring him. Her eyes locked onto the box, and she blinked twice.

"All right, gift first," I said and began unwrapping it. Inside was a gold wristband. Simple. Light. A small locket hung from it. I opened it carefully and turned it toward her so she could see my mom's picture inside. Young. Smiling. Alive.

"I hope you like it," I said as I slipped it around her stiff wrist. Her fingers curled slightly. The half smile deepened. A tear broke free and rolled down her cheek. That told me everything.

"That's beautiful," Amanda said softly, looking over my shoulder.

"Really great idea, and good call on giving the gift first," my dad said, overly friendly. He always was when he talked to me. He applauded everything I did or said. Kissing my ass twenty-four seven. Not because he wanted to repair our relationship but because of the guilt he carried over his own shitty behavior toward my mom and us. Lila and Ethan had been too young back then to understand what he'd done, but I remembered. And had no intention of forgiving him anytime soon.

"Were you able to get me my steroid cream for my rash?" Lila asked me with a mouthful of cake.

"What rash?" my dad asked.

"Nothing," she said, shrugging it off. "Just the same eczema that won't go away."

"Yeah," I said. "It's in the car. I'd better grab it now before I forget. Can somebody feed the cake to Grandma?"

"I'll do it!" Elizabeth shouted, already thundering back into the room.

It was the cutest thing, seeing how much she loved my grandma—who wasn't actually her grandma. But we never explained it like that. Grandma was Grandma.

I stood and stepped back to make room for Elizabeth. "Remember," I said.

"Slow and small bites," Elizabeth finished the sentence for me, serious and focused. I smiled and ran my hand over her golden-haired head.

"That's right. Slow and small bites."

I watched as Elizabeth lifted the fork and fed my grandma the first bite. She did really well. So I turned and headed for my car.

The cream was on my driver's seat. I'd called it in and picked it up two days ago.

I grabbed the paper bag and was about to walk back when something made me stop.

A black SUV.

It was parked just off to the side on our quiet, private road, right in front of the metal gate leading up to the house.

What the fuck?

My gaze flicked back to the house. Then to the SUV. Should I call the cops?

But before I fully realized what I was doing, I was already getting into my car. I closed the door and roared the engine to life. I drove slowly down the driveway, pretending like everything was normal. Like we'd run out of milk and I'd been sent to grab some.

The automatic gate opened.

But the SUV didn't move an inch.

It just sat there, engine running. A low hum in the quiet.

Shit. Now what?

Was it Myers? Had he finally come for us?

911 flashed through my mind again. But by the time the police would show up, he'd be gone. Should I get a knife, maybe? What if the car disappeared before I even made it back inside? I needed at least to get the plate number.

I turned onto the road where the SUV was parked and slowed. My hand shook as I pulled my phone from my pocket. I started to record a video of the plate, when the window of the SUV began to roll down.

Goddammit.

Was I about to get shot through the window? Better me than my family still inside the house. My jaw locked.

When nothing happened, as the seconds felt like minutes, I eased my car closer, inch by inch, and pulled up right next to the SUV. One foot stayed planted on the gas, ready to slam it and race off if I had to. I was also ready to throw myself sideways if bullets started flying. At least I'd see the driver's face. At least I'd know what Myers looked like.

But the second I rolled up beside him and saw who sat behind the wheel, my foot slammed the brake instead of the gas.

"No need to call 911, kid," Detective Nolan said calmly. "I'm already here."

He looked older than I remembered. Mid-thirties now. He had the kind of face that had seen too much and stopped pretending otherwise. His short dark hair had some gray in it. He had deep lines around his mouth. And his eyes still had that certain sparkle to them. A seasoned cop through and through.

I turned the video off and leaned toward the window. "What are you doing here?"

"Follow me" was all he said. Then he drove off.

I followed him and turned onto a narrow gravel road leading into a stretch of woods not far from my dad's house. The trees closed in on both sides. It looked like a place where hikers found bodies. Even knowing he was a cop, the whole thing felt wrong. Spooky.

He stopped suddenly and got out of his car.

I parked behind him, unlocked my door, and shifted into Park. My heart beat loudly in my ears as Nolan slid into the passenger seat of my car. His suit pants looked expensive but worn. A leather belt held his badge and gun. The door shut with a solid thump.

"Look at you, kid," he said, glancing over as he settled back. "Dr. Dylan Alderwyn, huh? Sure your grandma is proud as hell."

"She is," I said.

Silence followed. The small talk was done, and I felt like something ugly was coming.

"You're probably wondering what the hell I'm doing here," Nolan said. "I'll skip the crap and get right to it."

His gaze locked onto mine.

"They found John Myers."

I straightened. A cold wave rushed through my chest, sharp and sudden, like ice poured straight into my veins.

"What? Where?"

"We don't know for sure."

My head snapped back. "What do you mean you don't know for sure? Didn't you arrest him?"

Nolan's mouth tightened. He didn't look happy. Didn't look like this was the victory we all had hoped for.

"I need to clarify something," he said. "When I said we found him, it wasn't us. Not the police."

This didn't make any sense. "What do you mean? Who found him?"

He sighed. "Thomas Harlow."

My stomach dropped. "The AG who went after my mom to hurt my grandma?"

Nolan nodded. Slow. Somber. "Yeah," he said quietly. "That prick."

"But ... I thought he stepped down after my mom settled with the State."

The power of our million-dollar lawyer, Robert Goldberg, flashed through my mind. The way doors suddenly opened when he walked into a room. The system was so fucked, rotten to the core, but that time, for once, it had worked in our favor.

"He did step down," Nolan said. "The governor himself made sure of it. Quietly, on the outside. But it was a huge deal behind closed doors. Kara Belmont almost went down with Harlow. A few cops too. Then they decided it would be better to bury it all. To protect the so-called integrity of the State." His mouth twisted slightly. "In the end, Harlow was the only one taking the blame. He was removed and started his own private law firm. It was shit, of course. When you cross the system, the system won't take you back. You know how that works." He shifted in the seat, the leather creaking, and stared out the window for a moment, like he thought he'd heard something in the woods. "Harlow tried for years to stay relevant," he continued. "Did that interview for that crime show episode on Zach's murder. The one that landed him in hot water with the new AG and your big-shot lawyer again. After that, things really fell apart for him. Bad job here. Bad job there. He sank low. Last thing I heard in the office gossip mill was that he had to sell his fancy house and file for bankruptcy. After that, he dropped off the radar. Quiet for years."

"Until now," I said.

"Until now." Nolan nodded. "Gotta give the old bastard one thing. He's stubborn. Apparently, he went down the rabbit hole with Zach's case. Never let it go. Never gave up on his mission to destroy your grandma. All because she did the right thing with his rapist son." He shook his head slowly. In disgust. "People are nuts."

His words settled heavily in the car. I knew a thing or two about crazy people. The past pushed its way forward. Images stacked on top of each other. The hate from the people around us. The whispers. The bullying that followed us everywhere. My mom dying alone in jail. Months stolen from us. Time we never got back. My grandma fighting like hell for her until her body finally gave out and the stroke took her down. John Myers almost killing her. A broken nose. A shattered leg. Blood on the pavement.

People were nuts indeed.

My hands curled tightly in my lap.

I hated Myers. Just as much as I hated Thomas Harlow.

"So what does this all mean?" I asked. "If Thomas Harlow found John Myers, can't you force him to tell you where he is? So you can arrest him?"

Nolan let out a long sigh from deep within his chest. "We tried. But Harlow won't tell us where Myers is. He says he doesn't know. He claims that Myers contacted him from a blocked number to make a deal with the State. Using Harlow. Of course Harlow is lying. He knows where Myers is. And Myers didn't reach out to him. After all these years searching for him, Harlow found him. Maybe even blackmailed him to come back and reopen the case with him. To pin this on your mom somehow. Maybe with false testimony from Myers. A fake murder weapon. Who knows. This man is crazy. He didn't take his downfall well."

"False testimony?" My whole body shifted toward him. "To reopen the case?" The words came out hot. Exactly as intended.

"I know," Nolan said quietly. "The new AG's losing sleep over this. After the settlement, everyone just wanted all this to disappear. The State already looked like complete morons."

I opened my mouth, ready to argue.

"Rightfully so," Nolan added fast. "This case was fucked from the beginning. It'll always be that one case that sits wrong with me. Always." His jaw tightened. "But, right now, there's a real chance another shitstorm is about to hit. And it'll include your family again."

His eyes locked on to mine. No sugarcoating.

"If everything gets dug up again," he went on, "that means new documentaries. Crime shows tearing the case apart. Camera crews parked in front of your lawn and outside the station. Whatever Myers and Harlow are planning, it's nothing good." He exhaled hard. "Honestly, I thought the bastard was dead. Overdosed or stabbed in some bar fight. Who the fuck would've cared? God knows it would've been better that way. But, for some reason, the devil decided to send him back our way."

"So why don't you just put everything you have into finding him?" I demanded. "Finally do your damn job so my family doesn't have to suffer all over again."

Nolan let the insult slide. His gaze drifted out the window, toward the dark stretch of trees, as if answers might be waiting out there.

"I tried to find him," he said. "I really fucking did. But nobody knows where Myers is. And Harlow won't talk. Keeps lying." He rubbed a hand over his face. "We talked to Billy Dustin and interviewed customers at the Seacoast Inn, where he used to hide out. But it's not exactly the kind of place where cops are welcome or people feel like ratting. God. Maybe Myers isn't back. Maybe Harlow's full of shit and just wants attention before he dies alone, drunk in some piss-soaked alley muttering about the time he mattered."

"You don't believe that," I said. "Otherwise, you wouldn't be here."

Nolan looked back at me and gave a small nod. "You're as sharp as your grandma."

"So, what now?"

"Well"—he straightened in his seat—"I want to offer your grandma and Amanda an undercover cop as protection."

"That's great," I said, already dismissive. "But that won't fix the real problem. How the hell are you actually gonna find Myers and arrest him?"

Something flickered in Nolan's eyes. "Oh, believe me," he said, his gaze hardening, "I will find him this time. And I'll make him pay with everything the justice system legally puts into these hands." He lifted his palms, like he was weighing something heavy, then dropped them again. "But until we have him, I need you to be safe. And also ..."

Ah. Here it was. The thing he'd been circling this whole time.

"Also what?"

He scratched the side of his forehead. "And also ... call me if Myers or Harlow tries to reach out to you."

"Reach out to me? You mean like threats or blackmail?"

"Something like that."

A sarcastic, bitter laugh slipped past my lips. "But that's not all, is it?"

Our eyes locked.

"I mean, you wouldn't just follow me out here like this if there wasn't still icing left to put on this shit cake."

A thin smile tugged at his mouth. Not amusement. Something closer to admiration.

"You really are a lot like your grandma," he said.

I crossed my arms with an annoyed sigh.

"All right," Nolan said. "Let's just say it's important that I handle Myers' arrest myself."

I furrowed my brow.

"So that ... he can be interrogated properly. Statements recorded by me and by men I trust. Men I know who won't screw this up."

His eyes drifted forward. Almost ashamed. Then they came back to me.

"As crazy as it sounds," he said, "Harlow still has friends in the system. Even after all these years. And some of his crazy theories are starting to gain traction at the station."

My head lifted, and my mouth actually fell open too. Shock hit first. Then disbelief.

"What the actual fuck," I said, loud and clear. "You have to be kidding me."

Nolan's fingers tugged at the edge of his suit jacket like he didn't know what to do with his hands.

"Are you telling me," I said, my voice rising, "that after everything my mother and my family have already been through ..." The words backed up in my throat. Then they came out angrier. "After the incompetence of your department. After the personal mission of that asshole AG to destroy us. After all the little idiots who followed his illegal orders without once stopping to think for themselves …"

I shook my head in a sharp, disbelieving motion.

"After all that, you're now telling me that years after my mom died, the State is opening the gates to a new Alderwyn shitshow? And drag my family through hell again?"

I pointed at him. "How could you let all of this happen in the first place? Why the fuck didn't you arrest Myers when people first started telling you he murdered Zach? Why did all of you think it made more sense to throw a cancer-sick, traumatized mother in jail instead of going after a known violent man with a criminal record? Who was covered in blood that night, caught on an actual fucking video! And, and, and …" The words tripped over one another as I searched for more. "And now, all these years later, you're sitting here telling me you still can't find him. Still can't arrest him. That the State might make the same dumbass mistakes all over again. That some crazy man's conspiracy theories, fueled by his hate for my grandma, are gaining traction again."

I felt like I couldn't breathe. Anger sat hot in my chest, mixing with something darker.

Hate. Outrage. Disbelief.

"Oh, we will sue you fuckers to the moon and back," I announced. "And this time, no mercy, Nolan. No mercy. Not even for you."

My head shook as I turned toward the window. "Fucking John Myers is back, teaming up with Harlow's homeless drunk ass to destroy my family all over again."

A few more curses spilled out. Ugly ones. Then the car went quiet.

"You know," Nolan said after giving me some time to calm down, "if I were you, I'd do the same thing. Sue the State, I mean. And I hope you get whatever it is that'll make you feel better."

I waited for more. A but. A condition. Something.

Nothing came.

Nolan stared out the window. He shifted in his seat. His gaze was fixed on something in the distance. "I don't know if she ever told you," he finally said, "and you probably already know this, but your grandma was my teacher when I was a kid." A sad smile tugged at his lips.

"Some little rug rat who loved action figures and He-Man and all that stuff. I was full of hope for the world. For my family. For myself too, despite living in some … difficult circumstances. We don't have to get into all that, but let's just say everybody looked away. Ignored my mom's cries for help. Ignored mine. Ignored my sister's." His eyes stayed fixed on the trees. "Your grandma—she didn't look away. She saved us. She was the only one who didn't pretend that nothing was wrong." His jaw tightened. "She even lied for us. To the police. She put herself on the line, risked everything, just to help."

Silence settled between us.

"When your grandma was attacked and almost killed"—he shook his head slowly, like the memory was replaying right in front of him—"I let her down completely. I failed the woman who saved my life. Failed her family after she rescued mine."

His hands clenched in his lap.

"I could have stopped it. I know that now. If I'd listened to her. Followed the evidence. Done my job." His jaw tightened. "Instead, I buried my head. I was afraid of the AG like everyone else. And when I finally did the right thing, it felt too late, too little."

His eyes met mine.

"It haunts me," he said. "It really does. So if you want to sue the State, please do. I won't stop you. Actually, I'll help you however I can." His eyes darkened. "But please, I beg you, don't do anything until after I get my hands on John Myers."

He leaned closer.

"I know it's a lot to ask. But I need you to trust me. I need to be the one who arrests him and interrogates him. I need to be the first law enforcement his worthless ass sees. That's the only way I can make sure your grandma stays safe this time. That I don't put her through hell again. God knows she doesn't need that."

His mouth tightened.

"None of you do," he said. "Not her. Not the kids. Not Amanda, after losing her first husband like that. And Jesus, Dylan, you don't need this either. You don't need news crews camped outside your hospital, following your patients around, asking for interviews."

He was right. About all of it.

If Harlow still had support for his nonsense after all these years, more people would follow.

My head dropped into my hands. Fingers pressed against my face, rubbing hard, like I needed to feel something solid. To make sure this wasn't another nightmare. Another round of the same fucking hell.

Nolan's hand landed on my shoulder. Warm and firm, like it came from the dad I never had.

I looked up and met his eyes. There was compassion there. Sadness too. And guilt. The weight of failure.

In some twisted way, he was just another victim. Like my family.

It wasn't his fault that the system was the way it was. That Thomas Harlow had crossed paths with Grandma a long time ago. That he'd decided to destroy us for his rotten son's mistakes.

"That's not quite true," I said.

He shook his head, confused.

"I mean, that you completely failed my grandma and my family."

Something shifted in his face, and hope flickered to life in his eyes.

"You did help my grandma," I went on. "The gas station video. Remember? You got it even though you knew it could get you in trouble. And Mrs. Dustin—you helped her get away from her husband. She later gave testimony. Dead women can't do that." My voice steadied as the memories lined up. "It was also you who insisted the neighbor's statement be recorded that night when Myers attacked my grandma. The cops were told not to take it. Remember? You made them take it anyway. Even though it could've cost you your job." I paused. "You had a family to feed too, and you did it anyway. In the end, all of that became major evidence in court. Evidence we wouldn't have had without you. It helped get the charges dropped. And now here you are again, fighting for my family, making sure Thomas doesn't get the last word."

I held his gaze.

"So, yeah," I said. "You did more than you think."

He looked at me for a long moment. Then his shoulders eased a little. Like some weight had finally shifted.

"Will you call me," he asked, "if you hear from Harlow or Myers?"

"Even before 911?" I asked.

"Yes. Unless it's an emergency." He reached into his jacket. "We can't allow Harlow to make a deal for Myers. Or reopen the case on his terms. I've got my phone on me twenty-four seven."

He handed me a card.

I glanced at it, then tucked it into my pocket.

"Memorize my cell number," he said.

"I will."

His hand reached for the car door. Then he turned back toward me and looked me over from head to toe.

"Not surprised at all," he said with a genuine smile. "Knowing where the apple came from."

His smile faded, and his face hardened again. "Don't tell anybody about this meeting," he said. "Harlow can't know."

I nodded.

Then he stepped out and shut the door behind him.

I watched him hurry back to his SUV and drive off.

The forest closed in around me.

Trees stood tall like silent witnesses. Leaves rattled in the wind, red and yellow fall colors catching the light.

It was profoundly beautiful.

I sat there, alone, trying to understand what hell I'd just been pulled back into.

The man who attacked my mom and my grandma was back. The man who'd ruined our lives. Who stole months, maybe years, from my mom's life. He took that time from me and my siblings. Time we never got back. Who knew how long she might have lived without those months, rotting in jail?

And now he was back, teaming up with that other monster, Thomas Harlow. Like dung beetle buddies, rolling around in the same pile of shit together.

They wanted to finish what they'd started back then. And now my grandma wasn't able to continue the fight or win the final battle.

But she didn't have to.

I was here.

A grown-ass man, ready to do what I couldn't back then.

It was almost funny watching Detective Nolan offer to fight for us. I knew his intentions were real. His compassion too. Especially when it came to my grandma and the rest of my family.

But after everything that happened, how the hell could I trust him to handle the situation? This world wasn't built for good cops fighting the good fight anymore. Life had beaten that lesson into me early.

So, if Nolan thought I'd sit back and wait while Harlow or Myers played with my family, he was wrong.

I would find this bastard myself. By any means necessary. Then Nolan could do what he needed to do—ride in like a knight in shining armor and make sure Myers was treated like the monster he was. No deals. No favors. None of that shit. He would rot behind bars like my mom did.

Justice finally served.

Of course, that didn't mean a happy ending, not after what happened to Mom. But, God, with Myers rotting in prison, we could all sleep a little better at night.

My phone rang.

Dad.

"Hey," he said. "Did you go to the store or something?" His voice sounded fake. Too friendly. Like it should've followed with "I'm so sorry for everything I've done to you and your mom." Which, of course, it never would.

"No," I said. "I realized I'd left the steroid cream at my place." My eyes flicked to the dashboard clock. It made sense. My small, shitty apartment wasn't far.

"So I went to get it. Lila really needs it. I'm on my way back."

"Ah, yeah. Good call about the cream. You're so sma—"

I hung up before he could finish.

I slipped the car back into Drive.

Today was for my grandma. Opening gifts. Eating cake, surrounded by family. She deserved it.

After that, I'd work my night shift at the hospital. And the moment my shift ended, I would get right on it.

I would find fucking Myers.

39

DYLAN

I drove behind the abandoned gas station on Essex Street, heading north.

The area had turned bad a mile or so back. Houses sagging into themselves. Peeling paint. Boarded-up stores.

When my dad's Porsche rolled up to the group of waiting women, they all moved at once. Short mini-dresses. Bare legs despite the chilly evening air.

I tugged my baseball cap lower and pulled the COVID mask higher over my face. The brim shadowed my eyes. The mask hid the rest.

My gaze landed on a short woman. She was thinner than the others. Not young, not old either. Her face was blank. On her chest, right between her barely covered breasts, shiny blisters stood out against her pale skin.

She noticed my stare and tugged her dress higher, trying to hide what she could.

I pointed at her and leaned across to push the passenger door open.

She didn't hesitate. She slid in quickly as the others turned away without a word, already drifting back into their waiting positions.

Neither the mask nor the cap seemed to throw the woman off. Men hiding their faces was probably something she was used to. Perverted married guys. Cops. Worse.

"You got a room at the Seacoast Inn we can use?" I asked.

Everybody knew what the women behind this gas station were doing. Where they went. Prostitution was just a misdemeanor in Massachusetts. Not exactly a deterrent. Not for the buyers or for the women who didn't have better options.

"Yes," she said, pointing up the road. "It's right there. Ten minutes. Near the woods."

I nodded.

We drove in silence.

When I pulled into the Seacoast Inn parking lot, it looked exactly how I expected. A filthy old place beneath a gray sky. Paint chipped everywhere. Curtains were permanently drawn. The place smelled like urine and smoke.

As I put the car in Park, I could almost feel my grandmother sitting here all those years back. Looking for Myers. Same cracked pavement. Same shithole.

She had been stubborn and strong. But she was too kind to go as far as I would.

"We going in, or should I blow you here?" the prostitute asked. "I only do blow jobs right now. Personal reasons."

I glanced around.

A couple of shitty cars sat scattered across the lot. An older man stepped out of one of the rooms, pulling cash out of his pocket. A young woman followed him, eyes darting left, then right, before she slipped back inside and shut the door. With his cash, of course.

Everybody knew what the Seacoast Inn was for. Drugs. Prostitutes. If you could imagine it, it happened here. Most of the women waited behind the old gas station on Essex Street. Customers picked them up and brought them here for a quick fuck.

"Do those work?" I asked, nodding toward one of the security cameras mounted crookedly on the side of the building.

"No," she said. "So I can blow you here in the parking lot too."

I gave a half nod.

"Must be hard," I said. "This line of work."

Her head snapped toward me, and suspicion sharpened her features.

"Do you usually work at the inn?" I asked.

Her eyes narrowed. "What's with all the questions? You a pig or something?"

Her hand slid to the door handle.

"God, no," I said with a short, bitter laugh. "That's an insult, considering what they've done to me and my family. I can't stand the cops."

She studied me, her eyes searching my face for lies. She didn't seem to find any as she shifted in her seat and let go of the door handle.

"That rash of yours," I said, nodding at her chest. "That's shingles."

She laughed. "What, you a doctor or something like that?"

"Something like that." I kept my voice casual. "Shingles follows dermatomal distribution. It hides out in your ganglia, along the spine. Then it travels outward. That's why it shows up on your chest. Sometimes it goes away on its own. But sometimes it can also cause postherpetic neuralgia."

Her gaze dropped to the blisters on her chest.

"It can also make you blind if it spreads to the eye," I added. "You don't have HIV, do you? Because that can make the complications a lot worse."

She looked up fast. Eyes wide now. "What happens if somebody has HIV and shingles? I'm asking for a friend."

"That depends," I said.

"On what?"

"If people are on antivirals. And if they are generally healthy and willing to take medication to treat the shingles. And the HIV."

Her fingers played with the edge of her dress. "What if they can't afford their HIV meds?"

The fake designer purse. The cheap dress. The worn-down heels. My chest tightened for this woman.

"Then they should treat the shingles with antivirals as soon as possible," I said. "They're not expensive, even without insurance. And I could get them for free."

Our eyes met.

Shock flickered across her face, struggling to process what I just said. Like kindness was a language she didn't speak anymore. Seeing her this vulnerable made me hate Myers even more. As if he were responsible for her misery too.

"I … I have HIV," she confessed, like I didn't already know. "That's why I only give blow jobs right now. 'Cause I can't afford the meds to keep my count low."

I nodded. "Well, it's better if you don't do that either," I said as kindly as I could. "It's very, very rare, but if there's blood-to-blood contact, like a cut in your mouth and a wound on a client, it's possible to pass it along."

Her face drained fast.

"It's really unlikely," I added quickly. "Extremely unlikely. Have you had any injury in your mouth lately?"

Her head shook hard. "No. I haven't. I promise."

I reached for her hand before thinking. It was cold.

"As I said, it's unlikely. But we need to get you back on your meds. Not for the filthy bastards treating you like an animal. But for you. The Massachusetts HIV Drug Assistance Program pays for HIV meds for people who can't afford them. No questions asked."

She stared at me. "Why," she said slowly, "are you doing this? I mean … helping me."

I held her gaze. "Because almost nobody helped us when we needed it the most. And that was a terrible feeling."

My hand slipped from hers, and I looked out the window and back at the motel. The dirty curtains. A place that destroyed people.

"But I also need something," I said. "Information. About a bad, bad guy. Someone I need to take care of before he hurts more people. You think you can help me?"

She nodded. "Who are you looking for?"

"His name is John Myers," I said. "He has a big scar on his forehead."

Her lips pressed together as she looked out the window. When she looked back at me, something had hardened.

"I know that piece of shit," she said. "All the girls here do."

I straightened in my seat.

"We call him Gash," she went on. "Stopped fucking him because half of the time he doesn't pay. Gave Jody a broken nose when she refused to fuck him again. So now we avoid him."

The words landed hard. A real lead on Myers. I tried hard not to shake. He was so close!

"Does he live here?" I asked.

She shook her head. "No." Then tilted it sideways, considering. "Well … kinda. He's good friends with the owner of this shithole, Fat Bob. Went to school with him or something."

"Do you know where I can find Myers?"

She didn't hesitate. Not even for a second. It was amazing what treating people like human beings could do.

"Down there in the woods," she said, pointing toward the darkness beyond the motel lot. "There's a little hut. By the river. About a mile or so from here. He fucking broke Jody's nose in there when she asked for her money. That's where he stays when he's in the area. It's private property. Fat Bob owns it. Nobody knows about the hut but a few of us. And them. Why do you want to find him?"

"I . . . want to pay him a lot of money to leave and never come back."

For a moment, I let that sit. Made sure she would remember that part. She looked curious, but then just nodded.

"A lot of people want him gone."

My eyes followed the direction she'd pointed. The tree line swallowed a tiny path. No lights. Only leaves and dark secrets.

Then my hand shifted, and the car slipped back into Drive.

"Where are we going?" she asked. No panic or protest. Just curiosity.

"We'll get the antivirals for your shingles," I said. "Then I'll drop you off at the Massachusetts HIV Drug Assistance Program. We need to get you back on your meds as soon as possible. You don't want to die from HIV. It's a horrible death. It's just as bad as cancer if it's untreated."

The image of my mother flashed before me. When she was nothing more than skin and bones.

"Is that okay with you if we get you the meds now?"

She nodded, smiling faintly.

I was just about to pull out of the parking lot when her hand came down on my arm, right where it rested near the stick shift. Her touch was light. Careful. Like she was afraid she was crossing a line.

"Thank you," she said. "I'll never forget your kindness."

My eyes caught hers. And I smiled back under my mask.

"What's your name?" she asked.

I pulled onto the road, the motel shrinking behind us.

"Why don't you tell me yours first?" I asked.

40

DYLAN

Darkness pressed in on all sides as I stood completely still among the pitch-black trees of the forest. I'd parked my car on a gravel road about a mile away from Myers' hut in the woods near the Seacoast Inn. A glimmer of light coming through the hut's small window was proof that someone lived there.

Above me, the moon transformed everything around me into a painting of darkness and silver. It wasn't enough to see well. If anything, it made things spookier. Turned it into the kind of place where people got lost and never came back.

From where I stood, the hut looked small. Isolated. Swallowed by the woods pressing in from all sides.

My eyes narrowed when the door opened and Lucy, the kind prostitute, stepped out of the hut.

Warm light spilled from behind her. The glow outlined her skinny body and the edge of her mouth, showing she was talking.

She hesitated just outside the doorway, and a second figure stepped out.

John Myers.

My stomach turned, and adrenaline exploded through me.

It was him! It was actually fucking him!

The light from inside caught him too. He blocked part of the glow by standing there.

His face stayed mostly dark, but the edge of his nose and the large scar on his forehead flashed into view when he leaned forward.

He looked thin. Almost small. Short.

They exchanged a few brief words. I couldn't hear them, but suddenly Myers shoved her shoulder. Not hard enough to knock her down, but enough to make a point. Enough to remind her who had the power.

An argument.

I was about to bolt down and save her, when his arm moved again, reaching into his pocket. The light caught his hand as he pulled out money. He pressed it into her palm.

Lucy looked down at her hand, then turned and rushed off.

Her phone's beam flickered as she made her way along the narrow path toward the Seacoast Inn. Soon she was gone.

The door to the hut slammed shut again.

My body stayed rooted where it was, eyes locked on the dark outline of the hut. The place where the man who'd destroyed our lives now hid behind old wooden logs.

Something shifted deep in my chest. It wasn't the usual hot, explosive rage I felt whenever I thought about Myers. This was different. It was colder, quieter.

My breathing slowed. My shoulders relaxed, and my fingers hung loosely at my sides.

It surprised me how calm I was, considering how many times I'd replayed beating the shit out of him in my head. But standing here now, there was no sudden charge down the hill. No reckless rush over roots and slick stones to kick in the door and serve him some good old-fashioned justice.

For a moment, my hand moved toward my phone.

Detective Nolan had told me to call him the second Myers contacted me. And Nolan was only one tap away. I could call him right here, right now. Tell him I'd found Myers. Tell him it was over. That he could come get him and slap the cuffs on.

I left the phone in my pocket.

No.

This wasn't Nolan's time yet.

I had no doubt Lucy had told Myers everything about our meeting. It showed in the way she'd run. And the payment. She hadn't held anything back. Not my name. Not my visit. Not the questions I'd asked. Not the part where I said I would pay a lot of money for him to go away again. Every small detail about me had been handed over.

Soon, Myers would either run or come for me. And I had no doubt it was the second option. He was most likely tired of running and broke. Looking at him, his life was hell. And only dropped charges or a shit ton of money could make it better. But getting the charges dropped was getting more complicated now that people knew about his and Harlow's plans. Unless they had a smoking gun, this was a long shot in the first place. So taking the money and getting out of here was the better option than the insanity of reopening the case all over again. No matter what Harlow promised him.

Things would move fast from here on out. Myers would act soon. Men like him always did. And instead of handing him to incompetent cops or filthy pieces of shit like Thomas Harlow, I'd make sure things went differently this time. Nolan meant well. But Nolan hadn't gotten the job done before.

So it would be me taking over the reins.

I would watch.

I would wait.

And when he came for me, I'd be ready.

Now all I had to do was make him believe he'd get what he wanted. In return, I'd get what I needed.

The truth.

A confession.

And the fucking why.

Why he killed Zach. How my mom escaped.

She'd never been able to talk about it. Not only had she gone mute but her mind had seemed to collapse every time that night was brought up.

But Myers wasn't mute. Myers could talk.

Hopefully enough to clear my mother's name once and for all. Let her rest in peace. And keep my family from any more harm.

I stayed put, hidden in the darkness among the trees. The cold air carried the strong scent of moss and rain.

A slow breath in. Then out.

Now was not the time to confront him. Not here. Not like this. It needed planning.

And when Myers finally came for me, I wouldn't be running.

I'd be ready.

41

DYLAN

I'd noticed a shitty black truck following me the day before Thanksgiving. Not even two days after I watched Myers' hut in the woods.

The driver tried to be sneaky. Didn't park in my apartment complex parking lot but across the street.

Always waited at traffic stops.

And when I snatched up a parking spot on one of the side streets near the hospital, the driver didn't park anywhere close to me.

When I left my car on the dark street for my night shift, my head kept turning. I looked over my shoulder the whole time.

I'd asked my dad to hire security for the family, and silently thanked every higher power I could think of for that decision. He didn't hesitate. Probably even liked the idea. Buff guys walking around with him, watching his back, like he was somebody.

About halfway through the night shift with Erin on Thanksgiving, we finally sat at the table in the residence room.

"This fucking shift," Erin huffed as she leaned back in her chair. "I can't believe they let so many doctors and nurses take off."

I took a sip of my hospital coffee and instantly regretted it. It was bitter and nasty. The kind of coffee that only those on night shifts had to endure.

This shift had been nonstop fires until now. Calls. Chaos. No breaks. I was still wearing booties and a surgical cap, ready for the next emergency.

The clock on the wall read 12:02.

"It's Thanksgiving," I said. "People want to be with their families."

"I get that," she said. "But sick people don't just stop being sick. They could've at least left a bare-bones crew. This place feels like a graveyard."

My phone buzzed against the table.

A message from Kelley at the front desk.

Some guy left a note for you.

My fingers tightened around the phone, and I stood.

"Where are you going?" Erin asked.

"Front desk," I said. "Some patient is looking for me or something."

She nodded. "You coming back after?"

"Might be a bit. I'll do a few more rounds while I'm at it. ICU and the children's floor. Pediatric oncology's short today, so I'll help where I can. I'll see you later."

She hid her disappointment and nodded again.

Downstairs, Kelley sat at the front desk, reading a romance novel with a bare-chested guy on the cover. The ER waiting room to her left was nearly empty.

Without looking up, she handed me an envelope.

Her oversized pink glasses slid down her nose. She waited until I took the envelope before pushing them back up.

"Who left this?" I asked.

"I don't know," she said. "It wasn't the same guy as last time."

I nodded. Last time was Nolan.

"This one looked kinda homeless," she added.

"It was probably Willy," I said. "He's going through a rough patch again."

She shrugged, still not looking up. "Hard to say. He was wearing a baseball cap and one of those Florida sweaters. The tourist kind with bright colors and a big state logo on the front. It looked like something people buy on vacation and never stop wearing."

"Ah," I said, nodding like it all made sense. "Then it must be Willy. I got him a Florida sweater for colder days. He's always wearing that same T-shirt and thinks jackets have listening devices sewn into them."

She finally looked up at me and shook her head. "Listening devices? Oh God. I don't envy you."

She pointed at the envelope in my hand. "Probably a letter about him being a prophet or something."

"I hope I can get him back on his meds," I said. "He does so much better when he's on them."

"Let's hope," Kelley muttered, already turning back to her book.

"Happy Thanksgiving," I said and turned.

"Happy Thanksgiving," she mumbled.

I headed for the main stairs, then changed my mind and took the back stairwell instead. It was quiet, and the moment the door closed behind me, my legs gave out.

I fell on the stairs hard. Cold stone seeped through my scrubs. My phone slipped from my hand and landed next to me.

Thoughts flooded me, loud and fast. Too many to grab on to. And before I could slow them down, I ripped the envelope open and pulled out a picture ... of a bloody knife.

It looked like a regular kitchen knife. Nothing special. The kind anyone could buy at any store. Black handle. Silver blade. Except the blade was smeared with dark, crusted blood.

My stomach twisted hard.

I didn't need to wonder whose blood it was.

Zach's murder weapon had never been found. Now Zach's killer was sending me a picture of it.

This could mean only one thing.

Myers was done playing. Done hiding. Ready to move his pieces and start the game again.

Footsteps echoed in the stairwell.

"Happy Thanksgiving, Dylan," a woman said.

I looked up and faked a smile.

Tessa.

Her short white curls looked a little wild. Night shift on Thanksgiving.

"Happy Thanksgiving to you too!" I said, taking the first few steps up just as she took hers down.

"Almost done, huh?" I added, keeping my voice light.

"Just a few more hours," she hollered back. "We can do it."

Her footsteps faded, then the thud of the door two floors down echoed up through the stairwell.

I waited.

Then rushed down the stairs.

I had to act.

Fast.

I pushed through the back door by the trash cans and stepped into the back alley. The fall cold wrapped around me, biting through my scrubs. My whole body trembled. Maybe from the cold. Maybe not.

The street stretched out empty and dark. No cars. No people. Streetlights buzzed. Wind dragged leaves and trash across the street.

I turned more than once on the way back to the car. Stopped. Looked. Any flicker caught my eye and made my heart jump. The short walk felt endless.

The envelope and the picture were crumpled in my pocket. I unlocked my car, then spun around, scanning the street, half expecting Myers to jump me right there. To shove me inside. A gun to my head. A hand clamped over my mouth.

I waited and listened.

And when no one appeared, I yanked the door open and got inside. The engine roared to life, and the click of the locks sent a rush of relief through me.

But then a man's voice came from behind me.

"Don't turn around, or I'll blow your brains out."

My hands shot up without thinking. Fingers spread. My pulse slammed so hard it blurred my vision.

I glanced in the rearview mirror.

A man in a fucking ski mask sat in the backseat of my car!

I felt ice cold, like a bucket of ice water had been dumped on top of me.

"Start driving," he said.

Slowly, I lowered my hands to the steering wheel where he could see them.

My head raced. This was Myers. No doubt about it. The mask hid his face, but he was wearing the Florida sweater Kelley had mentioned.

Here I was. Finally. With *the* Myers.

"Where to?" The words barely made it out.

"You stupid or something?" he barked. "To the Seacoast Inn."

Of course.

I started driving. At the first stop sign, a cop pulled up next to us.

"Don't say a fucking word," Myers growled as he ducked lower in the back. "I've got nothing to lose anymore."

The way he said it left no room for doubt.

I waited. Forced myself to breathe. Watched the light turn green. Then drove, eyes locked ahead as the cop took a turn.

Once we hit the highway, Myers sat up straighter in the backseat. He twitched. Shifted. Sniffed hard. Over and over. His smell filled the car. Booze. Sweat. Something foul. He looked rough. Worse than I expected.

"I hear you've been fucking looking for me," he said.

The metal of his gun caught the highway lights as he pointed it at me. I kept my eyes forward. Said nothing.

"You fucking deaf or something?" he snapped.

"No. I just wasn't sure if you wanted me to say anything," I said fast.

"So why you looking for me?" He snorted. "Just like your fucking grandma back then," he added with hate.

"I-I was told you were in the area," I said. "And, all things considered, it's only logical I'd try to find you, no? To see if we can't make a deal that benefits us both."

Staying close to the truth felt smarter here. If he'd wanted me dead, I wouldn't still be breathing. So he wanted something else from me.

"That bitch cunt Harlow talks too much," he muttered. "Can't trust him."

"Nobody can trust Harlow," I said. "I'm sure he told you he will get your charges dropped. Said that if he can find you, the cops can find you too. And then it's too late for him to help you."

His knee bounced. His hand tightened around the gun, then loosened, then tightened again. Neurotic. Jittery. Not a good mix when someone points a gun at you.

"Well," I continued, "I guess we have one thing in common."

Our eyes met in the mirror.

"I mean, we both can't trust Harlow. He is a liar. Says whatever people want to hear to get what he wants."

He didn't respond.

We drove the rest of the way without talking. Buildings gave way to darker stretches of fields. It felt smarter to stay quiet. Let him feel in control. Which he was. He had the gun.

I took the county road leading to the Seacoast Inn, but as we got closer, he leaned forward again, close enough that I could feel his breath near my ear.

"Keep going," he ordered.

I knew exactly where he meant. The hut. Still, I played dumb.

"I thought you said we were going to—"

"Just fucking drive," he hissed. "About a mile down the road. Then take the dirt road on your right."

I did as he told me. My hands stayed steady on the wheel even though his gun moved in short, jerky motions every time he twitched.

The headlights brightened a narrow gravel road cutting into the woods. I eased onto it.

Trees closed in on both sides, tall and dense. I was driving straight through a gateway to my death.

At the end of the road, several large boulders blocked the way.

I put the car in Park.

"Turn the engine off and get out," he demanded.

The second we stepped outside, he shoved me forward, hard, sending me stumbling. It was nuts. All of it. I was still in my scrubs, booties, and even surgical cap.

"Move," he snapped, pushing me onto a narrow path. "This way."

At first, it was almost fully black. My foot caught on a root, and I hit the ground. He swore behind me, then turned on the flashlight on his phone. A weak beam cut through the darkness, lighting up the dirt path ahead.

I didn't have time to come up with an escape plan. But I noticed that he was much shorter than I was. At least a head. I was six four now.

My hands balled into fists.

Anger burned hot in my chest as reality really sank in.

Myers was fucking kidnapping me. Years after he killed Zach. Years after he let my mom rot for it. Years after he tried to kill my grandma. And he was much smaller than me. Skinny. Sickly. Like the substance abusers and alcoholics I saw in the hospital. ICU regulars. Shaking hands. One bottle away from kidney failure.

"Over there!" he barked.

He shoved me toward the little wooden hut I already knew was there. It sat in a small clearing, surrounded by trees. Clouds covered the sky, blocking any moonlight. A warm glow leaked through the hut's window.

He pulled out a set of keys and unlocked the door, never taking his eyes off me.

The door swung open, and he yanked me inside, rough, quick. One hand patted me down while the other kept the gun on me.

The hut was a tiny hellhole.

A couch he obviously slept on. A small table in the middle of the room. An old kitchenette straight out of the sixties, yellowed cabinets, and a filthy sink. Empty takeout boxes and beer cans were everywhere. It stank of stale alcohol, sweat, and mold. There was no bathroom. No shower. Just this one dirty room and a space heater humming in the corner.

"Can I sit?" I asked, nodding at the round wooden table buried under trash.

He hesitated. Thought about it. Then nodded.

I pulled the chair back and sat, taking in the space again.

Myers dropped onto the couch a few feet away. He stared at me, sniffing, restless. His leg bounced. His grip on the gun never relaxed.

"So," I said, folding my hands in my lap, "let's talk."

His eyes dragged over me, head to toe, as if I might be hiding a gun somewhere. As if that would even be possible in scrubs.

"You can take the mask off. I mean, I know who you—"

"Shut up!" he barked. "I'm not John Myers. I'm just a friend helping him negotiate things."

I nodded. Slow. Careful. "Makes sense. Then let's negotiate. Tell me what Myers wants. Obviously, he wouldn't be talking to Harlow or sending you after me if he didn't want something."

He rocked back and forth on the couch.

Finally, he locked eyes with me.

Brown eyes. Bloodshot.

"Myers needs money," he said. "A lot of it. Fucking Harlow found him and dragged this whole shitshow into the open again." A sharp sniff. "No way he trusts that piece of shit to get his charges dropped. This whore told Myers you will pay for him to leave."

I nodded, agreeing. "I would. How much does he want?"

Myers shrugged, the motion jerky. "Don't know. Maybe a hundred K?"

He watched my face closely. When I didn't laugh, he sat up straight.

"No, wait. More like five hundred K."

I stayed still. Kept nodding.

"No. Fucking wait, man." His voice rose. "One million. Yeah. He wants one million for this shit."

"Okay," I said. "One million."

Something loosened in him, and his lips formed into a crooked smile.

"Yeah," he said, lighter now. "Fucking one million. Yeah."

"Sounds fair," I said. "And what else does my family get in return for one million?"

"You stupid?" he snapped, arm stretching out, the barrel aimed at me. "He'll leave the area. Like you want him to. And I won't shoot you. After everything your fucking family put him through, I should blow your brains out. Let you join your mom in hell!"

I didn't flinch. Didn't look away. My gaze held his, steady, flat.

Finally, he scoffed and pulled the gun back a few inches.

"Fine," he said. "You also get the fucking murder weapon for a mill. How about that?"

My brows pulled together. "The one in this picture? May I?" I pointed toward my pockets, slow enough for him to see the movement.

When he didn't tense up, I slowly pulled out the picture of the knife. "This one?"

"Yeah. Fucking that one."

"Is that the smoking gun Thomas Harlow promised you in exchange for dropping your charges?"

His eyes widened.

"I see." I shook my head. "I can't believe you believed him. And how would buying the murder weapon from you benefit my family anyway?"

He shot up from the couch so fast the cushions fell. "You little shit! How about I just shoot you!"

I shrugged. "Yeah, maybe you should. Because that murder weapon you're trying to make a deal with here …"

Myers narrowed his eyes at me.

"Well," I continued, "you can't make a deal with it."

"And why the fuck not?" he yelled, stepping closer, the gun aimed straight at my chest.

"Because, Myers, you filthy piece of shit …"

Our eyes locked.

Time slowed.

The air felt heavy, pressing in from all sides.

"Because you don't have it anymore."

His head jerked. A twitch. Then his eyes shot to the kitchen drawer next to the filthy fridge.

"Go ahead," I said. "Go check."

I leaned forward in the chair as he rushed toward the kitchenette.

"You see, what Lucy didn't tell you, because I asked her not to, is that I knew about this little hiding place of yours."

He yanked open the drawer with one hand and started digging through it, tossing papers and junk onto the counter. An old battery fell to the floor. The gun stayed in his other hand, still pointing in my direction.

"Where the fuck is it!" he screamed, ripping through the drawer.

"Well … last night, when you left for the bar, I came here and took the knife."

I pulled the spare gloves from my scrub pocket and slid them on. "God. I couldn't believe how stupid you were when I found the murder weapon in a *kitchen drawer*. Considering how important it is to you."

Myers let out a raw scream, something between rage and panic, then spun around fast enough to knock over several beer cans on the counter.

"I'll kill you!"

"Nah, you won't," I said. "You're a head smaller than me. And when I came here last night, I also took the bullets out of your gun."

His eyes snapped to the weapon in his hand. Then to me. Then back to the gun. His fingers flexed around the grip.

"I knew there were fucking bullets in it when I checked this morning!" he said.

"So, you were smart enough to check," I countered.

"Fucking right, you asshole." He moved toward me fast and shoved the gun straight at my chest. "And I put new ones in."

The barrel hovered inches from me.

His hand shook. Not just his hand. His whole body trembled. If he had reloaded the gun, he would kill me. No doubt.

But not before he had his only bargaining chip back.

"Where's the fucking knife?" he screamed, spit flying from his mouth. The smell of foul breath filled my nose. My skin crawled, but I held his gaze.

This wasn't a bluff anymore.

There wasn't much time left.

Every jerk of his twitching movements told me he'd stopped caring a long time ago. He'd stepped over the edge years back. And now I had taken the only thing that gave him leverage.

"Where is the knife?" His gun shifted from my chest to my head.

The metal hovered inches from my forehead.

"Last chance, you little shit," he said, calm for the first time.

The calm of a man who'd made up his mind.

The calm of someone who didn't care anymore.

The calm of someone ready to kill.

This was it.

This was my only chance.

"It's right here," I said.

My hand slid under the table and wrapped around the gun I'd taped there last night. In one smooth motion, I pulled it free and fired.

He was too close for me to miss.

The shot exploded through the hut. It bounced off the old walls and rang in my ears.

Myers dropped hard.

He screamed as he hit the floor, a high, broken sound that didn't match the threats he'd been throwing seconds ago. His gun slid under the table. I kicked it out of reach and watched him whimper. Curled up tight. Arms wrapped around his stomach, rocking like a child.

"You shot me!" he cried. His body folded in on itself, arching, then collapsing again.

"Sorry about that," I said, "but when I came here last night to take the knife, I also left a gun under your table."

I shrugged. "You see, the trauma I've been through in life didn't kill me. But it changed me, I guess. It created an ice-cold corner deep inside my heart. One that surfaces when my loved ones are in danger." I watched him, emotionless. "I knew you'd come for me to get your money. I instructed Lucy to tell you that the oldest Alderwyn son was the one looking for you and was without protection. That I was the easiest target. Worked night shifts at the hospital. It was only logical that you'd come for me first and bring me here."

His breathing turned ragged. His hands pressed against his stomach, but blood still seeped through his fingers and soaked into his sweater.

I crouched next to him. The wound sat low in his abdomen.

"It's not an artery," I said, studying the way the blood flowed. "You could possibly live."

"Call 911," he gasped. "I need an ambulance."

A short laugh escaped me. Myers. The murderer. The monster. Begging for someone to save him. Like the countless other victims of his.

"Let's wait with that," I said.

I dragged the chair closer and turned it toward him. Placed my gun on the table within reach, then sat and faced him.

"There's still something we need to talk about."

"What?" Spit and saliva were collecting at the corner of his mouth. "Are you crazy? I'm dying!"

My brow lifted slowly. "Really? You're trying to play that card after everything you've done to my family and me?"

"Somebody heard the shot." He groaned. "The police will come soon."

"Nah." I shook my head. "Nobody calls the cops at the Seacoast Inn. Especially not when shots fly. And even if they did, you basically kidnapped me. I defended myself with an unregistered gun I found in your hut."

His face drained. Tears mixed with sweat and dirt.

"What do you want?" He sobbed.

His tears almost made me angrier than the threats.

"What do you think I want, Einstein?" I leaned forward, elbows on my knees. "My mom was found mute in the woods where her best friend's husband was murdered. And she was blamed for it."

My gaze locked onto his.

"You're the only person who knows what really happened that night."

My eyes dropped to his stomach wound. Blood kept seeping through his fingers. "A shot like that needs surgery. So you can be smart and talk, or play dumb and waste time. And time is something you don't really have, buddy."

Myers whimpered.

I leaned back in the chair. "Do the right thing for once in your life."

He bit down on his lip so hard I thought he might draw blood. His body trembled. Teeth chattering.

"Uh-oh," I said, cocking my head. "Starting to feel cold?"

His hands pressed harder against the wound.

"That's not a good sign. But what do I know? I'm only a doctor. Who, funny enough, could actually save your life."

A broken sound left him then. Maybe the weight of all the years had finally caught up. Or maybe it was just the pain of the bullet.

"Fine." He sobbed. "I'll tell you whatever you want."

"Good. Let's start with what happened that night. And don't leave anything out. Time's ticking."

He opened his mouth.

"Wait." I grabbed the edge of his ski mask and pulled it off in one sharp motion. "I want to see your filthy face."

And it was filthy.

Dear God.

His scar ran across his entire forehead, thick and raised, cutting through his eyebrow. His hair was greasy and flat, clumped together with white dandruff flakes. His skin looked dirty, and he was unshaven.

Such a nasty man ruined my mother's life. And hurt many others. His police report said he raped women and was a pedophile. He also almost killed my grandma.

"Now talk," I ordered.

Tears kept sliding down his face. His mouth opened and closed. But no words came.

"You still don't get that you'll die here if you don't start ta—"

"Fucking fine!" he snapped, coughing as pain cut through him. "I … I was there that night. Fucking happy?"

"No shit." My head shook slowly. "You better get to the important parts, or I'll leave."

His body flinched as another wave of pain hit him.

"You gonna call an ambulance if I talk?" he begged.

"It's probably already too late for that," I said. "We're too far from the hospital."

I crouched slightly, studying the wound again.

"But if you tell me the truth, I'll look at it myself."

"You will?" he whimpered.

"Yes. And I never break my promises."

Myers stared at me for a long moment. Then he flinched.

"I was there," he murmured.

"Rot in hell," I muttered under my breath and rose. Calmly, I walked toward the door.

"No, wait!" he shouted. "Please! Wait!"

I kept walking. "Piss off."

"I waited for them!" he blurted out.

That made me stop.

Slowly, I turned and looked at him lying there, blood pooling beneath him.

"On the country road to the lake," he said quickly. "It was already late. Nobody ever drives on that road that late. I waited there for them. For the fancy car."

I walked back to the chair and sat again. I flicked my hand, telling him to continue.

"I opened my hood," he said. "Pretended my car was broken down. When I saw the Mercedes drive down the road, I waved it over and asked for help."

He coughed.

"First, the man got out."

"You mean Zach?" I clarified.

"Yes, that guy. I walked up to him and told him my car wouldn't start. Said I might need help. But that asshole didn't want to help me."

"And the woman?" I asked.

"You mean your mother?"

My jaw tightened. "Yes. My mother."

"She offered to help," he said. "She said they couldn't just leave someone stranded."

That sounded like my kind mother.

"And then?"

"Then"—Myers' breathing turned rough again—"I pulled out a gun. I told the guy to get back in the car, or I'd shoot him. He did, and I got in the backseat behind them and told him to start driving down a gravel road not far from there. He did everything I told him to. Even pissed himself when we stopped at the end of the gravel road in the woods."

"And my mother was there with you?" I asked quietly.

The image cut through me. Her in that car. Trapped. Terrified.

"Yes," he said. "Yes, she was."

"What then?"

He hesitated. Started crying again. Harder this time.

"What then, Myers!" I shouted.

He flinched, and a groan escaped him as he clutched his bleeding stomach tighter.

"Then … I raised my gun to the back of the guy's head, right here." His shaking finger pointed to the back of his own skull. "And … and …"

The words wouldn't come. A dark stain spread across his crotch.

Jesus.

He'd actually peed himself. Just like Zach did back then. The irony.

I stood up. Ready to leave.

"No, please," he begged. "Please."

"Then fucking talk!" I leaned over him, close enough to smell the sour mix of sweat, blood, and urine. "Talk, or I'll leave you here to bleed out like the pig you are!"

He cried harder but didn't say a word.

"I swear to God," I shouted, my rage breaking free. "This is your last—"

"Then I got out of the car!" he shouted back at me.

I stared at him.

His forehead glistened under the weak yellow light. Tears cut dirty tracks through the grime on his face. His lips trembled.

"You what?" I asked.

"I got out!" he repeated. "I got out of the fucking car."

"To get the knife?" I asked.

"No! To fucking run!"

I straightened slowly, still staring at him.

"I couldn't do it," he rambled on, words spilling out fast now. "I just couldn't. She'd offered so much money, but I couldn't do it. So I got out."

I heard him say the words. I really did. But my mind refused to let them in. As if they were so utterly ridiculous that they would be a waste of space in my brain.

"You're lying."

"I swear it's the truth!" he sobbed. "I told her I couldn't go through with it. I … I never killed anybody before. I just needed the money. My friend Billy told me about some woman he knew from his AA meetings years back. She knew about Billy's record and contacted him all these years later. She asked if he knew somebody who could help her take care of some bad dude. Billy never told me we'd actually kill this guy. I thought we were just gonna hurt him a little. Scare him."

It was like reality and some other dimension blurred together right in front of me. The walls felt closer all of a sudden. Then farther. Then closer again.

Every instinct in me screamed that Myers was lying.

I tried to sit on the chair but missed it. My legs folded, and I hit the floor hard. My shoulder knocked against the table's leg. The wood scraped across the floor.

"After I got out of the car and told her I couldn't do it," he went on, "she got so mad. Started yelling at everybody. Then they got into it. The dude and your mom. In the car. Everything happened so fast. The shouting. The shoving. And then, all of a sudden, the dude screamed. He screamed so fucking loud!" Myers' head shook as if it were happening in front of him all over again. "That's when I realized what she was doing. She was fucking stabbing him. Two times. Three. Four. He fought back. Got on top of her. But she screamed for me to help her. Said if he survived, we'd both go down. So I pulled him off of her, and she stabbed him again. Over and over. There was so much blood. His guts fell out of him right in front of us …"

I just sat there on the floor.

Feeling so fucking empty.

I couldn't tell anymore who was dying in this hut. Him or me.

Memories flooded me, like a tsunami hitting the shore with full force. My mom brushing chocolate smears off my cheek with her thumb. The way she warmed my clothes with her hairdryer in the winter. All those times she checked if I was breathing when she thought I was asleep. The warmth of her arms around me whenever I needed a hug. I could almost feel its warmth again, sitting here on this cold, nasty floor.

My mother was so full of love. Always had my back. No matter what. She was superwoman.

Not a monster.

"Then after she was done with him, she suddenly charged at me," Myers whimpered. "I stumbled backward and fell, and she cut me with the knife right here on my forehead."

"Stop," I ordered.

My eyes were fixed on the dirty floor in front of me. Its empty beer cans suddenly merged with the memory of my mom and Zach fighting in the bowling parking lot. I saw it now right in front of me. At first, the flashback felt distant. Fuzzy. Their words blurred together.

Then something shifted. And the scene sharpened.

"That guy was already dead," Myers continued somewhere in the background. "But she just kept stabbing him."

"I said stop," I warned Myers as the conversation between Mom and Zach in my flashback now became crystal clear:

"You can't force her to come with you!" my mom yelled at Zach. "This isn't the 1500s. Amanda wants to stay with the kids. My family needs her. Brian won't be able to keep it together, and my mom has heart problems. My death will kill her. Please, just wait with the move for a few years. I'm freaking dying. Please."

"That's not my problem," Zach shot back, shrugging like it meant nothing. "We're moving to California. She's my wife. She's coming with me, or I'll divorce her and sue her into financial ruin. And after I'm done with her, I'll come for your family. I'll drag your useless husband and mother through the courts for years. Tie them up in hearings and motions until every last penny they have is wasted on lawyers."

"If you hurt them, I'll kill you!" my mom threatened.

"Just die faster, you stupid bitch!" Zach yelled back.

The flashback stopped abruptly, and I was back in the hut with Myers.

"I was able to grab a rock and hit her on the head," Myers continued, now sobbing uncontrollably. "She fell, and I took the knife and ran. It wasn't me who gutted that dude. I didn't kill him. It was your m—"

"I said *STOOOOOP!*"

My scream ripped out of me like another bullet. It came from somewhere deep and dark. It was so loud, it hurt my ears.

Myers flinched and curled up on the floor.

Silence fell after that. Except for his quiet whimpers.

We sat there. Him bleeding and crying. Me staring at nothing.

I didn't know how much time had passed.

Seconds. Maybe minutes.

But he finally spoke again.

"You have to believe me. Please. I didn't kill him."

"Why should I believe a filthy liar who tried to kill my grandma?" I shot back.

Something inside me pushed against his story. Myers was nothing but filthy scum. A rapist and liar. And my mother was so innocent and sweet. Had always been there for me. Unconditionally loving me. How could that person have done such a thing?

"If what you're saying is true," I asked slowly, "why did you attack my grandma?"

He flinched.

"I … I didn't mean to hurt her," he said. "I just wanted to scare her. Make her stop looking for me. The police had no idea who I was and that I was at the crime scene, and your grandma was changing all that."

"You broke her nose and her leg," I countered with hate.

"Things got out of hand!" he cried. "I wanted to scare her a little. Then she fell out of the window, and the dog came after me. I … I—"

I stood quickly. Two steps and I was in front of him. Towering.

He looked up at me with wide eyes, shaking. Like some abused victim. Like he was the one wronged by life.

"I didn't do it," he begged. "Please. Please help me. I'm dying. I didn't do it. The knife … it wasn't mine. It wasn't me."

Slowly, I reached into my pocket and pulled out the picture of the knife again. And looked at it. Really looked at it. The paper trembled between my fingers as something clicked.

That knife in the picture.

It was our garage knife.

The one we used to cut boxes open on recycling day. The one that sat in the drawer by the workbench. That unique chip in its handle from when Dad dropped it while cutting up boxes after Christmas left no doubt.

My breath grew shallow.

Then another memory hit.

In the elevator, Dr. Rothchild said he remembered seeing a patient named Alderwyn. If I did the math, it lined up. It would have been right before the murder happened.

Before everything.

Which would mean she knew. My mom knew about the cancer. She had known all along she was going to die.

I shook my head and put the picture back into my pocket.

If there was a moment to feel hate for my mother, this should've been it. But, instead, a tear slid down my cheek. Hot and burning. Not for me. For my mom.

All that endless pain she carried. It must have been so scary to get the cancer diagnosis, knowing my dad would destroy us kids after she was gone. With his drinking. And weak selfishness. He would fight my grandma over custody even if he didn't want us. Just out of spite. Unless someone like Amanda took care of him. Contained him. Mothered him like he was a big child. So his kids had a chance to grow up somewhat normally.

And Zach was a problem in all this, as he was trying to take Amanda away. Wouldn't even let her leave. Threatened to destroy her if she divorced him to be with us.

Who knew where we all would be right now if it hadn't been for Zach's death? If Amanda hadn't been able to marry my dad and hold everything together after my mom died and my grandma had a stroke, nothing would be as it is right now. And thinking about all this, all I could feel for my mom was love. The boundless love of a son for his mother. A woman who had sacrificed her eternal soul to save her kids. And her useless husband.

Sure, Zach didn't deserve to die. But he was an abusive piece of shit who would have destroyed us all if Amanda chose us over him. And blaming Myers for his murder …

My gaze dropped to the filthy man bleeding in front of me.

This man had broken my grandma's nose and leg. Broke into an elderly woman's house with a knife. Did he really think I'd believe he went there to chat? He also hurt the prostitutes. Raped them without paying. Broke one of their noses as well. The list of violent charges on his record was a mile long, including the rape of a young college student in a grocery store parking lot. And he possessed child pornography.

So, no.

My mom did nothing wrong when it came to this man.

And yet.

As I looked down at him, begging for his life, a different question crept in.

Was I a monster if I let him bleed out here? Would it haunt me for the rest of my life?

I leaned over him.

"Take off your sweater," I told him.

He obeyed instantly. It took effort. He winced, teeth grinding, hands shaking as he peeled the blood-soaked sweater over his head. It dropped to the floor next to him.

"Move your hands so I can see your wound."

He hesitated for a moment, then did that too.

Crimson blood kept pushing out of the small, round entry wound in his stomach. Not spraying. Not spurting. Just steady. Thick. It had pooled beneath him.

My fingers pressed into his abdomen.

He screamed.

The muscle felt tight. Hard.

"No artery was hit," I said calmly. "Or you'd be dead already."

His breathing came fast and shallow, but he looked relieved.

"But with that blood loss," I continued, watching the way it kept seeping out, "I'd say an organ was hit. It's not going to stop bleeding on its own. You've got maybe one, two hours tops without help."

"Then help me," he begged. "Stitch me up. Or call 911. *Call* them."

I rose and looked for his phone.

Mine was still at the hospital. On the stairs.

I walked over to the couch and grabbed his phone. His keys lay beside it, so I took them as well.

Then I turned and walked back to him.

"Call 911!" he groaned. "Quick!"

And I could. Tell them he kidnapped me. Tell them there was a weapon on the kitchen counter, and I took it and shot him when he got distracted. The gun wasn't registered. Nobody would question my story. I was the one kidnapped.

The only problem was … that wasn't the story I wanted to tell. Not after what I'd just heard in here.

So, I just stood there, staring at him. Phone and keys resting in my hands.

Blood pooled under his body. The smell grew stronger.

"What are you doing?" he gasped. "You said you'd call an ambulance!"

My mouth tightened. "That's not what I said. I said I would look at your wound." I gave a small shrug. "And I did. It doesn't look good. An hour. Two, absolute tops. So good luck. You really need it."

His face drained.

I bent, picked up the Florida sweater beside him, and stepped around him in a wide circle. Then I walked toward the door.

"No! Please!" Myers begged. He dragged himself across the floor, leaving a thick smear behind him. "Please help me! I didn't do it! I didn't do it!"

The door handle felt cold, even through my latex gloves.

I opened it.

And left.

There wasn't much more left to say about all this.

Behind me, his screaming shifted. Meaner. Hateful.

"You're a fucking murderer just like your whore mother!" he yelled.

The door shut.

"Fuck you, murderer!"

I locked it with the keys.

"Fuck you and that cunt!"

Outside, the night breeze hit my face. Cold and fresh.

I threw the keys deep into the bushes. They vanished somewhere in the dark with a jingle.

For a moment, I just stood there, breathing.

Strangely, it felt like something bad had finally ended. Like I had finally cut loose a horrible piece of the past.

As I rushed back to my car, Myers' screams faded about a quarter mile down the path.

The night was silent now.

When I got to my car, I pulled off the hospital booties first, then the gloves, then the surgical cap, and shoved everything inside a plastic bag I grabbed from my car. Including the Florida sweater. I put Myers' phone in a different plastic bag, so I could later wipe it clean and throw it away in a public trash can.

Everything now had to happen fast. Time was not on my side.

The engine roared to life, and I drove back toward the hospital.

My thoughts ran wild as I drove.

But not with guilt.

I probably was supposed to feel horrible about Myers, but I didn't. The hate was still there. Solid. Heavy. If he had just come forward and confessed from the beginning, maybe things would've been different. But attacking my grandmother and almost killing her, no matter what story he fed me in that hut, wasn't something a man who deserved to live would do.

And parts of me doubted Myers' story.

A man who raped women could murder just as easily. And lie, of course. That much was obvious. So maybe my mom was innocent. She could've still been the victim who fled that night. And the trauma broke her. Stole her voice forever.

Another thought forced itself into my head.

My father.

God, I hated him.

If he had been stronger. Less of a liar. Less of a drunk. Less of a cheater. Less of everything. Then maybe my mom wouldn't have worried so much about leaving us behind with him.

I tried to picture it. A scared mom sitting in a sterile doctor's office, hearing she was dying. The cold air. The ticking clock. The word *cancer* stabbing her like a knife. Then thinking of her children. Knowing she'd leave them in the hands of a man who would destroy them.

That kind of fear probably hurt more than the disease.

So, what choice did she have with a father like mine?

Thinking about it now, I saw it all more clearly.

My dad had spun an abusive web around her. Not with fists. Not with bruises anyone could see. But with passive-aggressive hate. Insults disguised as jokes. Cheating. Lying. Drinking. Wearing her down until there was nothing left.

He would apologize afterward. Promise the moon. Swear it would never happen again. For a while, there'd be peace. A honeymoon phase. Then the drinking. The lies. The cheating. Again.

A cycle of hell my mother was trapped in.

I hated him. I really did.

Why didn't she leave?

I'd asked myself that question so many times before. Late at night, lying in my bed awake.

But who was I to judge?

After years of mental terror and abuse, she probably didn't even think she deserved better. Maybe she stopped believing she was worth anything. She kept smiling for us and kept the house running. Cooked dinners. Went to work to pay the bills, then helped with homework after that. All while swallowing mental abuse from the only man she ever loved. A broken heart suffering quietly for years.

People in abusive relationships often feel that the mental abuse is worse than the physical. It slowly drives them mad. Quietly. Day by day. Until they started questioning their own thoughts. Their own memories. The abuse takes their self-esteem away first. Then the inner flame. That flame inside all of us that keeps us upright and warms us from within. The part that lets you love others. And love yourself.

Destroyed by some worthless piece of shit.

Gone.

Courts and the police didn't do shit for women who were beaten black and blue or got stalked and killed. Of course, they wouldn't do shit for a woman like my mom, reporting psychological abuse and trauma without ever being able to show a black eye.

So no. I refused to blame the victim in this story. Like those idiots asking what a woman was wearing when she got raped. Always the victim's fault. Never the abuser's.

My mother fought the only way she could in a world where women were treated like objects and the courts were ruled by money over justice. She wasn't at fault in this. Not to me, at least.

The highway lights flashed past the windshield.

As the hospital grew closer, something inside me hardened.

What if it was my dad?

What if he paid Myers to kill Zach?

Myers said it was my mom. But what if he'd lied to protect my dad, to keep a card in his pocket for later? For blackmail. For money.

My hands tightened around the steering wheel until my knuckles turned white.

It made sense.

He'd loved Amanda since they were kids. That cat had been out of the bag for years. He only married Mom when she got pregnant with me. I was a mistake in his eyes.

Then Amanda married Zach. A man my dad never liked. Never respected. He ranted about him constantly. Zach this. Zach that. That asshole. His Porsche.

Zach had money. Stability. A polished life. The pretty wife my dad always wanted.

Then my mom was dying.

The path to Amanda would've been clear—if Zach hadn't been in the way.

And of course he'd blame my mom. Or stay quiet when she was accused. Too much of a coward to step forward. Better her than him.

That's how it always was.

I arrived at the hospital and parked my car in the same spot as before. The plastic bag felt light in my hand as I stepped out.

I entered the hospital from the back. Inside, the hallways were quiet at this hour.

Quickly, I walked to the red biohazard waste bin, lifted the lid, then dropped in the plastic bag.

It disappeared among other discarded hospital waste that would never be seen again.

The lid closed with a dull thud.

And, just like that, it was done.

I walked down the hallway, past the occasional nurse pushing a cart or flipping through a chart, and stepped into the resident room.

Erin was sitting at the table with my phone in her hand.

"There you are," she said, relief flashing across her face. "I was looking for you."

"Oh, thank God somebody found it," I said and took the phone from her. "I was looking for it everywhere. I even checked my car and every bathroom I ever used."

She didn't look suspicious. Just nodded.

"Are you done with your rounds?" I asked, slipping the phone into my pocket. "I need to finish mine now that I found my phone. You're welcome to join me."

Her eyes widened, and her lips curved into a huge smile. "I'd love to."

I smiled back. "Just wait here. I'll be right back. Gonna use the bathroom real quick."

"Okay."

The bathroom was right around the corner. I slipped inside and checked the stalls. Empty.

Quickly, I pulled my phone out.

My dad's number lit up the screen. It rang longer than usual.

"Dylan, you okay?" His voice came through, tired but alert.

"Yes," I said. My tone sounded completely normal. Friendly. Like I hadn't spent years resenting him. "Sorry for calling this late. Hey, listen, can you do me a big one?"

"Yeah. Of course."

"Well, my car broke down at the gas station near the Seacoast Inn."

"That shithole?"

"Yeah." I sighed. "Don't tell Amanda, but I was trying to get something to help me sleep. The nightmares are back. I needed some Valium off the books. Some guy sells it behind a liquor store near the motel. Nothing you need to worry about. But my car started acting up and … I feel horrible asking this, but can you come get me?"

There was the sound of movement on his end. Keys. Clothes.

"Yeah, of course. I'm already on my way."

"Thanks, Dad."

"You bet."

He sounded pleased. Too pleased. Like this small rescue erased everything. Like showing up tonight could cancel out years of cheating, lying, and abuse.

"Oh, and Dad?" I said before he could hang up.

"Yeah?"

"Can you please bring the Porsche? I'd love to drive that thing again."

He chuckled. "You bet, buddy. I'll be there in a minute."

I hung up.

For a moment, I just stood there in the bathroom, staring at my reflection in the mirror.

Then I unlocked the door and walked back to get Erin.

42

DYLAN

It was Christmas Eve, and we were all sitting around the dinner table, eating and laughing.

The tree lights blinked colorfully, and pumpkin-spice candles mingled with the smell of roasted meat and cookies.

Elizabeth and Markus were going on and on to Lila about how good they had been all year, constantly glancing at the elf on the shelf on the sideboard. As if that elf would decide whether they woke up to gifts or tears.

Ethan sat across from them, one hand on his fork, the other scrolling on his phone under the table.

Amanda wore a red mini dress and a Christmas apron printed with the words "Best Stepmom Ever." Lila's birthday gift from last year. The contrast between the apron and her outfit was bizarre. Her fake boobs, heavy makeup, and high heels made her look like something straight out of OnlyFans. Which was fine, if only that was who she wanted to be.

Grandma sat in her wheelchair at the side of the table. Next to me. Watching with a blanket over her legs.

She'd had a stomach bug all week and barely touched her food. Just sipped tea and followed the conversation with tired eyes.

At the head of the table, my dad leaned back in his chair, waiting for Amanda to refill his wine like he was some old king being served at court. I was about to say as much when my phone rang.

Nolan.

I froze. Then picked up quickly. "Yes?"

"It's me. Detective Nolan."

"I know. What happened?"

"Are you sitting?"

"Yes."

"Good, cuz I think I have some really good news for you all."

I paused. The laughter around the table kept going over the Christmas music.

"John Myers …" he said. "He was found dead in a cabin near the Seacoast Inn."

"What?" The word came out loud and intense.

The whole room went quiet.

The music kept playing until I gestured at the Bluetooth speaker. Lila reached over and turned it off.

"Is everything okay?" Amanda asked.

"What happened?" I asked Nolan, forcing shock into my voice.

"We don't know," Nolan said. "He was shot a few weeks ago but wasn't found until this morning."

"Holy shit," I said.

"Holy shit indeed."

"Do you know who did it?" I asked.

"Who the fuck knows. Apparently, the owner of the Seacoast Inn hid him there. But considering where he was found and the fact that he messed around with some of the prostitutes, it could've been a pimp. Or someone the ladies hired. A drug dealer. He also had gambling debts. The crime scene is littered with DNA of prostitutes. The murder weapon was left on the table, but it's an unregistered gun, and there were no prints on it. Nobody's talking. We don't expect to find much more."

"What the actual fuck," I muttered, shaking my head.

"What is it?" my dad asked now. Everyone was staring at me. Tense. Fearful.

"They found John Myers," I said. "He's dead."

"What?" Amanda gasped.

"No way!" my dad shouted.

"Holy shit!" Lila covered her mouth.

"Hell yeah!" Ethan grinned.

My eyes moved to Grandma.

Her fingers twitched against the armrest of the wheelchair. Small movements but frantic. The only ones her body allowed. Then her lips curved. Not wide. Just that half smile on the right side of her face.

Then a tear rolled down her cheek.

I leaned over and put my arm around her shoulders.

"It's over, Grandma," I said, pulling her closer. "That monster is finally dead."

The Christmas tree lights kept blinking behind me. The room smelled of cookies. People were mumbling and gasping. Yet, for the first time in years, the house felt quiet in a different way.

"Is your grandma there? Did she hear the good news?" Nolan asked as Amanda started crying.

My dad pulled her into his arms to comfort her. Lila and Ethan mumbled excitedly while Elizabeth and Markus looked lost and confused.

It was a scene of chaos.

In all the best ways.

The faces of the people I loved looked like they had just woken from a long, heavy nightmare. Like their lives could finally resume, free from the monster of our past. The worst chapters of our lives were finally closing with a dull thud.

"Hello?" Nolan asked again.

"Sorry. Yeah, my grandma knows. She's here."

Silence hung on the other end for a moment.

"Good," he finally said. "Tell her I'm happy for her."

"I will."

"Did … he ever reach out to you?" Nolan asked out of the blue.

"Who? Myers?" I asked back, even though I knew exactly who he meant.

"Yeah."

I shook my head. "Nope. Nothing."

My turn. "Do you know anything about what happened?"

"No. I told you all I know. The AG wants this to go away quietly to avoid any more lawsuits against the State. Harlow is being shut up now that his last lifeline is gone. There won't be much digging. It all points to a fight between scum at the Seacoast Inn. That shithole had two shootings in the last six months alone. Both deadly."

"You said he was shot?" I asked.

"Yeah. Around Thanksgiving."

"Shot around Thanksgiving at the Seacoast Inn," I repeated loudly and watched my dad freeze. He was still holding Amanda, who cried into his broad shoulder.

Slowly, almost carefully, his eyes lifted and met mine.

"Hey, listen, I'll call you back later," Nolan said. "I just wanted to call you as soon as I could."

"Thank you," I said. "I really appreciate it."

"Merry Christmas," Nolan added. "You'll all sleep in peace tonight."

"We will. Thank you. And merry Christmas to you too."

The call ended.

Phone still in hand, I stared at my dad. The world continued around us. Amanda sniffled. Lila hugged Markus. Ethan laughed too loudly at something. Plates clinked again. Life resumed.

But my dad and I didn't move an inch.

"They said they don't know who did it," I said, still looking at him. I could see the shock in his eyes. The disbelief. The tightness in his jaw.

He understood. Thanksgiving. The Seacoast Inn. Myers dead.

I narrowed my eyes, trying to look deeper. Deep into that dark corner where a man would hide his secrets.

For a moment, the room faded. The Christmas lights blurred. The laughter sounded far away.

And all that existed was him and me.

And the ultimate question.

Did he do it? Did he have Zach killed?

Because if he did, I'd be the first to call Nolan and tell him about my dad acting strange after Thanksgiving. About the way he disappeared with his Porsche that night.

And my dad wasn't stupid.

He knew that going to the gas station I'd sent him to, the same one where Myers had been caught years ago after Zach was murdered, meant cameras. Recording every license plate and face. And, in this case, also recording the same Porsche Lucy had seen me pull up in.

The same Porsche I'd used to take her to the HIV center.

That day I told her my name was Brian. My dad's name.

I'd worn a baseball cap. A COVID mask. We had the same height and muscular build.

When he got to the gas station the night I killed Myers, I wasn't there, of course. So he called, asking where I was. I apologized and said my car started again, said my phone battery died, and I couldn't call him sooner. Told him I had to rush back to the hospital for an emergency and couldn't wait for him at the motel.

Best part was that I had an alibi nobody would tear apart.

Hospital cameras caught me walking down certain hallways. I chose the ones with cameras when I needed to be seen. Took the back stairs and service doors when I needed to disappear. Even parked my car in a dark alley instead of the parking garage so no one could trace the exact times.

Plenty of witnesses too.

Any gaps would be explained by my searching for my phone. Bathroom stalls. The showers. My car.

It all fit.

I even went further. I bought Willy, the homeless patient, a Florida sweater and a baseball cap. The exact kind Myers wore when he dropped off the note. Made sure people noticed Willy in those clothes. Mentioned it casually. Let it stick.

Willy wore them proudly as he insisted he was Jesus. Said it was winter in summer and summer in winter. Talked about voices. Nobody would question that it wasn't him who dropped something off for me. Nobody would ever connect me to Myers that night he died.

The pieces were in place. They were rock solid.

The expression on my dad's face as he put one and one together was almost as satisfying as knowing Myers would never hurt anybody ever again.

It was almost as satisfying as knowing my mother could finally rest in peace. Free from new murder allegations. And my grandmother would close her eyes one day without wondering where Myers was.

Amanda. Lila. Ethan. They would sleep again too. No more waking up wondering if Myers would show up to hurt us. No more glancing over shoulders in parking lots. The people I loved were finally breathing again.

My grandma's fingers trembled as she clutched the wristband with my mother's picture in her hand. As if she was saying, "Sweetheart, it's over. We won. Rest now. I'll see you soon."

My eyes went back to my dad.

"The police say they'll close the case quietly," I said, my voice steady. "They think it was some drug dealer or pimp who shot Myers. And unless somebody steps forward with tips or new evidence—I don't know, like some gas station footage or something—the case is pretty much closed. So we can finally move on. Right, Dad?"

Was it fear flickering over his tense face? Fear from thinking I had found out the truth? That he was the one who got Zach killed? Or fear that I killed Myers and made it look like he did?

"Aren't we, Dad?" I repeated, slower this time. "Moving on? Living the best life we possibly can?"

His mouth opened.

Nothing came out.

"Dad?" Lila asked. "You okay?"

"Oh, uh, yes," he said, forcing a smile. "Sorry. All this is just so shocking."

"It is," Amanda said, nodding. "Would it be wrong to get some champagne? I mean … someone died. Even if that someone was a monster."

"No," I said. "I think that's a great idea. Very fitting. Celebrating the death of a monster. Right, Dad?"

"Y-yes," he said.

Amanda rushed toward the kitchen, but I stopped her. "Amanda."

She turned, curious.

"Do you remember that Christmas dress you used to wear years ago? The one with that ugly reindeer stitched on it?"

"My ugly Christmas dress! Of course I do. My mom made it for me before she died. For our ugly sweater party."

"Do you still have it?" I asked.

"I ... do." She looked at my dad. A quick glance. "But your dad kinda hates it. He likes when I wear short—"

"Nah," I cut in gently. "Dad just told me the other day he'd love to see you wear some of your old clothes again. The ones you chose for yourself."

She laughed awkwardly. "You're funny."

Not funny.

Changing things.

Poor Amanda.

Sure, what she did back then, cheating with him while he was still married to my mom, wasn't right. And we were angry with her for a long time. But, God, she'd paid for it. Her husband murdered. And my dad had also cheated on her after childbirth changed her body. As if stretch marks were sins in the Bible.

Like my mom, Amanda had given him everything. Her money. Her time. Her youth. Raised his kids with the kind of love a real mom gives. School lunches packed before sunrise, homework checked at the kitchen table, sitting through fevers and nightmares and teenage tantrums while he went on golf trips. Doing those ridiculous plastic surgeries for him too.

And still it wasn't enough.

This pig.

The audacity.

"I'm not joking," I said loud and clear. "Isn't that right?" I asked, looking straight at my dad. "Didn't you say you miss Amanda's old style?"

He held my gaze like a man staring at a loaded gun.

He wasn't stupid. The fear in his eyes told me he understood the shift in this house. The new orchestra playing.

I could have ended him right here. One call to Nolan. One mention of Dad missing that night. He and his Porsche caught on the gas station footage near the Seacoast Inn, the night of the murder. And Lucy thought my name was Brian.

If I made that call, Dad would be gone for good. Part of me wanted it so bad. I wanted him to suffer. For my mom. For Grandma. For me too.

But Dad going to jail would hurt my siblings more than it would ever satisfy me. The news would rip through the country and tear open every old wound. Reporters outside again. New documentaries. More gossip at school. A new hell. And my family had been through enough.

So, instead, I would take over for my mom. I would protect this family now. Just like she did. But, unlike my mom, I'd protect it from him too. I'd watch his every move. Every word. I'd allow him to stay for as long as he made my family happy. The moment he hurt them, cheating, yelling, slapping Markus ever again, anything, he'd be done.

Gone.

Bye-bye.

"Right, Dad?" I asked once more. "Didn't you say that? How much you miss Amanda's old style?"

Everyone was watching now. Curious.

"Yes," he finally said, smiling too wide. "I did say that. I'd love to see the ugly Christmas dress on you."

Amanda lit up like someone had opened a window to a sunny spring after months of gray winter.

She hurried off toward the bedroom. Ecstatic.

It was strange. She seemed happier with permission to wear what she wanted than with the news of Myers' death.

"I was also thinking …" I added casually. "Maybe Grandma could move in here with you guys."

His eyes widened even more. Not surprised. Horrified.

"I mean, you've got three guest rooms. One of them is on the first floor. We could hire an in-home nurse too. Amanda once told me she'd love that. For the kids. And for Grandma."

"Yaaay!" the kids shouted. "Grandma's gonna live here!"

"That would be amazing," Ethan said, already smiling.

"Dad, you really okay with this?" Lila asked. Her smile was hopeful but cautious.

"Of course he is," I said. "It was his idea, right, Dad?"

There it was again. That tiny pause of shock. But then he laughed. A little too loud. A little too forced.

"Yes," he said. "I did suggest that. I was just thinking how blessed we are and how much Nicole has done for all of us."

The kids erupted, cheering like they'd just won something.

"How kind of you, Dad," I said. "Why don't you get the champagne now to celebrate all this amazing change around here?"

I hugged Grandma again. The kind of hug that says I love you. Thank you. I'm here.

Little arms wrapped around us. Elizabeth first. Then Markus jumping in. Lila and Ethan followed. Warm bodies encircling me.

We stood like that for a while.

Amanda joined too, in her ugly sweater dress, wrapping her arms around all of us. A knot of love and soft smiles.

It felt incredible.

My family.

Just like my mom, my love had no limits when it came to them.

I would protect them. Take their pain. Carry their burdens. Let them live happy and carefree lives. Even if it meant I was the one drowning for them. Even if it meant my tears had to come later, when I was all alone, when no one was watching.

My eyes drifted to my dad. He fumbled with the champagne cork. The bottle popped, and he flinched nervously.

And he had every right to be nervous, because I would do anything for the people I loved.

The phone in my pocket vibrated.

The hug loosened as I got the phone out of my pocket.

For a second, I thought it was Detective Nolan again. But the display read Dr. Rothchild.

"Hello?" I answered, stepping away from the table. I dreaded what came next. His calls usually meant one thing.

"Hey, it's me," he said. "I'm sorry to do this to you, but I really need you to come in. We don't have a single physician on the oncology floor. Two have COVID, one has the flu, one's wife is in labor, and Greg has to leave in an hour after a twenty-two-hour shift. I'm really sorry, but we have two patients in oncology who might pass away tonight. I really need you."

My hand dragged through my hair. "Shit … Ummm … yeah. Yeah, of course."

"Thanks, kid."

The line crackled faintly, but he wasn't done.

"Oh, before I forget."

"Yeah?"

"Remember I told you about the Alderwyn patient I met all those years back?"

"Yes."

"I finally remembered her name. It was Lacey Alderwyn."

I froze briefly, then nodded. I'd already suspected it. Still, hearing my mother's name spoken like that unsettled me.

"It was right after that snowstorm," he went on. "End of March. Eleven years ago."

March.

Before Zach's murder.

There it was. No more space left for denial. My mom knew about the cancer before Zach was killed.

"She came in with another woman," he added.

That made my head lift.

Another woman?

My grandmother was the first thought.

"Was she older?" I asked quietly, eyes drifting toward Grandma in her wheelchair. My heart began to hammer against my ribs. If she'd been there with my mom before Zach was killed … then that would mean she knew about the cancer before my mom went to jail.

"No," he said.

The word didn't register at first. Made no sense.

"She came in with a woman in her early thirties," he said.

As if in slow motion, I turned, and my gaze landed on Amanda.

She stood by the table, laughing as she filled champagne glasses for the adults and sparkling apple cider for the kids. The ugly Christmas sweater dress made her look so innocent. Red knit fabric. A ridiculous stitched reindeer across the chest with dangling wool antlers.

"She had blond hair," Dr. Rothchild said.

My throat tightened.

Amanda's hair caught the glow of the lights, almost golden.

"Kinda petite," he added. "Pretty. Sweet voice. Don't get me wrong. I'm not saying this in a creepy way. So don't get me canceled on social media or something like that."

His attempt to joke floated past me.

The room felt both too small and too large at the same time. Sound dulled. Markus giggling. Dad's low chuckle. All of it far away.

Amanda tipped her head back and laughed at something Lila said.

"Hello?" Dr. Rothchild asked.

I heard him.

But for a second, I was mute.

Amanda.

She had been there with my mom. At her cancer appointment. Before Zach was murdered. She knew. She fucking knew!

Myers' last words looped in my head.

Some woman his friend knew from his AA meetings years back, Myers had said in the hut. Not your mother.

Thinking about it now, it made sense. My mom once told me how much Amanda helped the family when she had to attend college classes and Grandma worked. There was nobody to drive Dad to his AA meetings when he lost his driver's license for a while after another DUI. So Amanda stepped in. Smiling. Helpful. Always there for us. It was Amanda who had been taking Dad to his AA meetings in the morning. Waiting outside. Chatting with other members. Drinking coffee and eating doughnuts while listening to sad stories.

"Hello?" Dr. Rothchild said again. This time sharper.

"Y-yes. Sorry."

"Do you know any Lacey Alderwyn?" he asked.

Across the room, Amanda laughed at something. She always looked so sweet.

I stared at her.

The woman I thought I knew. The woman who never raised her voice. Who made cookies for school events and volunteered at the homeless shelter.

Her gaze lifted and found mine.

The clink of glasses and the voices around us faded into the background.

Her smile faded first. Then her shoulders froze. Eyes sharpened.

There it was.

Not panic. Not guilt.

Recognition.

And something all-knowing behind it. As if she understood exactly what I'd just learned.

"Do you know these two women?" Dr. Rothchild asked.

My mouth moved before the rest of me caught up.

"I," I said, still looking at Amanda. "I don't think so."

"Yeah, I thought so," he replied. "See you in a few."

The line clicked, and I put my phone back into my pocket.

Amanda hadn't looked away. Her blue eyes were wide now. Searching. Questions in them. And answers at the same time.

"Everything okay?" she finally asked.

I stared at her a moment longer, then smiled warmly.

"Yeah," I said. "Everything's okay. But I gotta go in for a shift."

Protests came from all directions at once. Lila groaned. Ethan shook his head. Elizabeth shouted that Santa was coming.

"I know, I'm sorry," I said and picked up a glass of apple cider since I had to drive. "But before I go, I want to offer a toast."

I lifted my glass, and the room turned quiet.

"To Ethan," I said and looked at my teenage brother. He tried to act cool, leaning back in his chair, but his eyes softened when they met mine. "You have a heart of gold. I love you."

"Eeeew, back off," he joked, making a face.

"To Lila," I said, turning to her. "May your kind heart and sharp wits lead you on the greatest journey in Europe next year. I love you."

Love you too, she mouthed without sound, pressing her lips together to keep from crying.

"To Markus and Elizabeth." They both giggled. "May Santa bring you twice as many toys because you're the best little rug rats walking this earth. I love you."

"To Dad." I turned to him. He stood there with the champagne bottle in his hand.

"And better choices," was all I could get out.

"To Grandma." I walked over to her so she could see me better. I bent down to her level. "We all owe you our lives. Without you, none of us would be here. I love you so much."

A tear slid down her cheek. I wiped it away with my thumb.

"To Mom," I added.

The room grew extra quiet. All eyes on me.

"I know you're in heaven. Someone with a heart that big can't be anywhere else. You did everything for us, always putting yourself last. I love you, and I can't wait to see you again someday."

Then I lifted the glass once more.

After a slight pause, I said, "And to Amanda."

All eyes turned to her as she stood there in that ugly Christmas sweater dress.

Our eyes met.

"Who helped my mom when she needed her most. In good times and in really dark ones. We love you."

Amanda wiped away a tear, careful not to smudge her mascara.

I drank the apple cider, then set the glass on the table. "Well, I gotta go."

We all hugged. Kissed cheeks. I promised I'd be back right after the shift. Markus clung to my leg all the way to the door.

I stepped outside.

The cold winter night wrapped around me. It smelled faintly of wood smoke from the fireplace. Snow crunched under my shoes as I walked down the path to my car.

The moon stood silver and high in a cloudless sky.

I unlocked my car and was about to get in, when the front door opened and Amanda came after me.

"Dylan, wait!"

She stopped a few feet away from me, as if to give me space to process what I had just learned. Her arms were wrapped tight around her body as she shivered in the cold without a jacket. At first, she looked like she would try to pretend, make up some story that would cut her loose from this web of lies and murder. But then she nodded, and her blue eyes found mine.

"Your mom and I begged Zach to agree to stay for a few years after she died. So I could be with you until you all were older. And make sure your dad would be all right." She looked over her shoulder to make sure nobody had followed her.

"But Zach didn't even consider it. He always hated your dad, and it brought him joy to think about your dad's struggles and what would become of you kids after Lacey was gone."

She paused, weighing her words carefully.

"That confrontation between your mom and Zach in the parking lot happened after he'd threatened me. I told him I would leave him. Which, to a man like Zach who had everything handed to him in life, was unthinkable. You don't leave Zach. Not without his permission. He had a prenup and would've left me penniless. And he swore he would destroy me and your family in court if I ever left him. Make me look mentally unfit to be around you kids. He would get the best lawyers in the nation who could keep us in court until we lost everything."

Her blond hair shimmered silver in the moonlight as she paused.

"One day," she said, "when I was throwing away some old clothes of mine, I found an AA meeting sign-in sheet from one of your dad's sessions. It was in an old coat." She shook her head. "I mean, what are the odds of that?"

She looked down at the snow. "I remembered your dad telling me at one of the meetings to stay away from this Dustin guy. That he was dangerous and had a record."

She didn't have to elaborate more on that point. After she and my mom had come up with the plan to get rid of Zach, Amanda had contacted Billy Dustin to ask if he knew someone who could get the job done. And Billy connected her to Myers. He probably made money off the whole thing too.

"So it was all planned?"

"Yes and no. Not like it happened, I mean. Your mom isn't some calculating monster. This guy, Myers, lied to us and completely changed the plan. Your mom was supposed to get out of the car at the side of the road. Myers was supposed to take only Zach into the woods. But he took her too and tried to blackmail her for more money. Said he would back out. Right in front of Zach. He overheard the whole thing and attacked your mom."

I nodded. Of course Myers had left all of this out. Lying scum.

"Things happened so fast from there. She only brought the knife in case she had to defend herself."

"Why did you stop talking to us and not help my mom sooner?" I asked.

Amanda looked up at me, then her gaze dropped again in shame.

"It was a lot, you know. The pictures of him. The way Zach died and your mom at the center of it all …"

"Did Dad know?"

She shook her head hard. "No. I swear. He doesn't even remember Dustin from his AA meetings back then."

I watched her as she stood shaking in the cold. She was shivering dramatically, her teeth chattering.

I had so many reasons to be mad at her. But, in the end, just like my mom, Amanda had saved our lives. She was now no more than another tragic woman destroyed by my dad, and Zach before him. And deep down I believed that she didn't do all this just to finally be with my dad. She did it to save us. The kids she loved as much as her own.

I walked up to her and put my jacket over her shoulders. Tucked her into it like she was the child and I the parent.

"Go inside now. It's cold."

Her eyes and mouth widened. "You're … not mad?"

I smiled gently. "No. Not one bit. Go now. We'll never talk about this ever again."

She smiled back at me as a tear rolled down her cheek.

"Your mom was right to keep you when everybody told her to get an abortion. It's like she knew how badly a world full of Zachs and Brians would need a man like you."

She gently ran her hand over my cheek, the way only a mother does with her child, then turned and rushed back. She was already at the door and reaching for the handle to get back inside when I stopped her.

"Amanda!"

She turned around, and our eyes met.

"If… my mom couldn't talk after the incident, how do you know what happened that night?"

She stared at me, the smile on her lips never fading.

And I knew the meaning of it.

"Everything your mom ever did was for you. When she died, she had only one wish. That in her next life, she could be your mom again."

Then she opened the door, stepped inside, and closed it behind her.

All the warmth drained out of me, and ice-cold needles stabbed every inch of my heart.

Maybe because I didn't have a jacket.

Maybe because the cruelest twist of all had just revealed itself to me.

My mom had been able to talk all along.

But in the end, what did it matter?

My mom had sacrificed her soul for me. And I would find her in the next life and be her son again. And the one after that.

I stared through the window and watched Amanda join the others. Filling everyone's glasses with laughs and jokes.

The world wanted clean stories. Good guys. Bad guys.

But love and family weren't clean. They weren't black and white.

We were broken glass.

Shattered by life.

Glittering beautifully when the sun hit us. Yet sharp enough to cut anyone who tried to touch us.

Nothing that happened tonight would change my commitment or my love for my family and mom.

I'd do anything for the people I loved.
And when I said anything …
Just like my mom.
Just like my grandma.
And, apparently, just like Amanda.
I meant it.
"Rest now, Mom. I've got it from here."

ASHMAN'S OTHER BOOKS

Dive into the brilliance of *Criminal Minds* and the haunting edge of

***Gone Girl* in one of the highest-rated psychological thrillers on the market.**

There is a serial killer the FBI can't find.

There is another serial killer who has been watching him work for years.

And now they are hunting each other.

Leah Nachtnebel only kills killers. To the world, she is one of the greatest pianists of our time. Behind the curtain, she hunts predators who slipped through the cracks and makes sure they never hurt anyone again.

But when Leah targets the wrong man, she becomes the obsession of a killer who doesn't run from monsters.

He is one.

He doesn't just see her as a traitor. He sees her as a trophy he must possess.

And he isn't the only one closing in. FBI Special Agent Liam Richter is following a trail of murders that don't make sense.

Now Leah is fighting a war on two fronts.

One man wants to expose her. The other wants to end her.

And on a killer's playground, there's one rule: win and live, or lose and die.

Read here (FREE with Kindle Unlimited):

I Kill Killers READ HERE

FREE Excerpt from I Kill Killers:

Prologue

When I was eight years old, I stabbed a boy.

He came from a troubled home, the kind where violence was the solution to any problem. His piercing eyes were a window to his sadistic soul, revealing a weariness far beyond his years. At thirteen years old, he tortured and killed cats and dogs. There were also rumors that he had molested a kindergartner in the school's bathroom.

I did my best to avoid him until one day, after school, I saw him lingering in front of the grocery store. At the time, he'd been suspended from school. He looked unkempt. His brown hair was sticky and long, and his face was smudged with dirt. Our eyes met for a split second before I stepped past him and into the store.

I was on my way home when I felt the unmistakable sensation of being followed. Glancing around, I saw his shadowy figure darting between cars, keeping pace with my strides. I felt no fear, only a nagging annoyance that he might make me late for my piano lesson.

I kept walking and entered a quiet street, where he managed to pull me behind a small patch of rosebushes. Concealed from the road, he threw me onto the leaf-littered ground and pulled out a knife, its blade glinting in the September sunlight. He told me he'd cut me open if I screamed. I nodded and asked him what he wanted.

"Kiss it," he said, grabbing his crotch.

I agreed but asked him to sit on the ground. "You're too tall," I said, which seemed to make sense to him.

He sat down in front of me. I knelt between his outstretched legs and waited for him to put the knife on the ground to unzip his pants. As soon as he did, I snatched up the blade and slashed his neck with a single smooth movement.

I'll never forget the look of horror on his face as he frantically pressed his hands against the deep crimson that gushed relentlessly from the wound in his neck. I'll also never forget the odd sense of emptiness I felt as I stood there watching him. No sadness or joy. Just a numb void that left me feeling detached from myself and the world.

When the first group of people gathered around the scene, gasping and screaming, I calmly walked straight to the police station and told them everything, bloody knife still in hand.

The boy survived, but my parents left me to rot in the Kim Arundel Psychiatric Hospital for the Severely Mentally Ill for the rest of the school year. I'd told the police that it was self-defense, and they'd believed me. But the composed and emotionless way I'd handled myself created a ripple effect in my small town, and CPS branded me a high-risk child in need of immediate intervention.

The therapeutic period that followed was mostly unremarkable. There were the standard programs designed to help normalize me: the grippy socks, the endless talk sessions. But what really left its indelible mark on my mind was the time I spent in the treatment center's library, a space shared by the children and adult units.

It was there, between the picture books and cleavage-filled romance novels, that I discovered a book about German National Socialism during World War II. Judge me how you want, but strangely, this book, as thick and heavy as three books combined, gave me hope.

My fascination with the book wasn't related to the horrific atrocities committed by the Nazis, nor was I fool enough to admire one of the greatest mass murderers in history. My obsession with Hitler stemmed from the peculiar fact that the same monster who was responsible for sending millions of people to concentration camps was also a vegetarian who had a deep affection for his dog, Blondi. At a time when a human's life meant close to nothing, Hitler passed some of the strictest animal protection laws ever written. He introduced penalties for animal cruelty and banned free hunting rights.

As I sat there on the library's torn and dusty couch, the worn book spread open on my lap, something stirred inside me. This, by itself, was shocking because I rarely felt any kind of emotion—hatred, joy, contentment, nothing. I understood the difference between right and wrong and derived no pleasure from witnessing animals or people suffer. Yet, on most days, I simply felt nothing—as if my inner world was a merciless desert devoid of even the slightest hint of life. Feeling that warm flicker inside me meant everything. Eventually I realized what it was: It was hope.

If a man as evil as Hitler could unearth the slightest bit of love within the depths of his icy, rotten heart—even if it was for animals—then perhaps, one day, I might be able to do the same.

Chapter
One

I'm here, Tim texted.

My phone's bright light illuminated the glass of water sitting beside it. It was 5:36 p.m. Tim was thirty-six minutes late. Men like him often were.

I was in a cheap Chinese restaurant, listening to the sounds of forks clinking against plates, the occasional peal of laughter, and the sizzling of grease against hot pans in the kitchen.

I picked up my phone.

About time, I texted. Waiting inside. Blonde girl with short hair, holding a red rose.

The familiar bouncing three dots indicated Tim was answering.

I'm late, and you got me a rose? That was my job. Want me to grab one real quick? Feel like a douche now. LOL

I took a sip of my ice water. Just kidding. No rose. But I'm the only one in a red dress. Get your sexy butt in here.

Exhaling deeply, more out of annoyance than anything else, I turned toward the window overlooking the parking lot. The sky was a canvas of fading orange and purple hues fighting against the encroaching gray of the night. Several streetlights illuminated the handful of scattered cars in the dim parking lot of the small shopping mall, which consisted of nine-to-five businesses such as an outdated fitness studio and a shabby tattoo parlor.

As I scanned the cars, my phone remained silent. A whole two minutes ticked by without a response.

He's debating leaving.

Many debated internally over whether to do 'it' just one more time, each motivated by their own reasons, in a constant back-and-forth.

I glanced at my phone, noticing the three dots bouncing again.

Shit, Tim texted. I'm so sorry, but work just called me in.

Oh no, I replied, hoping I could persuade him to change his mind. If he backed out now, it would complicate things significantly. My upcoming weeks were packed with concerts.

This late? I texted.

My boss says some older woman has a major leak in her ceiling, and our on-call guy won't pick up the phone. I'm so sorry. I feel terrible.

That's a shame. But don't feel bad. Work pays the bills. I get it. It's nice you're helping that elderly lady. You sound like a keeper.

There was another silence. Disappointed, I continued to stare out the window. I needed something to push him—quickly—or he might not bite. Something that preyed on his most primal instincts as a man.

Possessiveness. Jealousy.

My friend Mike is having a beer close by anyway, I texted. He begged me to meet up tonight. I'll just join him. No biggie.

Suddenly a pair of headlights turned on from the far end of the parking lot.

Bingo.

He'd been watching all along. I knew it.

He texted again: Hey, this might seem super weird...but do you want to tag along?

My green eyes narrowed at the headlights. Attaboy.

I just really want to get to know you, he continued. Could be a fun story at our wedding reception. LOL

Wedding reception? That was a little forward. He was attempting to exploit the loneliness of the type of woman I was pretending to be. A sweet and kind soul. One that longed for love and stability like a flower craves the sunlight.

Won't you get in trouble for that? I asked. Bringing me along to work?

Nah. It won't take me long to fix the leak. We could bring donuts and coffee and just talk in the car. Or grab dinner after. I know a fancy place and could make a reservation for nine thirty.

I waved at the young Asian waitress and reached inside my purse to grab twenty dollars. She hurried over. "Are you ready to order?"

"Sorry, but I have to go." I placed the twenty on the table. The soft fabric of my knee-length red dress slid over my thighs as I rose. I was wearing matching red ballerina shoes.

"Thank you," the waitress said, fingering the bill.

The door's bell tinkled as I stepped out into the parking lot and inhaled the cool autumn breeze. It smelled like a mixture of Chinese food and the fake floral scent of detergent from a nearby Laundromat. I waited a moment, then texted:

I'm outside. Just promise me you're not a serial killer. LOL

More dancing dots.

I promise.

The vehicle with the bright headlights at the far end of the parking lot started rolling toward me. Slowly. Under the dim light of a nearby streetlight, it revealed itself as a gray van that read East Coast Plumbing. We Do It Right! on its side. The van came to a stop in front of me. For a moment I stood there, waiting for Tim to get out. When he didn't, I walked around the front to the passenger's side. The door stuck a bit when I opened it.

As I got a closer look at Tim, I noticed the overwhelming difference between his dating-app pictures and reality. The photos were fake, of course. His once handsome cheekbones were now hidden beneath quite a few extra pounds. The striking blue eyes that could ignite a woman's wildest fantasies had lost their luster, appearing weary and dull. He was clean-shaven with an obscenely wide nose; only his brown hair and tall, imposing stature matched his photos. He wore a white protective coverall. Brand-new. Industrial, disposable.

He's a two out of ten, I thought and climbed up onto the seat.

"Wow," Tim said as I closed the door and strapped on my seat belt. It tightened against my chest, outlining my small breasts. Tim stared at them. Shameless. "You look even prettier than in the pictures," he continued.

I forced a playful giggle. "Stop it."

"No, really." Tim grinned, shifting the van into gear. "I'm a lucky man." His eyes lingered on me. "I don't think I've ever been with a woman as pretty as you." His gaze dropped to my legs before traveling back up to my breasts. "You could be a model."

He conveniently didn't address his own looks—or more the lack of them when compared to his pictures. Many of his kind were like this. Manipulative, dishonest, and yet with an air of entitlement, always prepared with an excuse to justify their self-serving actions.

Tim maneuvered his van out of the parking lot, smoothly merging with the flow of traffic as he joined the bustling street.

"Is the woman's house far?" I asked as the van snaked its way through the southern Boston suburb of Dorchester without stopping. I peeked over my shoulder into the back of the van—rusty toolboxes, pieces of white PVC piping, sponges, and buckets. Then my eyes settled on a very familiar five-gallon white-and-blue bucket of Fixx. The cleaning detergent used oxygen instead of chlorine. It was a fairly new cleaning product that erased all traces of hemoglobin, the oxygen-transporting protein in blood that was crucial in forensic tests.

Tim focused on the road. "No, not far at all. She lives close to the Blue Hills Reservation State Park."

The forest.

I stayed quiet. He laughed. "Don't worry. I promised not to be a serial killer, remember?"

Adjusting my dress, I forced out a chuckle. "Yeah, you did."

The houses gradually spread apart until the dark silhouettes of trees rose in the distance, marking the entrance to the large state park. I shifted in my seat. He glanced at me out of the side of his eye but didn't say anything.

Tim's headlights beamed into the darkness as he steered the van onto a dark road leading into the park. It was a smaller road, not the one that passed through the park's entrance and parking lot.

"She's pretty secluded out here," I commented, looking out my window at the endless black trunks of the trees now surrounding us. I sensed Tim smiling beside me, but he remained silent, driving deeper into the darkness of the woods until the road transitioned from concrete to gravel.

The stuffy air in the van grew even thicker, almost unbreathable. My heart started pounding against my chest as an icy adrenaline rush raced through my veins. This was the only time I felt excitement, and I often wondered why. Why did I feel this way before the storm hit? Why not later when his sweaty body violently pressed against mine?

I snapped out of my thoughts before Tim became suspicious of my silence.

"I...I think I want to turn back," I said in a weak, trembling voice. My fingers fumbled with the leather strap of my purse.

Tim remained silent, his dark profile starkly outlined against the window.

"Are we almost there?" I asked. "I think it's better if I go home. It's getting late."

Nothing but that stupid grin.

The van shook on the uneven gravel road as we ventured deeper and deeper into the woods. No one would ever come this way tonight. No one would be here to save me.

"I...I have to go home. Can we please turn around?" I pleaded, my voice rising in desperation.

His grin persisted, but he still offered no response.

Suddenly Tim stopped the van at a small bend in the road. End of the line. The headlights illuminated the never-ending rows of dense bushes and trees. To the left of the van, I could barely make out a narrow, overgrown path obstructed by branches, leaves, and rocks.

Turning toward his window, Tim gazed out into the night. Abruptly his hand jerked up to his hair, and he ran his fingers through it repeatedly, mumbling something to himself that sounded like "You're all the same."

"Tim?" My voice was a frightened whisper.

"Be quiet."

My throat started burning, suddenly dry, and I rubbed my hand against it.

There was nothing normal about any of this, and he not only knew it, but he loved it. He lived for these moments, craved my fear like a drug.

"Please," I said in a shaky voice. "I want to go—"

"I said shut up!" he snapped. His wide eyes locked with mine, and I noticed something flickering in his pitch-black pupils. Hate. Rage. Lust for pain.

Ah, the crude savage. Among the myriad of killers, I detested his kind the most, with their raw ferocity and absence of finesse.

Helpless whimpers escaped my lips.

"Stop that," Tim demanded, balling a fist.

I bit my lower lip and covered my mouth with my hand. The first tear rolled down my cheek, landing wetly on my dress. Whimpers emerged once more.

"I said shut up!" he yelled, slamming his fist onto the steering wheel. The loud honk of the horn echoed through the still night, making me jump in my seat.

"Please," I begged. "I won't tell anybody."

"Tell anybody what?" Tim yelled, pounding his fist on the horn again and again. "Tell anybody what, what, what, you cunt!"

I reached for the door handle, but just as my fingers wrapped around the metal, Tim grasped my arm and yanked me toward him.

"No!" I screamed. "Help! Help!"

In a matter of seconds, Tim was on top of me, his heavy body like a boulder crushing me into the soft seat. My stomach churned at his stale body odor and onion breath.

"No!" I screamed again as his large hand found my throat and wrapped around it. He used his free hand to lift up my dress and tear at my panties. The fabric cut into my skin until it finally snapped.

Scratching, biting, kicking, I fought every second, but it was no use.

"Please," I begged, my eyes beginning to water. "Please!"

But the hand around my throat tightened, cutting off all air. My eyes felt like they were bursting from my skull.

"You loose little whore," he huffed above me. "Want to abandon me to fuck that Mike, huh?" His dark eyes met mine, and I saw the evil flicker of a monster in them.

Trembling with excitement, he pushed my legs open with his knee and maneuvered his hips between them.

"A cunt is a cunt," he mumbled over and over again as if summoning a demon.

I thought about screaming once more. For help, to make him stop, but I knew it was futile. So I didn't scream. And he didn't stop.

I waited until he was fumbling with the coverall's zipper on his chest. Then I went still, dropping my arms abruptly like a puppet without strings.

That was when I started to laugh.

At first a weak chuckle escaped my lips, tentative and shy, but as soon as he loosened his grip around my neck, my giggles rose in volume and turned into a burst of uncontrollable, full-bellied laughter.

Tim's eyebrows furrowed in confusion as he removed his hand from my neck and pushed himself into a sitting position. Disbelief was written all over his face as he struggled to process the situation unfolding in front of him.

"What...what's so funny?"

I just kept laughing, gasping for air, my chest heaving up and down.

"What's so funny?" he yelled. The anger in his voice had returned, but this time it was the rage of a pissed-off man, not a manic psychopath.

With practiced ease, my hand reached into the pocket of my dress, finding the syringe. I slid it out and removed the needle cap with one hand, almost poking myself.

"You want to know...," I said, steadying my voice, "what's so funny?"

For a moment, the van lay in complete silence, as if time itself had stopped. Neither of our sweat-slicked bodies moved.

I narrowed my eyes at Tim. Emotionless. Cold.

"It's amusing that most of your kind share the same traits. Not one of you keeps going when I laugh. You need the screaming to feel powerful, don't you? But the truth is, there's nothing powerful about you."

I rammed the syringe into the side of Tim's neck and pushed the contents into him. Tim jerked as if he'd been shot. Then he grabbed for my hand, yanked the needle out, and stared at it.

Quickly, from underneath him, I tugged at the door handle and kicked it open. Before he realized what was happening, I angled my legs and kicked him backward out of the van so he wouldn't collapse on top of me. With a heavy thud, Tim's large body crashed onto the ground, snapping a branch underneath it.

I scooted to the edge of the seat and carefully smoothed out the creases in my dress with my hands. "The propofol acts fast," I said. "We'll talk some more when you wake up again."

I stepped out of the van and onto Tim's chest. He coughed under my weight.

"Then you'll tell me where the bodies of Kimberly Horne and Janet Potts are."

Gasping for air, Tim somehow managed to squirm onto his side before he stopped moving. His vacant eyes stared into nothingness while his mouth was torn open, as if frozen in a scream.

I reached into my purse for my gloves and carefully slipped my hands into them. Bending down, I took off Tim's leather boots and slid them onto my feet. They were too large for me, and I was slightly unsteady in them, but I made my way to the back of his van just fine.

"Let's see what we're working with here," I said, adjusting the short blonde wig on my head. It had shifted to the side a little during the fight. Short-haired wigs were my first choice when hunting. They perfectly covered my long hair, disguising one of my most identifiable features. The police rarely considered a good wig when searching for their persons of interest.

"You still with me, Tim?" I asked as I opened the doors of his van and climbed in.

No answer.

"Good."

Want to know what happens next?

You can find the full book on Amazon, Barnes & Noble, or at your local bookstore.

FREE with Kindle Unlimited:

I Kill Killers READ HERE

AFTERWORD

Dear Reader,

Thank you for reading "Her Silence." If you enjoyed the book, please consider leaving a review on your preferred retailer's website (like Amazon, Goodreads, Barnes & Noble, etc.). Every review, share, and kind word makes a huge difference and means the world to me.

Review Her Silence on Amazon

Join Ashman's Facebook Group to Meet the Author:

https://www.facebook.com/groups/295886162846929

Newsletter:

https://www.ashmanbooks.com

Instagram:

https://www.instagram.com/booksbyashman/

TikTok:

https://www.tiktok.com/@ashmanbooks

Contact: hello@ashmanbooks.com

I'm so excited to meet you on one of these platforms!

Thank you!

S. T. Ashman

ABOUT THE AUTHOR

S. T. Ashman is a writer who once delved into the criminal justice system as a psychotherapist. This role gifted her with a unique insight into the human psyche—both the beautiful and the deeply shadowed. She considers herself a crime-solving enthusiast, often daydreaming about being the female version of Columbo, solving mysteries while rocking a trench coat. Her writing promises to keep readers engrossed in a nail-biting adventure.

When she's not busy crafting suspenseful tales, she's chasing after her nap-resistant kids, binge-watching TV with her husband, or … actually, that pretty much covers it.

Come join her on her book journeys.

www.ingramcontent.com/pod-product-compliance
Lightning Source LLC
LaVergne TN
LVHW090131160826
845673LV00017B/1410

9798995857709